MW00491450

TALES FROM TAYLOR STREET
Volume 1

MONEY FOR NOTHING

by Aaron Palmer

Copyright © 2023 by Aaron Palmer

All rights reserved.

This book is a work of fiction. Any references to historical events, real people, or real places are used fictitiously. Other names, characters, places, and events are products of the author's imagination, and any resemblance to actual events or places or persons, living or dead, is entirely coincidental.

ISBN 978-1-960378-08-8   (paperback)
ISBN 978-1-960378-07-1   (hardcover)
ISBN 978-1-960378-09-5   (eBook)

1st Edition

moneyfornothing-book.com
aaron@moneyfornothing-book.com

Book design by Anna Hall

MONEY FOR NOTHING

A NOTE FROM THE AUTHOR
TO THE PEOPLE OF TAYLOR STREET

Please keep in mind that this is a work of fiction. It is not about you or anyone you know. Most of the settings are real, but the characters have been completely imagined and then imbued with some of the traits of people in the neighborhood that I have heard stories about. Many of the settings, situations, and characters will be familiar to you, and many may seem incorrect. But they are not meant to be real. They are purposely jumbled composites of the people and places I have heard about and the stories I have been told, all wrapped up into a larger fictional narrative. I hope you have fun reading this book. If it makes you smile, even a little bit, I will consider it a success.

CHAPTER 1

CAPO'S LEATHER JACKET

BEANS CAME TO a stop at the light. He rolled up the windows, turned off the radio, and glanced from mirror to mirror. Left side-view, rear-view, right side-view. Repeat.

The gangbangers around here could be unpredictable.

When on the job, he felt the municipal license plates on his city vehicle provided a layer of protection. But now, after work, driving his own car, he felt vulnerable—just an ordinary citizen. He continued through the intersection, left hand on the steering wheel, right hand on the butt of the revolver in his waistband. Why had he agreed to meet this junkie on Eighteenth Street? For that matter, why had he agreed to meet him at all? The guy's tips rarely panned out.

He rolled slowly past La Playa Restaurant.

Perched on the stoop of the building next door was Billy "the Goat" Godina.

Beans pulled to the curb and climbed out of the Olds.

"Yo, Beans," Billy said.

Billy looked as he always did. Overweight and unkempt. Jeans wrinkled and soiled. Black canvas All-Stars with holes in the toes.

His usual self, save for one thing.

"Nice fuckin' jacket," Beans said, eyeing the three-quarter length black leather. "Looks brand new."

Billy gripped the lapel. "You like it? It's for sale. Just boosted it from Marshall Field's." He held out an elbow. "Go on, feel how soft this leather is."

"I'm good, thanks. What'd you want to tell me?"

"You're gonna love it, Beans," Billy said. "There's this old Black guy they call Rooster. Works for the gas company. He's got his whole crew on juice."

"A loan shark? You brought me here for a loan shark?" Beans looked off, exhaling loudly, and came back. "I don't have time for this shit."

"No, wait." A greasy lock of black hair swagged down Billy's forehead and stuck there. "He's the boss. He gets their checks before they do, cashes 'em, then takes his cut and gives 'em what's left."

A loud three-note squeal, almost like a baby's cry, echoed through the area.

Beans glanced around. "What the fuck was that?"

"Who cares?" Billy said. "Whattaya think?"

"I think you're wasting my fuckin' time."

"This ain't no small potatoes, Beans. He's got twenty guys on the arm—construction workers, equipment operators. With all the overtime and shit, these guys make a G-note a week, at least. That's forty grand, twice a month."

"Yike, yike, yike!"

"Son of a bitch." Beans eyed the gangway between the two buildings. "What the fuck *is* that?"

"Yo, Beans," Billy said, stepping into his line of sight. "Whattaya think—about the guy?"

After a third round of wails, Beans dug a hand into his breast pocket and came up with a pen and notepad. He tore off a sheet and handed it and the pen over to Billy. "Write down his name. I'll be right back."

Beans pulled his gun and concealed it behind his leg as he jogged into the alley. There, he came face to face with a man clutching a two-foot length of sawed-off broom handle.

As Beans drew nearer, he spotted a dog, bloodied and whimpering, lying on the ground at the guy's feet. "Motherfucker! What the fuck is wrong with you?" Beans ran at him.

The guy raised the makeshift weapon and cocked back his arm, preparing to take a swing at Beans. "Mind your fuckin' business, *cabrón.*"

Before the asshole could get off a blow, Beans brought down his gun like a sledgehammer, the barrel crashing hard across the bridge of the guy's nose, which split open and gushed. He dropped to his knees. Beans brought down the gun again, this time squarely atop the man's head, and he fell sideways onto the pavement, unconscious.

Beans knelt beside the German shepherd pup—about six months old, by his estimation. The dog lay on its side and was bleeding from his ear and mouth. His right foreleg appeared misshapen.

Beans gently dug his hands under the dog's torso, scooped him up to his chest, and walked, gingerly, up the gangway and around to the front of the building. "Billy!"

The Goat waddled over to meet him. "What the fuck?"

"Some scumbag motherfucker back there was beating this dog. I fucked the guy up pretty good." Beans shifted sideways. "Go in my jacket pocket. Get my keys. Open my car."

Billy did as told, unlocking and pulling open the passenger-side door.

Beans started to put the dog in the car, then paused, glancing at his tan Member's Only jacket, now spotted with blood, then stared down at the Ninety Eight's immaculate gray velour seats. "How much do you want for that jacket?" he asked Billy.

"I dunno—a C-note?"

"I'll give you fifty. Take it off and lay it there on the seat."

"Seriously?" Billy's blemished face contorted. "You're gonna waste this beautiful leather on a dog?"

"Just fuckin' do it. Where's the closest vet?"

"How the fuck should I know?"

After Billy surrendered the coat and spread it over the passenger seat, Beans, as delicately as possible, transferred the ailing pup into the car. "And call an ambulance for that piece of shit in the alley."

"Are you kidding?" Billy asked. "Who gives a fuck about him?"

"He's bleeding pretty bad, and I'm no murderer."

"What about the other guy?"

"What other guy? Oh, that. Did you write his name down?"

Billy handed him the sheet of paper and the pen, and Beans pocketed it. He then slipped off his jacket, turned it inside out, and tossed it onto the floor below the front seat before sliding behind the steering wheel.

As Beans pulled away from the curb, he heard Billy shout, "Hey! What about my fifty bucks?"

4

CHAPTER 2

A FISTFUL OF ... COTTON BALLS?

BEANS ABSENTLY DRUMMED his fingers on the steering wheel. *If Rooster carries a gun, things could go sideways fast. What time is it?* He had to squint against the blaze of the midday sun, through waves of undulating heat rising from the windshield, to read the red-lighted digital clock on the bank sign. The numbers blinked, alternating between time and temperature—*11:37, 86 degrees.*

This was the worst part, the waiting.

Beans and his partners, Izzy and Cosh, despite their "plain" clothes, were obviously not residents of this neighborhood. Nonetheless, they sat in the unmarked charcoal-gray Chevy Caprice as it idled at the bus stop kitty-corner to Illinois Mutual, intently studying the people walking into, out of, and around the bank. On the dashboard was a walkie-talkie, its volume set so low the dispatcher's voice crackled and hissed nearly inaudibly through the sticky ozone.

Beans shifted his weight from one butt cheek to the other and back again. He checked his mustache in the rear-view mirror.

Where is this motherfucker? Should be here by now.

He studied the faces and body language of the street-savvy locals as they passed, easily able to detect the moment each noticed the conspicuous car. What had been a hurried or casual gait became at once slow and deliberate. Chins tucked to chest as if ducking through a too-low doorway. Eyes, formerly preoccupied, began a furtive dance of suspicion, from their own feet to the three people in the car. Beans considered it a feat of the human mind that one could, in an instant, sort out the significant, telltale subtleties and spit out the appropriate conclusion faster than any computer.

In truth, it wasn't that difficult. What to the unaware were mere nuances, to the streetwise were buzzing neon signs. Now that they were well into the eighties, Chevy sedans had all but replaced the Plymouths of the seventies as the most commonly used cars by Chicago detectives. This one was dirty, with no pinstriping or hubcaps, and Beans had parked in an obvious tow zone. What the experienced eye was inevitably alerted to was the license plate, with its bright-green lettering, starting with *M*, denoting a municipal vehicle.

Cosh, in the shotgun seat, sniffled, snorted, and scratched at the red blotch on his neck.

"Whatsa matter?" Beans asked.

"Don't you see all the fuckin' pollen flying around out there?" Cosh reached into his shirt pocket, plucked out a loose Benadryl tablet, and swallowed it down dry.

"Hey, Beans," Izzy said. "You some kind of environmentalist or somethin'?"

"What?"

Beans glanced in the rear-view mirror to the back seat, where Izzy sat alone, sweat dripping from his forehead.

"Are you trying to conserve gasoline, or what?" Izzy could never just ask a simple question. Always had to wind around to his point.

Beans had no idea where this was going. "What the fuck are you talkin' about?" he asked.

"Turn on the AC! I'm fuckin' melting back here!" Izzy yelled this so loud his voice went hoarse midsentence.

Beans glanced at Cosh, and together they busted up laughing. Even in the most precarious of situations, they could count on Izzy to relieve the tension.

Beans slapped at the air-conditioning controls with his right hand, and with his left, depressed the silver buttons on the driver's side door two at a time to close all four windows.

Cosh fumbled into his back pants pocket and pulled out a neatly folded handkerchief. He snapped it open with a flick of his wrist and held it out to Izzy. "Here. Wipe your face."

Tiny beads of sweat had sequined into the creases of Izzy's forehead, forming a collection of parallel horizontal lines. "Put that thing away," he said. "I ain't puttin' no dirty snot-rag of yours on my face!"

"What the hell's wrong with you?" Cosh shot back. "You think I'd give you a used hanky?"

A large gray droplet inched its way down from Izzy's temple to his chin, leaving a trail through the hair on his unshaven cheek. Cosh flung the handkerchief, which landed on and stuck to Izzy's sweaty stubble.

Now all three of them were laughing.

"Where is this guy?" Izzy said, wiping his face with the cloth. "He's late. You sure you got his habits down right, Cosh?"

"I know how to do my job," Cosh returned. "The last six times, he arrived here between 11:11 and 11:18. I only used the same car twice, and I'm sure he didn't spot me. You got a problem with that, you handle the recon next time."

"Let me see the book again," Izzy said.

Cosh handed him the blue pocket-sized spiral notebook where he jotted down all the particulars of his surveillance.

Izzy mumbled as he read. "Roosevelt Davis—aka, Rooster. Black, sixty-two years old, works at People's Gas, twenty-four years, payroll department. Drives a powder-blue '76 Buick LeSabre, Illinois plate *ROOSTR*. Lunch eleven to twelve. Payday, first and fifteenth of month. Goes to the bank—"

"Twice a month for the last three months," Cosh said. "We watched him walk into that fuckin' bank with one of them accordion folders—flat when he walked in and bulging when he walked out. Same time, every time, only a few minutes either way. Where he's at now, I don't know. Maybe he got a flat tire."

"You guys are a couple of regular fuckin' Columbos," Izzy said. "I'm getting hungry sittin' around doin' nothing. I'm goin' across the street to get a doughnut. You guys want somethin'?"

Beans pulled the door handle. "I'll go with you."

"Are you nuts?" Cosh's face flushed red hot. "Un-fucking-believable. You guys are gonna blow the whole operation. What if he comes while you're over there? What if he sees you crossing the fuckin' street? You're gonna spook him, and he won't go into the bank!"

"Relax," Izzy said. "He won't see us. And if he comes while we're there, just handcuff him and blow the horn. We'll be right out."

"Fuck!" Cosh thrust a meaty fist upward and punched the velvety roof liner, leaving an imprint of his knuckles. "Fuckin' smartasses—both of you."

Izzy and Beans jumped out of the car, slammed their respective doors, and strutted across the street.

Their appearance, Beans acknowledged, was as much of a giveaway as the car. For him, blue jeans, black Reeboks, and a silver hip-length baseball jacket with black stripes on the collar and cuffs. On his head was a matching White Sox cap. Who but a cop would wear this kind of bushy black mustache, offset by a three-day beard? His .38 hung at his right hip, visible just below the bottom of his jacket, and a single shiny shackle of a pair of handcuffs dangled indiscreetly from his back pants pocket.

For Izzy it was jeans and white Reeboks. His dark-blue three-quarter-length nylon windbreaker with orange Chicago Bears logo hung open, exposing the leather straps of his shoulder holster and the butt of his .45. He had contained, barely, a head of frizzy black hair under a plain-blue baseball cap. They looked like every other plainclothes cop in Chicago. They might as well have been in uniform.

• • •

Beans set his coffee on the roof and dusted the powdered sugar from his hands before reclaiming his seat behind the wheel.

"Anything?" he asked, taking a sip from the Styrofoam cup.

"Nothing," Cosh reported. "I'm ready to give up on this one."

Beans gave a shrug. "Good things come to those who wait."

Izzy, clutching a brown cardboard carryout tray holding two cups and a small grease-soaked bag, maneuvered his muscular bulk into the roomy back seat. Once settled, he reached into the bag, came up with a cruller, and shoved the entire thing into his mouth. After three chews and a swallow, he plucked up one of the cups and thrust it at Cosh. "Relax. You got something better to do? Here, I got you a Boston."

Cosh crossed his arms over his chest, his bulging biceps straining the seams of his Chicago Cubs jersey. "Did you dump out some of the coffee to make room for the cream?"

"Yeees."

"How many sugars?"

"Five. Just how you like it, princess."

"Okay." Cosh reached back and grabbed the cup, mumbling, "Last time you got me coffee it tasted like fuckin' roofing tar."

"You don't like coffee," Izzy returned. "You like coffee-flavored milkshakes."

Beans chuckled, then his eyes locked on the left side-view mirror. As the big Buick drew closer, he was just able to make out the plate. *ROOSTR.*

Beans crowed like a cock at 5:00 a.m. "Okay, boys," he said. "It's showtime."

Cosh made the sign of the cross.

Beans didn't have to remind them of the plan. He, Izzy, and Cosh had worked together for years and by now had grown to know each other so well they could do the entire job without a single word spoken between them. They were professionals. Partners. The closest of friends. But more than any of that, when it came to business, they worked together like three well-oiled parts of the same machine.

When the Buick rolled through the intersection and into the parking lot of Illinois Mutual, Beans shifted the Chevy into gear, but kept his foot on the brake. He watched as Roosevelt Davis, orangey-brown faux leather accordion file tucked under his bony left arm, climbed out of the car and walked inside the bank.

The traffic light at the intersection had turned red.

Izzy shoved in a second doughnut and washed it down with a slug of coffee.

When the light turned green, Beans casually pulled away from the bus stop and into westbound traffic. As the Chevy moved across the intersection, three of its windows descended simultaneously and three nearly full cups of coffee sailed out and exploded onto the pavement of Chicago Avenue.

Beans turned left into the small parking lot, which was sandwiched between a three-story apartment building and the bank itself on the corner. He backed into an empty spot across the aisle from the Buick—one that also gave them a clear view of the bank's glass entrance doors. He then put the car in drive while again keeping his foot on the brake.

More waiting.

Beans, heart thumping, drummed his fingers on the steering wheel. It had taken three tedious months of diligence to get to this point. Now, in just a few minutes, they'd be at the climax of the job. Excitement, uncertainty, danger, adventure—this is what made it all worth it. Adrenaline pumped through his veins, vibrating every nerve ending and bringing with it an acute sense of awareness for every detail of their surroundings.

A sudden wave of emotion washed over him—a peculiar empathy for all the drug addicts he had known. Beans was, without a doubt, an adrenaline junkie. Though he had no personal experience with drugs, he couldn't imagine one that could make him feel this good. *The thrill of the hunt.*

He glanced in the rear-view mirror.

Dark streaks of perspiration had begun a trek from Izzy's temples to his neck. Crumpled beside him on the back seat was Cosh's handkerchief. Izzy snatched it up and wiped at his face.

Beans cocked his head toward Cosh, whose chin was tucked to his collarbone, his eyes sunken into his brow, like a boxer. His lips were pursed, and his jaw was clenched so tight the muscles shook under his skin. He was like a Neanderthal preparing to pounce on some unsuspecting bison. Beans knew the look. Though short in stature, Cosh was powerfully built and carried an inner rage just below the surface that, if allowed to rise, made him capable of tremendous violence. One wrong move and Roosevelt Davis would be in trouble.

Beans caught Izzy's eye in the rear-view mirror and motioned with his head toward Cosh.

Izzy scooted to center and poked his head forward into the space above the armrest. "Can you believe that guy charged me for the coffee?"

The question hung in the air momentarily until Beans said, "That bastard!"

"What?" Cosh said. "He didn't realize that you're Izzy the Great?"

"You know what I mean." Izzy hooked his hands on the back of the front seat. "Remember when we were kids? The cops would go up and down Taylor Street and get all kinds of free shit. We can't even get a fuckin' cup of coffee."

"People got no respect for authority these days," Beans said.

They were all smiling now, and the time passed without another word. But this was an easy silence. Their banter acted like a release valve on a steam boiler.

They returned their attention to the bank, where Rooster was walking out—this time with a much fatter file under his left arm.

Beans and his partners waited patiently while Rooster dug into his pocket with his right hand, came up with a set of keys, and raised one to the lock.

If the guy had a weapon, he'd be hard pressed to reach for it now.

Beans shifted his foot from the brake to the accelerator and stomped on it. The distance between the two cars closed with a leap, and it took all of Beans's strength back on the brake to keep from crashing into the Buick. The two cars now sat nose to nose, their front bumpers only inches apart. Rooster's face twisted in shock as he eyed the Chevy's municipal plate, white with green lettering.

The Chevy was still rocking when the doors flung open and the three of them sprung out. Cosh and Izzy, exiting from the passenger side, were on Rooster in an instant. Beans's job was to run interference for any possible variables, such as a previously unnoticed cohort of Rooster's or a curious citizen. He remained on the driver's side, right hand resting on the butt of his revolver as he surveyed the scene.

Izzy took control of the action. "Roosevelt Davis?" It was more a statement than a question.

"Yessir," came the frightened response.

"Set the package on the ground, and put your hands on the hood."

Izzy, when called upon, could be very authoritative.

Rooster did as he was told, and Cosh squatted behind him and frisked, starting at the ankles. As Cosh worked his way up the first leg, Rooster lost control of his bowels, which, thankfully, were empty, except for a lot of gas. His bladder, however, had been full. Urine soaked and darkened the front of his beige polyester pants.

"Motherfucker!" Cosh pulled his hands away.

Izzy's hand went to his .45. "Whatsa matter?"

"He's fartin' right in my face!" Cosh straightened and backed up. Beans, unable to suppress it, bowed his head and laughed.

Izzy joined in for a moment, then composed himself, stepping closer to Rooster. He moved his hand from the .45 and set it on Rooster's bony shoulder. "Please try to relax, Mr. Davis," he said, meeting Rooster's terrified gaze. "Nobody's going to hurt you. We just need you to take a ride with us, that's all."

Beans pulled himself together and reassessed Roosevelt Davis. He was just a fragile old man. Brown wingtip shoes. White, short-sleeved terrycloth shirt. Taller than Izzy's six feet, but skinny, his gaunt face shadowed under a faded brown fedora. His skin, where visible, was wrinkled like a deflated balloon.

Izzy nodded for Cosh to continue frisking.

"Fine. Hold on." Cosh pulled on a pair of black leather gloves and proceeded to empty the contents of Rooster's pockets onto the hood of the Buick: tattered wallet, some loose change, three paper clips, an open pack of Halls cough drops, and an ivory-handled straight razor. He patted down Rooster's torso, snatched the hat from his head, and searched the inside of it before tossing it beside the rest. Cosh then placed his left palm on the space between Rooster's shoulder blades and gave Rooster a shove while at the same time jerking his right hand off the hood and bending it behind him.

Rooster's face thunked onto the hood.

In one seamless motion, Cosh pulled back Rooster's left arm and roughly slapped on the cuffs, then stepped back. Beans almost expected him to curtsy like a dancer after a well-performed routine.

"Hey, that's not Dillinger we got there," Izzy said, establishing the good-cop-bad-cop routine. "No need to be so rough."

"Aw-right," Cosh replied, using the voice of a dejected child. He then leaned toward Rooster and whispered, "That was for using biological warfare against me."

Beans let out a quiet sigh of relief. With Rooster cuffed, the worst of the potential danger was over. As he moved to slip back behind the wheel of the Chevy, a blue-and-white patrol car cruised by the lot's apron. The uniformed officers inside, who looked to be engaged in a heated discussion, drove out of sight without any notice of them.

"Way to be on your toes, boys," he mumbled.

Beans climbed in behind the wheel, while Izzy led Rooster by the elbow to the back seat. Cosh, meanwhile, loaded Rooster's belongings—including his car keys, which had been left dangling from the lock—into the fedora, and carefully lifted the accordion folder from the asphalt. He then assumed his position in the shotgun seat, dropped Rooster's hatful of miscellany on the floor between his feet, and held the file on his lap.

Izzy slid into the back seat, next to Rooster.

When all looked secure, Beans executed a three-point turn, backing the Chevy away from Rooster's Buick, and turned right out of the lot, heading eastbound on Chicago Avenue. He glanced in the rear-view mirror to where Rooster sat fidgeting in the back beside Izzy.

"Wh-where you takin' me?"

"Harrison and Kedzie," Cosh said, not bothering to turn around. "You can call your lawyer when we get there."

"But I didn't do nothin' wrong."

"Nothing wrong, huh?" Cosh said. "How about embezzlement, forgery, and usury? You know what usury is, right?"

Izzy and Beans kept mum, while Cosh played it tough.

"No. And whatever it means, I didn't do it."

"Let me tell you what we know. Stop me when I'm wrong. You work for People's Gas. You handle payroll for the construction department. Mostly young men working those jobs, and you realized most of 'em blow their paychecks as soon as they cash 'em. So you're more than happy to loan 'em money, at a hundred percent interest, 'til the next paych—"

"Not a hundred percent!" Rooster cut in. "Only double what they borrow."

Cosh looked skyward as if seeking guidance from above. "That, my friend, is usury. Then, if they complain that they can't afford to pay you, you just tack on enough phony overtime to cover it. That's embezzlement. And just to make sure you get your money, you intercept their checks, sign 'em yourself, and bring 'em to your little Puerto Rican girlfriend at the bank—the one who doesn't bother to verify signatures—and you cash 'em all, taking what they owe you off the top before they see any of it. That's forgery. You're going to jail, and so is whatsername—Dolores?—for being your accomplice."

"I'm gonna lose my job, my pension, my wife . . ."

Cosh dug a hand into the accordion folder and came up with a stack of cash-stuffed envelopes. "Well, well," he said, shooting Beans a side-eye. "Will you look at this. Each with its very own check stub."

"My partner's a little upset," Izzy said. "We're actually really nice guys. It doesn't have to be like this."

"I swear, I'll quit. Right now. Today. You let me go, I never do it again."

"Well, we're not *that* nice." Izzy chuckled. There was a pause, and then, "It's gonna take a little more than that."

16

"Whachu want?" Rooster's tone had shifted. He was beginning to understand.

"The money."

"How much?"

"All of it."

"Take it. Fuck. Take it all. Fuck. Thank you. I promise, I quit. You let me go an' I quit. Promise."

"I knew we could work this out." Izzy patted Rooster's knee. "You're a smart guy. Let's take Rooster back to his car, boys."

"That's okay," Rooster said. "I'll get out right here. Just take these cuffs offa me an' I'll jump out right here."

"Now hold on a sec." Cosh turned to kneel backward on the front seat. "We ain't done with you yet. Fuck quittin'. Don't even think about it. Matter of fact, you need to increase your business 'cause now you got three new partners. Every payday from now on, somebody'll contact you, and you're gonna give the guy five hundred. Got that?"

"I don' want no trouble." Rooster's voice trembled.

"Don't worry," Cosh continued. "Anyone fucks with you, we'll handle it. Cops, Outfit guys—anyone." He smiled. "We're your friends now."

Beans caught Izzy's eye in the rear-view mirror. This wasn't part of the plan. Cosh was improvising.

They held their collective breath, waiting for Rooster's answer.

"You guys are gonna protect me?" Rooster said after a lengthy moment of contemplation. "I don't have to worry about getting caught anymore? My daddy always said the choices you make sets your destiny." Rooster sounded delighted by this shiny new prospect. "Okay. But I'll need them check stubs back so's I can pay everyone like nothin' happened."

Cosh turned back around and flipped through the envelopes, pulling out the stubs. "You get these, and that's all. You pay 'em with your own money."

Beans pulled the Chevy to the curb.

Izzy set Rooster free of the cuffs and passed him his fedora. When Cosh handed over the stubs, Rooster tucked them inside the hat with his other belongings. Then, with a quick nod to good-cop Izzy, Rooster scooted out of the back seat and started walking back toward the bank.

"Someone will contact you in the next two weeks!" Cosh called out of the passenger-side window.

"You motherfucker!" Beans slapped Cosh's knee. "That was fuckin' brilliant!"

"Why didn't we think of that before?" Izzy asked.

Cosh raised the cash-filled accordion folder over his head. "Because we were too focused on all *this*!"

They laughed and congratulated each other for a job well done.

Beans drove to Pulaski Street, turned right, then drove south another two blocks to the self-service car wash—ten side-by-side stalls, separated by walls made of cinder block, like a series of garages but all under one roof. An eight-foot staggered-plank fence ran along the alley at the back of the building, sequestering it from outside traffic.

Beans drove around back and pulled into the last stall, where Jimmy Pope was washing Izzy's red Ford pickup. When Jimmy saw the Chevy approaching, he turned off his Sony Walkman, yanked the headphones down around his neck like a clamper necklace, and jumped in the truck, pulling it forward just enough for Beans to slip in behind but still blocking the front entrance—and any view into the stall from Pulaski Street.

Jimmy lifted a hockey gym bag from the bed of the pickup and walked it over to Beans, who, like Cosh and Izzy, was stripping off his clothes. "How'd it go?"

"Like fuckin' clockwork," Izzy replied, standing beside the Chevy wearing nothing but a pair of maroon-and-white striped boxers. His shoes, socks, and other "plain" clothes, topped with his .45, had been piled neatly on the floor a few feet away.

Beans and Cosh, too, were down to their underwear, their discarded disguises and weapons laid out in similar fashion.

Jimmy dropped the gym bag in the center of the circle they had formed and opened it. He handed Beans a bottle of rubbing alcohol and a small package of cotton balls. Beans ripped open the plastic bag, pulled out a fistful of cotton balls, then passed the bag to Cosh, who did the same. They held their cotton balls together as Beans doused them, sending alcohol over their hands and splashing onto the cement below. Once the cotton was thoroughly saturated, they cupped their respective handfuls and wiped at the area between their nose and upper lip. Within seconds, the spirit gum dissolved and their mustaches dropped to the floor amid a litter of soiled cotton balls.

Beans looked down and grimaced. "Looks like two mutant centipedes guarding an egg nest."

"Gimme the hose," Izzy called to Jimmy.

Jimmy handed it over, and Izzy bent forward, holding the nozzle to his head. Streams of icy dark water ran off, staining the floor, as Izzy's black hair gradually returned to its natural dirty blond.

"Is it all out?" Izzy rotated his head for Jimmy to inspect.

"Looks good to me."

Izzy whipped the still-running hose toward the front mouth of the stall, where it wriggled and hissed before landing near the pickup's rear wheels. He snatched a clean white towel from the gym bag and rubbed at his head of coarse, wavy hair, checking the towel periodically for any remnants of the Halloween dye. "Start working on the car," he barked.

Jimmy, who had been standing there, staring in awe, dropped to his knees and shoved both hands into the gym bag and came up with four hubcaps. He dug in again up to his elbows, fished out a rubber mallet, a screwdriver, and the Chevy's real license plates, which he quickly got to work swapping out, removing the *M* plates Beans had stolen from a garbage truck.

Cosh reached in and pulled out three kitchen trash bags. Inside of each was a change of clothes and an electric shaver. He tossed one each to Beans and Izzy. Before long, Izzy was naked, holding a shaver to his cheek with his right hand while hopping on his right leg and pulling on a pair of palm-tree patterned shorts with the other. Cosh and Beans were in various stages of similar activity.

Jimmy glanced up from his work and laughed so hard he fell backward from his squatting position at the back of the Chevy.

Izzy looked at Beans and motioned with his head toward Jimmy.

"What is this kid?" he said. "A fuckin' hyena?"

Beans chuckled and pulled a blue polo shirt over his head.

"Hey, Giggles," Izzy said, still hopping away. "What's your fuckin' problem?"

"You guys look like the Three fuckin' Stooges." Jimmy, overtaken by another fit of laughter, lay back on the cement, gripping his middle.

Jimmy was a kid from the neighborhood and would never disrespect an "older" guy, especially one of their caliber. It was their fondness for the kid that allowed for a little latitude now and again. Besides, any remark comparing them to the highly revered Three Stooges could never be considered an insult.

"'Remind me to kill you later,'" Beans said, quoting Moe.

Jimmy took a breath between giggles to offer Curly's famous retort, "'I'll make a note of it.'"

Cosh dumped the contents of the accordion file into a brown paper bag, tossed the folder by their piles of discarded clothes, and rolled up the top of the bag tightly before tucking it under the passenger side of the pickup's bench seat.

"When you're done with the car," Izzy said to Jimmy, "clean up this place good. Stash the guns and clothes and shit at your house and park the Chevy on Lexington Street. Then, meet us at the club when you're done. We'll be there after one o'clock."

"Okay, this won't take long at all." Jimmy positioned his headphones back over his ears and moved on to the hubcaps.

After that and a thorough washing, the full-sized sedan would look sufficiently different from earlier when it was used in the crime. In any case, anyone looking for it would have good cause to doubt themselves because Chevy Caprices were so common.

"What are you listening to?" Beans asked.

Jimmy pulled one side of his headphones away, and Beans leaned in. "Car Wash" by Rose Royce was playing.

Beans came away with a chuckle and a shake of his head. "I should've known."

CHAPTER 3

GUGOOTZ

THERE WAS NO available parking on Taylor Street in front of the club, so Izzy parked around the corner on Bishop Street. When they climbed out of the truck, Beans could only marvel at the transformation. Where mere minutes ago they had looked like gritty Chicago police detectives, they were now clean-shaven suburbanites on their way to the beach, complete with shorts, polos, and flip-flops.

Cosh snagged the paper bag from under the seat, tucked it under his arm like a newspaper, and they casually walked down and around the corner.

As they approached the club, Beans couldn't help but feel a burst of pride.

It had been six years since he, Izzy, and Cosh, just sixteen at the time, had conceived the idea, and since then, they had put a lot of work into the place—which had turned out to be well worth the effort. He remembered the day they first walked in and negotiated the rent. Back then, it was still occupied by a small restaurant named Nailati that had gone out of business. The boys liked the name—Italian spelled backward—so they left that painted on the windows on either side of the entrance door. After that, the place was unofficially dubbed the Nailati Club.

There was a full kitchen and bathroom in the back, as well as an old storage pantry the boys converted into a small bedroom. The walls of the main room were dark wood panel and the floors parquet. They left both as is, brought in a full-sized leather couch, several nonmatching recliner chairs, and a console television. There were also three large tables, round, surrounded by folding chairs—for card games. Although eclectic, the furnishings were far from shabby. They were either donated or they had fallen off a truck. Along the entire length of the back wall they had constructed a bar with an opening at the center to allow passage to the kitchen, bathroom, and bedroom. The wall behind the bar was plastered, neatly, with covers of *Playboy* magazine—the Bernadette Peters issue.

Beans had been elected treasurer on the very first day and had held the position ever since. It was his job to make sure the rent and other bills were paid, and he did this efficiently and inventively, calculating that each member would have to pay monthly dues of twenty dollars. (He had to count on roughly half the members to be consistently in arrears, but they all paid up eventually.) His uncle Skinny provided a jukebox and a slot machine, and Skinny had a guy come in once a week to empty them both, handing 50 percent of the take over to the club.

Beans had nailed to the top of the bar a sizable tin box with a slot opening in the top and a sign on the side that read *All Drinks $1.00*. Even at that low price, and little to no supervision, the bar always showed a profit.

They held bimonthly games of poker and craps, reserving

a cut of the pot for the club—and of course for Uncle Skinny. Beans had made a deal with fifty-year-old bachelor and longtime neighborhood bookie, Willy the Wiz. Few people besides Beans knew that the Wiz, who was a quarter Polish, was called this because his last name was Wisniewski. Most people figured it was a nod to his mathematical prowess. It was rumored that he could figure baseball parlay payouts in his head. For a fee of a hundred dollars a week, Willy would sit in the club and ply his trade daily until one o'clock in the afternoon when first-post time came around.

Thanks to all this collaborative effort, the club's budget ran at a surplus—most of which was used to finance the wild parties they'd become known for.

Beans turned the key in the lock, stepped inside the club, and froze. About six feet in from the door, Capo sat at full attention, as if he were about to pounce on Beans if he took another step. Capo. That's what Beans had named him. They locked eyes. The battered German Shepherd pup had made a full recovery in the months since the unfortunate incident in the alley. He was also enormous, having grown to his full adult size. He was a perfect breed specimen, complete with big, bushy ears that stood erect at all times.

Beans patted himself on the chest and blasted a short whistle through his teeth. "C'mon, boy!" he said, then braced himself.

Capo went from sitting to airborne to in Beans's arms as if shot from a cannon.

The dog's forelegs draped over Beans's shoulders, and his hind legs clutched and clawed at Beans's hips, working for a foothold. Beans bent a knee to the floor and set down the dog, who was now profusely licking his face.

"Okay, okay! Good boy. Relax."

When Capo continued his ardent display of affection, Beans laughed and stroked his ears.

Capo lived at the club now—had, in fact, become the club's official mascot.

Beans stood. "Okay. That's all. Go lie down. I'll be right there."

The dog turned and trotted into the back.

"Lock that mutt in the bedroom before I start sneezing." Cosh fished into his pocket for a Benadryl and popped it into his mouth.

Beans dragged a folding chair from one of the poker tables and moved it in front of the doorway behind the bar.

"Sorry, buddy," he called back to Capo, who had already curled up on the leather jacket that had become his dog bed. "I'll leave the door open, so you can see us."

Izzy snagged the two-by-four leaning against the wall to the right of the front door and slid it into two brackets mounted halfway down on either side of the doorframe.

It was after one now, so the Wiz had gone for the day, and with him his usual round of customers. It was still too early for most of the regulars, who typically stopped in after work.

Izzy moved behind the bar, opened a bottle of sambuca, and poured three shots. Then they all filed into the back, where Beans emptied a cup of kibble into Capo's bowl just outside the bedroom door, and Cosh dumped the cash-filled envelopes from the sack onto the kitchen table.

Izzy handed each of them a glass and raised his own. "To Rooster!" He brought the glass to his lips. "I still can't believe he pissed his pants."

Beans nodded. "I gotta admit, I kinda feel sorry for the guy."

"Yeah," Cosh said. "Poor bastard. To Rooster."

They drained their glasses and slammed them down on the table. Beans's throat burned as the syrupy, anise-flavored liquid sunk into his chest.

"Eh, fuck 'im," Cosh said through a cough. "Puttin' out juice without a license. If we tried that shit, we'd get whistled in by your uncle Skinny."

"Good point," Beans said. And it was true enough. Rooster was loan-sharking without paying the street tax to the Outfit.

Izzy, busy licking sambuca off his fingers, added a nod and a shrug.

They pulled up a trio of wooden chairs, sat at the table, and emptied the contents of the envelopes. They were stacking the cash into neat piles when a "Shave and a Haircut" knock came at the door.

"Probably Jimmy. I'll get it." Beans pushed away from the table. "You guys get to countin.'" Beans returned to the front of the club and put his eye to the "peephole," which was actually just a scratch in the black paint they'd sprayed over the door's diamond-shaped window.

Standing on the sidewalk outside was Jimmy, wearing a wide grin.

"You alone?" Beans shouted.

A muffled "yeah," came through the door.

Beans let him in and resecured the premises. "Sit down. You want a drink?"

"Sure." Jimmy took a seat on the couch.

Beans stepped behind the bar, poured a shot of sambuca, then swiped his own glass from the kitchen and poured a second shot for himself.

"Thanks," Jimmy said when Beans rejoined him. "I coulda got

it myself." He threw back his head and swallowed. "Eee-yuch! Was that anisette?"

"Sambuca."

"It's fuckin' horrible!"

Beans laughed. "You're just a pup. You'll get used to it." He downed his own and held on to the glass. "You did real good today, kid."

"Thanks. I gotta admit, though, I'm always a little nervous."

"That's okay. A little nervous is good. Keeps you alert. Matter of fact, don't ever go on a job with a guy who ain't a little nervous. Means he's not scared of getting caught. Something wrong about a guy like that. Might be a stool pigeon who knows he can snitch his way out of it. Or he might be one of those maniacs who actually likes prison. Either way, it don't matter. Just keep those guys at a distance."

"Okay," Jimmy said.

Beans wasn't convinced the kid was getting the message. "That don't mean you should be so nervous you can't think straight. That's no good either. So, remember, if you lose your head, your ass goes with it."

"Hey, Beans!" Cosh called from the kitchen. "C'mere a minute."

Beans left Jimmy, mumbling to himself. "Stay away from maniacs. Nervous, but not too nervous. Lose your ass . . . no, wait."

Back in the kitchen, Beans found a pair of dissatisfied faces.

"Thirteen-six," Izzy said, frowning.

"Get the fuck outta here!" Beans said. "That's all there is? How many envelopes were there?"

"Twelve," Cosh said. "The tipster said there'd be over forty grand. This is the second time that guy's fucked us. Fuckin' junkie.

What the fuck does he care how much is there? He don't have to take no risks, and he gets enough money to get high 'til whenever."

Izzy brought a fist down on the table. "I oughta open that Billy Goat's head with a nine iron."

"And while you're on his head," Cosh chimed in, "I'm gonna work his kneecaps."

"Think about it, guys," Beans said, looking to calm the two. "Billy's an addict—a fuckin' junkie. Whattaya think he's gonna do if we give him a beating and don't kill him? He's gonna rat us out."

Izzy and Cosh exchanged a look. "Okay," they said.

Beans looked from one to the other, making sure to meet their eyes. "You guys know I'm up for pretty much anything. But I have one rule. I do not kill people."

"Well, he ain't getting his end," Izzy said. "Fuck him. There ain't enough to go around."

"Let me give him a grand," Beans reasoned. "He'll go smoke dope or shoot dope or whatever the fuck he does with the stuff and forget all about us. That way, he don't even know we're mad. And then"—Beans cleared his throat—"if a few weeks or a few months from now someone happens to give him a beating, he won't know where it came from. He gets what's coming to him, keeps his mouth shut and, as a bonus, we keep most of his end." Beans smiled. "It's a win-win-win."

"I'd rather break his kneecaps," Cosh said. "Today. But it sounds like a good plan."

Beans looked at Izzy. "What about you?"

"I guess it makes sense," he conceded with a sigh. "But you know I'd rather open his head right fuckin' now."

"Okay," Cosh said, looking over the stacks. "That leaves twelve-six for us to split three ways."

"Uh, guys." Beans pointed with his thumb toward the front. "What about the kid?"

Izzy and Cosh went momentarily silent, then Cosh spoke up.

"How about we give him the six hundred and the three of us can split the even twelve grand?"

"I guess that's okay. But I was hoping to start working him up to an even cut."

Cosh lit on an idea. "Let's give him Rooster. He can go meet the guy every two weeks, and we'll split the nickel four ways even. That's a fuckin' car payment."

Until now, Beans had completely forgotten about the deal they'd made with the aging loan shark.

"Sounds good to me," Izzy said, looking to Beans.

"I'll go talk to him." Beans counted off six hundred-dollar bills from the pile and took them to the front. "I've got some bad news, kid."

The color drained from Jimmy's face.

"There was a lot less there today than we expected. Your end only came to six hundred." Beans handed Jimmy the money and set a hand on his shoulder. "But there's something else. I'm gonna give you a phone number. I want you to call this guy and arrange a regular meeting. He's gonna have five hundred dollars for us every two weeks. All you gotta do is go pick it up, bring it here, and you get a buck and a quarter every time. That okay with you?"

Jimmy's brow shot up, and his eyes went wide. "Are you kidding? It's fuckin' great! Six hundred bucks for driving some cars around, plus two-fifty a month? I thought you were mad at me."

"Why would I be mad at you?"

"I dunno," Jimmy said, sounding a little sheepish. "Thought I heard something back there."

"Oh, that? Just workin' out a little problem. Nothing to do with you."

"What are we gonna do next?" Jimmy asked.

Beans couldn't help but smile at Jimmy's enthusiasm. Nonetheless, he felt compelled to tap the brakes. "Listen, kid," he said, taking a seat on the couch. "So far everything we've done together—things have gone right. But it doesn't always go that way. We do our best to plan, of course, but there's always a chance you're gonna get caught. You know the drill: Don't do the crime if you can't do the time."

"I remember," Jimmy said. "You told me that a long time ago."

"Yeah, but it's not just some catchy rhyme. Sometimes it's a deciding factor—one that separates a stand-up guy from a stool pigeon. Know what I mean?"

Jimmy shook his head. "Not really."

Beans snagged a cigarette from the half-empty pack of Winstons in his shorts pocket and put it to his lips. "A lot of guys walk around like big shots, thinking they're invincible, like they'll never get caught. And then they do get caught. And when the shock wears off and reality sets in, they might find themselves willing to do anything to get out of doing time. That's when they turn stool pigeon."

"I ain't no fuckin' rat."

"I know that," Beans said. "And I believe that you believe that. But when you're separated from your crew and handcuffed to a steel table in an interrogation room with two cops taking turns beating you with a phone book, well . . . someday remind me to tell you what happened to Cosh and Izzy."

"What happened to them?" Jimmy asked. "Can you tell me now?"

Beans lit his cigarette, took a drag, then blew out a long stream of smoke. "A few years ago, we did a jewelry store. Long story short, I got away, and Cosh and Izzy got pinched. Turns out, the store was owned by the brother-in-law of a Chicago police captain."

"Oh, fuck."

"Yeah," Beans said. "Police held 'em for three days without booking 'em. You see, the cops knew they had a partner. For three days, they beat the fuck out of 'em, trying to get 'em to rat. Then they moved 'em to a different precinct every eight hours so we couldn't locate 'em. Every time they arrived at a new station, they got a new beating from a fresh pair of cops. And every time we got any word about their location and attempted to bail 'em out, they'd be gone before the lawyer could even get there."

"Jeez." Jimmy looked like he might just welcome a second shot of sambuca, despite his distaste for the stuff.

"We finally found 'em at County, where they'd put 'em in a holding cell with prisoners awaiting trial that day. Then they fucked with them some more."

"What'd they do?"

"They turned off the heat and turned up the AC, full blast."

"That's it? Why is that a big deal?"

"Well, it was January, for one. And the prisoners were only wearing their jumpsuits." Beans took another drag and exhaled. "Cosh and Izzy, on the other hand, had been allowed to wear their winter jackets. You get me?"

"Cosh and Iz had to fight every one of those guys, didn't they?"

"Very perceptive, kid. By the time we got 'em out, they were black and blue and bloodied. Miles beyond exhausted. But they never ratted. And they were still wearing those jackets."

"Damn," Jimmy said.

"So, something all three of us do"—Beans glanced toward the kitchen—"every time before we go out . . . assume that if you do this thing, you are *going* to get caught. You ever see *Scared Straight*?"

"Uh-uh."

Beans pulled an ashtray from one of the tables and flicked off an inch-long ash. "Watch it. That's an order. And then here's what you do: every time you decide to do a thing, you imagine you're gonna get caught and thrown in a goddamned sewer where you have to fight off a hundred ax murderers all trying to fuck you in the ass. You gotta fight for your life. Every day. All day long. For ten fuckin' years."

"Is it really that bad in there?" Jimmy asked.

"Can be. We have friends who can make your life easier, but you gotta prepare yourself."

Jimmy put his hand out. "Lemme get a pull offa that."

Beans passed him the mostly gone Winston.

Jimmy took an extended pull, exhaled toward the ceiling, and then, looking Beans in the eye, ground the tip into his opposite palm.

There was a brief hiss before the smell of burnt flesh wafted into the air around them.

Jimmy didn't flinch. "I ain't no fuckin' rat," he said.

Beans smiled. "As long as you stay strong, kid, you'll be all right. One of these days we're gonna find the big score. That's all I want—that one big, perfect score." Beans stood, offered a hand, and pulled Jimmy to his feet. "Let's go have another drink."

Izzy and Cosh emerged from the kitchen.

"Good job today, kid," Izzy said.

He brushed past Beans without pausing and slipped a wad of bills into his hand.

Beans's four thousand for the day's work, which he nonchalantly shoved into the pocket of his khaki Bermudas.

Izzy continued on to Jimmy and threw his arms around the kid—a short but fierce embrace. Then he pushed him into the arms of Cosh, who did the same.

Beans walked behind the bar, and the other three took up stools on the other side.

"What'll it be, boys?" Beans asked, Old West-style.

Cosh pounded on the mahogany bar top. "Sambuca all around!"

"Oh, no," Jimmy said. "Not for me. I'll have a light beer."

"Sorry, Jimmy," Beans said, winking at Cosh. "You wanna run with us, you gotta play by our rules." Beans slid a shot glass in front of the kid and the other two, then poured one for himself. "To Rooster."

They raised their glasses and tossed back their shots.

Jimmy gagged, and they laughed.

"Hey, Beans, can I join the club?" Jimmy was looking at the dues roster, which was posted behind the bar on a three-by-four piece of white poster board and drawn up in black Magic Marker. There were thirteen columns in all, and reading left to right, starting with each member's name, one could see the dues paid—or owed—by each for every month of the year.

Truth told, it was Beans's way of shaming people into keeping current.

"Your crew don't have their own club?" Beans said. "Hell, we were younger than you when we started this one."

"All my friends care about is sports. They don't care about this stuff. They don't even care about girls. If it ain't baseball, it's basketball, or football, or hockey. If they aren't playing it, they're watching it on TV."

"Well, it's okay by me." Beans looked to Izzy and Cosh. "How 'bout you guys?"

His partners exchanged a shrug.

Beans swiped the marker from the counter behind him and put it to the roster. "What's your nickname, kid?"

"Don't have one. Everyone just calls me Jimmy."

Beans dropped his arm and turned around. "What do you mean you don't have one? You gotta have a nickname. Everyone has a nickname."

"I don't. Really. Always been just Jimmy. Jimmy Pope."

"Well, I can't put your real name up here. See." Beans ran the other end of the marker down the left side of the roster. "All nicknames, in case we get raided. What do your friends call you?"

"Jimmy."

Who goes through life without a nickname? "Okay, then. What do you *want* me to put for your name?"

"Jimmy?"

Beans threw up his hands, and the marker sailed from his fingers, bouncing off the ceiling and landing somewhere behind the bar. "What're we gonna do with this kid?" He looked to Izzy then to Cosh.

"We gotta give him a name, I guess," Cosh said.

"You're a lucky guy, Jimmy Pope." Beans rested an arm on the bar. "Most guys don't get to pick their own nickname. It just happens. So, whattaya wanna be called?"

"Fuck if I know," Jimmy said. "How'd you get yours?"

"My real name's Ralph Trombino. My friends called me Bino as far back as I can remember. Then somewhere along the line someone squeezed it down further, started callin' me Beans, and it just stuck. Then there's Izzy here. Richard Tonsi. In grammar school someone figured out that Tonsi spelled backward is 'Is not.' So we started callin' him that, 'til one day it just turned into Izzy."

Jimmy turned to Cosh. "What about you?"

Izzy jumped in. "You ever heard of caciocavallo cheese?"

"Yeah."

"*Cavallo* means horse. We call him that 'cause he's hung like a horse." Izzy dropped his right shoulder and let his arm hang loose like a swinging pendulum.

Cosh shook his head. "Don't listen to him, kid. It's just regular."

"His family owns Geraldi's Deli," Beans explained. "They specialize in cheese, and Cosh's favorite is caciocavallo. When we were kids, he used to eat the stuff all fuckin' day. Lots of times we just called him Cheese. Sometimes, even a nickname has a nickname. Confuses the fuck out of the cops."

"Who comes up with the names?"

"Nobody. Everybody." Beans dropped to his hands and knees and began searching the floor for the Magic Marker. "It just happens. Could be part of your real name, or something you do all the time, or some stupid thing you said or did that just sticks to you."

"I get it, I think. Like Vinnie Virrina is called Step because he limps."

"Exactly. We used to call him Step-and-a-Half. Now it's just Step." Beans snatched the marker from under the sink and jumped back up, holding it over his head like a trophy.

"Well, my last name's Pope, so how 'bout 'Your Holiness'?"

"Well, at least you're thinking now. But try again."

"I got it!" Cosh reached to his left and pulled Jimmy into a headlock, then dragged him to Izzy for inspection. "Look at this head."

36

"Hey!" Jimmy's hands went to his neck. "Don't break my headphones!"

Jimmy's body, dangling under Cosh's tight grip, followed his head around like the tail of a kite.

"Just look at it," Cosh said. "It's shaped like a fuckin' peanut. Let's call him Mr. Peanut."

Izzy's mouth curved into a thoughtful frown. "I kinda see it."

"Let me see." Beans leaned over the bar.

Cosh thrust Jimmy's head so close Beans could smell the kid's shampoo.

"From this angle," Beans said, "looks more like a pickle. I think we should call him Jadrool."

"Gimme another look, Cosh," Izzy said.

With a yank, Jimmy's head was butted up against Izzy's chest. By now, the poor kid's face was beet red, and he was gasping for air. He grabbed Cosh's wrists and attempted to pry them away—a fruitless effort, if ever there was one.

"I don't know," Izzy said. "I don't see a pickle." He held Jimmy's ears and rotated the kid's head back and forth against Cosh's grip. "Maybe a peanut . . ."

Jimmy gurgled and grunted, trying to speak—another fruitless effort.

"Wait!" Izzy said. "I got it! It's a fuckin' gugootz!"

Cosh looked down. "I think you nailed it, Iz. Here, Beans. You check."

Again Cosh thrust Jimmy's head toward him, while Jimmy's body, folded over the bar, went limp, his toes barely touching the floor.

"Gotta give credit where credit is due." Beans looked up. "Izzy, you really got an eye for this sort of thing. Gugootz, it is."

The tip of the Magic Marker squeaked against the poster board as Beans turned and scribbled in Jimmy's new name at the start of the next available row.

"You really are lucky, kid," Izzy said, tousling the hair on Jimmy's imprisoned head. "Got your nickname and initiation over with all at once."

Cosh laughed and released his grip, and Jimmy slumped to the floor. From that day forward, Jimmy Pope was Jimmy Gugootz.

CHAPTER 4

GRAVY

IT WAS A typical Sunday at the Trombino residence.

Beans had been out all Saturday night, and had just awakened at a little past one. He'd been coaxed from his slumber by the aroma of frying meatballs and simmering gravy, which was what they called spaghetti sauce here on Taylor Street. Something to do with the way the word *sugo* was translated from Italian to English. Or maybe that it was a sauce made with meat. Or something. Beans wasn't really sure why. Whatever the case, gravy was delicious. And if you didn't call it gravy, you didn't know what gravy was.

The balmy, spicy scent crept from his mother's kitchen on the third floor all the way to his apartment in the basement, pulling him from his bed as if in a trance. Beans shuffled as far as his leather recliner, plopped into it, and promptly fell back to sleep.

He was awakened by the sound of someone entering his apartment.

Debbie strode in carrying a plate with a slice of Italian bread smothered in gravy and topped with a meatball.

"Mornin', sis."

"What time did you get home last night?"

"No fuckin' idea."

"Five a.m. Wanna know how I know?"

"How?"

"Because Mom told me," she said, fixing him with a pointed stare. "You know she won't let herself fall asleep until she hears you come in."

Debbie's olive complexion, big brown eyes, and striking Romanesque features mirrored his. Good looks ran in the family.

"I told her not to do that."

"Like she's going to listen to you."

Debbie set the plate on the table. "Come. Eat something. You'll feel better."

He pushed forward the lever on the side of the chair and sat up, his head pounding in the effort. "Thanks." He trudged into the kitchen and sat down. "Can you grab me a fork? I can't get up again."

She was already ahead of him and slapped one into his palm.

"And the cheese?" Beans lifted the glass shaker Debbie put beside him and shook it over the sandwich, but the cheese wasn't coming out fast enough. He unscrewed the lid and dumped a pyramid of grated Pecorino Romano in the center of the sandwich, then used the fork to spread it around.

"Would you like some gravy with your cheese?" she said.

"Don't be a smartass. Sit down. Don't make me eat alone."

She slid into the chair across from him.

"Hey," he said, "remember when you were in the third grade, and I stole the lunch money from the cafeteria? They tried to make you rat me out, but you held strong. Eight years old. Unbelievable. Bigger balls than most grown men I know, even then."

"Thanks for the compliment—I think." She rested her arms on the table. "Know what I remember about the third grade? Breaking my leg a few days after Christmas and you giving me piggyback rides to school and back for two months."

This was a common topic for them—recalling who had done what for who.

"How about that time you looked out the window and saw those five Puerto Ricans doing the tarantell' on my head. You ran out in the middle of biology class to get Cosh. You got detention for that."

"Thank God for Cosh." She chuckled. "You were getting smoked."

"What the fuck—there were five of 'em."

"And Cosh put three of them in the hospital."

"Yeah, he got pinched for that. Almost went to juvie. Speaking of Cosh, how about the time I saw the two of you playin' spin the bottle? I never said a word about that."

"Because you never saw it!"

He smiled. "Yeah, you think I don't know things, but I know. I'm watching you even when I'm not around." He pointed to his blind right eye. "I see things with this that normal people can't see."

"Yeah," she said, "you got some kind of magic there. But don't forget, I know how you got that magic eye."

She had him there. He finished the rest of his meal in silence.

He was scraping up the last of the gravy from the plate when he heard a shrill whistle from outside.

"Yo, Beans!"

The whistle was Izzy, but the voice belonged to Cosh.

"Can you let 'em in, please?"

"Sure." Debbie went to the door and opened it. "Come on in, guys."

41

Izzy walked in ahead of Cosh. "Hiya, cutie."

"Hi, Iz." They pecked each other's cheeks.

Cosh paused in the doorway. "Hi, Deb."

"Nicholas."

Cosh set a hand on her arm and gave her a wink. Debbie winked back and gave him a peck on the cheek. Beans paid close attention to this encounter. Cosh's mom and Debbie were the only ones who called Cosh by his real name, and Debbie had had a crush on him since grade school.

Izzy moved behind Beans and briskly massaged his shoulders. "How you feelin' there, buddy boy? You ready to go?"

"Go? Where?"

"You don't remember?" Izzy said. "We gotta go find your car. You forgot where you parked it last night. Your friend Izzy had to drive you home."

"Oh, fuck. Yeah, I remember."

Cosh chuckled through his nose. "Do you remember doin' shots with the bartender?"

"Yeah."

Cosh chuckled again. "You remember makin' out with that beast?"

Izzy rubbed harder. "Deb, you should have seen the beast your brother was with last night."

"What the fuck are you guys talkin' about?" Beans searched his fuzzy mind. "She wasn't bad looking."

"Cosh?" Izzy said. "Was she a beast?"

"Oh, she was a beast, all right. I think her name was Wilda. Wilda Fuckin' Beast. And you two were makin' L-U-V like she was Sophia Loren."

Debbie stomped her foot. "What's wrong with you guys?

You're supposed to be his friends. Why would you let him go off with some ugly chick?"

Izzy shrugged. "'Cause it was fuckin' hilarious?"

Beans stood and pitched his plate in the sink.

"Hey," Debbie said, "aren't you going to read it?"

"Oh, yeah. Sorry." Beans pulled the plate back out and turned it over. He peeled off the piece of paper taped to the bottom. "What did Mr. and Mrs. Fish name their son?" He looked up at Debbie. "I don't know."

"You give up?"

"Yes. Just tell me."

Debbie looked to Cosh and Izzy. "You guys wanna take a shot?"

They both shook their heads.

She paused for effect, then flashed a smile. "Gill."

"Damn." Beans slapped his forehead. "I shoulda got that."

"I don't get it," Cosh said.

Debbie cocked an eyebrow. "Seriously? They're fish. Fish have gills . . ."

"No, no. I get the joke. What I don't get is why there was a joke taped to the bottom of the plate."

"It's just a thing we do." Beans moved back to the recliner. "You remember how skinny Debbie was in grammar school?"

"Yeah."

"That's because she never ate. She would sit at the table and make circles in her food with a fork or spoon. So when I used to get her ready for school, I would tape a joke or a riddle on the bottom of her bowl before I filled it with cereal and milk. She would have to eat all the cereal and drink all the milk for her to be able to turn the bowl over and read it. Now she's getting even with me."

"Well, it worked," Cosh said, "'cause she eats like a horse now." He threw his hands up to block the incoming punches from Debbie.

"You calling me fat? Son of a bitch." Debbie was not fat. She was five feet seven—tall for an Italian girl—and svelte.

"I didn't say that," Cosh said. "Stop hitting me!"

Debbie relented, and he lowered his hands.

"Don't do that"—a sly smile appeared on Cosh's face—"you know I'm ticklish."

Debbie landed one final punch—right in the solar plexus.

"Ow! That one really hurt. That's quite an arm you got there."

Beans closed his eyes and rubbed at his temples. "Can you guys come back in a half-hour? I need a shower."

"Good idea," Cosh said. "Get that wilda-stink off ya before you get in my car."

• • •

Beans sat on the front stoop, waiting for Cosh and Izzy.

He ground out his cigarette when a neighbor, Mrs. DiMarco, pushed the wheelchair holding her son, Mickey, up to the stoop and snapped on the brake.

"Hi, Mrs. D."

"Hi, Beans," she said.

Mickey held out a hand, which Beans shook. Then he honked Mickey's nose. "Is that your nose?" Beans asked. "Or are you eatin' a banana?"

His old friend let out a deep, guttural giggle. Mickey hadn't been the same since the accident thirteen years ago when they'd all been in the fourth grade together.

"Take me for a ride," Mickey said.

"A ride? Where you wanna go?"

"'Round the block."

"Around the block, huh? Okay. But only if you guess correctly." Beans turned his back and reached into his pants pocket, taking out two watermelon-flavored Jolly Ranchers. He grasped one in each hand and spun back around, palms down. "Which one?"

Mickey's eyes darted from fist to fist. Finally, he tapped the left one.

Beans turned over his hand and opened it. "Holy cow!" he exclaimed, discreetly slipping the other candy back into his pocket. "You do it every time!"

Mickey unwrapped his prize and popped it into his mouth. "Okay, ride."

Beans released the brake on the chair, and gave Mrs. DiMarco a wink as he and Mickey started down the block.

As they headed into the turn at the corner, Mickey glanced over his shoulder to make sure they were out of sight of his mother. "Wheelie!" he yelled.

"Okay," Beans said. "But don't choke on that Rancher or your mother will kill me." He pushed down on the handles, lifted the front wheels, and two-wheeled Mickey most of the way around, setting down the front wheels only as they came around to the top of the block.

He was parking Mickey at the stoop next to his mom when Cosh and Izzy pulled up, double-parked, and got out.

"Hi, Mrs. D," they both said in unison.

"Hello, boys."

"Hey, Mickey." Izzy honked Mickey's nose. "Is that your nose, or are you eating a banana?"

Mickey responded with his usual low, throaty laugh.

"What's up, Mick?" Cosh honked his nose. "Is that your nose, or are you eating a banana?"

Mickey giggled like he had never heard that one before.

Izzy turned to Beans. "Ready to go?"

"Yeah."

"I go with yous," Mickey said.

"You wanna come?" Beans looked at Mrs. DiMarco.

Whenever and wherever possible, Beans and the boys took Mickey along with them. Back in the day, before he had landed in the chair, Mickey had been one of the gang, after all.

Mrs. DiMarco looked at her watch. "He needs to be home at five—sharp. Last time, he missed his pills and was all off schedule."

Beans and Izzy each slipped a hand under Mickey's armpits, and Cosh grabbed his ankles. They lifted him out of the chair and positioned him in the front seat of the car. Mickey smiled and waved to his mom as they started off in search of Beans's cherished Ninety-Eight.

CHAPTER 5

MAGGOTS

MAGGOTS. WHY DID there have to be maggots?

Beans dry-heaved at the sight inside the trunk of the '73 Ford Maverick, where a pulsating mound of wriggling, writhing larvae feasted on the decaying body of a dead cat. The putrid smell blasted him in the face, penetrating his nostrils and soaking his mucous membranes with foulness. The main reason he'd had himself transferred from sanitation to towing was that he hated bugs.

And rats. And foul odors.

He covered his mouth and gagged again as he slammed the trunk closed, not failing to notice that, except for the carcass of a rotting feline, the trunk was empty.

"Motherfucker!"

He had already riffled through the glove box and searched under the seats. Nothing there either. The radio, too, was already gone.

Working the abandoned section of the Chicago Police Towing Unit wasn't exactly lucrative, but every once in a while he got lucky. One good thing about it was that, since the cars had been abandoned, usually stolen, no one could say whether things had gone missing before or after he had gotten there. Often the car had been snagged by some kids just looking for a joyride, who left it intact after it ran out of gas—without ever bothering to look in the trunk.

Among his finds were guns, sets of golf clubs, even jewelry. And then, if the car hadn't been gutted, sound systems, radar detectors, tires, and wheels. Petty stuff when compared to his usual scores, but he wasn't one to pass up an opportunity, however insignificant. He was a pathological thief. No score thus far had been able to scratch that itch. So he would keep on scratching until he came across that one score, scam, or scheme that would stop the itch forever. Riffling through cars didn't amount to much, but at least it gave temporary relief. Like calamine for crooks. To that end, he had devised a plan that would provide him with an endless supply of soothing pink lotion—metaphorically speaking.

Unable to get the gory scene in the Maverick's trunk out of his mind, Beans sought refuge back inside his tow truck. The pristine condition of the cab, along with the faint aroma of vanilla wafting from the little yellow Christmas tree hanging from the mirror, helped ease his nausea. He was proud of the way he cared for his truck. Not like some of the other drivers who would let a film of impound yard dust blanket the interior or who would kick their lunch scraps under the seat. Beans wasn't a neat freak like Cosh. He just liked things clean and orderly.

He reached into the glove box, where he kept his black leather pouch of cassette tapes, and pulled out one of his favorites, then fumbled under the passenger seat for the Blaupunkt he had hooked up under there. He bounced the tape against the face of the player until it found the slot and was sucked inside. Then he reclined the driver's seat, lit a cigarette, and composed himself to the sound of Frankie Valli's falsetto rendition of "Under My Skin."

When the song was over, he glanced at his watch—10:45 a.m.

• • •

It took Beans all of eight minutes to drive to the Lucky Star Café, where, at eleven o'clock most mornings of the week, he met Pat Gibbons, the officer in charge of abandoned vehicles in the twelfth district, to turn in his completed tow reports and receive new orders. Pat was about as straight as a bolt of lightning and one of the few cops Beans liked.

The street outside was lined with squad cars, unmarked vehicles, garbage trucks, and sewer department trucks. City workers, especially cops, were notorious cheapskates, and the Lucky Star served a mountain of fried rice for three dollars and seventy-five cents, or two dollars for a bowl of Yet Ca Mein soup. Beans cruised past slowly. When he spotted Pat's car—number 1212—he double-parked the truck, grabbed his clipboard, and walked inside the restaurant.

The interior of the place hadn't been updated since the fifties, when it was still a malt shop. To the left of the door was a white Formica counter, speckled with gold, that ran the length the room, bordered by a long row of chrome swivel stools topped with tired red vinyl that sprouted from the floor like mushrooms. Sitting along the counter were men in various types of uniforms and street clothes, some with pistols hanging at their sides. To Beans's right were eight rectangular tables topped with green plastic, where men wearing similar garb were gathered. Chinese waiters wearing soiled white aprons bustled between the tables and the counter. Two televisions, tuned to two different stations and volume blaring, were mounted near the embossed tin ceiling at opposite corners of the room. He couldn't hear either one above the din of garbled conversation coming from what sounded like a hundred mouths full of eggrolls.

Beans scanned the room for Pat, who caught his attention by waving a fork in the air and pointing it toward the empty seat across from him. As Beans threaded his way between the crowded tables, a waiter squeezed by him holding a plate of rice that reminded him a little too much of this morning's maggots. His stomach convulsed, and he paused to compose himself before continuing on to the table.

"Siddown, Ralphie." Pat flashed his usual welcoming smile. That he used Beans's real name somehow made him more endearing. "How ya doin'?"

Pat's easy way made him the kind of guy people liked to be around, and he always seemed happy to see Beans. But Beans's cautious nature made him wonder sometimes if it was just a tactic to gain his confidence. Beans dismissed the thought. Pat had a long-standing reputation for being loved by cops and crooks alike. Hell, even some of the Outfit guys in the neighborhood were fond of the guy.

"Paddy," Beans said, taking a seat, "if I were any better I'd have to be twins."

"That's what I like to hear," Pat said. He broke open an eggroll with his fork.

"So what's new on the beat?"

Officer Pat Gibbons was a barrel-chested, stocky middle-ager who sported a perfectly groomed head of white hair that he rarely, if ever, covered with his policeman's cap. He also had a fondness for gossiping about police business, and Beans was always plenty interested in what the other team was up to.

To his surprise today, however, Pat hesitated, his expression growing dark.

Finally, he set down his fork and said, "We had a bad one yesterday. Just three doors down from here. Very disturbing. I almost called in sick today."

"Damn. What the hell happened?"

"You gonna eat today?"

"Nah, no appetite. Maybe just a cup of coffee."

Pat motioned to the owner's wife behind the counter, holding his left hand under his chin like a saucer while drinking from an invisible cup in his right hand. Beans noticed Pat's pinkie, which stuck out as he mimed, held a gold ring with an enormous solitaire diamond.

When Pat caught him looking, Beans swiftly shifted gears, sticking out his own pinkie and wiggling it. "Very dainty."

"Yeah, well," Pat returned, "I'm a regular Emily Post, don't you know?"

Beans chuckled. "So, as you were saying . . ."

"Some sicko's been going around doin' some really weird shit. Yesterday, he tortured and killed a poor Chinese girl. By the time I got the call and raced out of here, there was nothing to be done."

"No shit? A serial killer, you think?"

"Nah. We think he's a burglar, a home invader, always after the money. But he seems to prefer to strike when people are at home."

"That's pretty ballsy."

"You're tellin' me. He tied the poor girl to a chair and burned circles around her nipples with a cigarette. Stole the family's money. And that's not all . . ."

"What?"

Pat leaned over the table. "Then he took a shit on the kitchen floor."

Beans had seen and heard about a lot of sick shit in this business, but this was a new one even for him. "Some people just need to be removed from society."

"He will be," Pat said, pushing his mostly full plate aside. "Doesn't seem too smart. He had to have seen the storm of squad cars pull up to the house. Must have been twenty of 'em before the ambulance even arrived. I think we just missed him."

Beans leaned back. "How long you been a cop, Paddy?"

"Twenty-two years. Three more, and I'll be fifty-five with twenty-five years on. Then it's Arizona, here I come."

"Good for you. Fifty-five's a good age to retire." *But twenty-five is better.*

"Yeah, I ain't gonna be like these guys." Pat looked around the room. "They stay on the job 'til their dicks don't work anymore. I'm gonna have a whole lotta life in me left to enjoy."

Beans hoped this was true as he studied Pat's once chiseled features, now barely discernable amid the bloated flesh of decades-long overindulgence. Thanks to a virtual network of broken blood vessels, his cheeks and nose were permanently ruddy.

The woman from the counter came up from behind Beans, set a hand on his shoulder, and bent close, pushing a cup of coffee onto the table.

"Hi, Sara." Beans smiled, but didn't turn around.

She ran her hand gently from his shoulder to his neck. "Nice tan."

Beans had known Sara before she was married. Half-Chinese, half-French, and petite, she was a stunner then and, so far, aging well. Every city worker in the place tried to flirt with her, but only Beans, it seemed, stood a chance.

"Still hangin' out at Oak Street Beach?" she asked him.

"Nah, just on the corner under the pump," Beans said, referencing their first encounter when he had hoisted her onto his shoulder before running through the spray of a fire hydrant.

She dragged her fingernails across his back as she walked away.

Beans glanced sideways and came back to Pat. "So, twenty-two years, huh? How many arrests do you think you've made in that time?"

"None."

"Seriously, Pat," he said. "How many?"

"None," Pat repeated.

"How the fuck could you be a cop twenty-two years and not make a single arrest?"

"Traffic duty, man. I write tickets. I ain't Dirty Harry."

Beans laughed. "Didn't you just tell me two weeks ago you caught a purse snatcher who beat up an old lady?"

"Yeah, so?"

"So..."

"I said I caught him. I didn't say I arrested him."

"Well, then what'd you do with the guy?"

A sly grin stretched Pat's lips. "He resisted arrest."

Beans leaned in close and whispered, "Come on. Whadja do?"

"I left that motherfucker in a dumpster, bleeding from every orifice." Pat said it loudly enough for anyone in the room to hear.

Beans looked around, expecting at least some reproach from the other cops.

There was none.

I like this guy. Beans dumped a pack of sugar in his coffee and stirred, looking up at Pat. It was still hard to believe he hadn't made a single arrest in twenty-two years. "Okay," Beans said. "Let's say you stop a guy for speeding and you realize he's drunk?"

"Is he belligerent?"

"No."

"Then I make him pay a fine. If the guy's really fucked-up, I might park his car and drive him home."

Beans fixed the cop with a knowing look. "How much?"

"Whatever he's got, less a few bucks. It's bad manners to leave a guy broke."

Pat's entree arrived—a Hong Kong steak, the most expensive item on the menu. Beans nursed his coffee while Pat wolfed down his meal, chatting between bites and sips. When Pat was finished, Beans pulled his completed tow reports from the clipboard and pushed them across the table to Pat, who handed him four new tow sheets.

"That top one has four flats," he warned. "I hope you got air in your tank."

"No problem." Beans stared down at the paperwork in his hand. "You know, these tow orders . . ."

"Yeah?"

"How hard would it be to get some blank ones?"

CHAPTER 6

SWEET BERNADETTE

CLUNK. CLUNK. CLUNK.

"Hold on!" Beans yelled through the closed door. "I'll be right out!"

He gathered up the sheet around his body and stood, urinating carefully while examining the walls of the club's bathroom.

One of his side enterprises was distributing around town the latest issue of *Playboy*. Of course, they were hot. He had a connection with a worker on the company's loading dock who passed him bundles of the magazine every month. He sold them half-price to newsstands around town, and whatever he didn't sell were used for club wallpaper. Whereas the bar was dedicated to Bernadette Peters, nearly every inch of the club's bathroom walls was covered with centerfolds featuring other women. Bernadette, put up in 1981, was too good for the bathroom and, to wit, was the only girl in the place who never got rotated out.

Presently, Beans was trying to decide which girl would have to come down this month when the new issue came out. It was a matter of personal taste, rather than chronology.

"I love all you girls," he said to the gallery. "But one of you has to go."

He shook, flushed, and checked himself in the mirror. Even though it was already Halloween, his complexion still held much of its summer tan. He straightened the laurels on his head to evenly encircle his thick, black waves, then cinched the gold-colored rope around his waist. After wiggling his toes in his slightly snug gladiator sandals, Beans, as Julius Caesar, turned to the wall and pressed his face against Miss July's crotch.

He peered through the pinhole in her crotch, and through the hole drilled in the wall behind it. The hole went clear through the shared wall between the bathroom and the main room, behind the bar. He was able to see almost the entire width of the main room. (The hole was also plenty useful in reverse when, say, some unsuspecting girl was using the bathroom.)

He smiled to see the older guys from the Headquarters Club around the corner had abandoned their own party to join this one. Even including them, females outnumbered males two to one.

Beans wondered which one, or ones, he'd be with tonight.

The bathroom's old wood door did little to dampen the too-loud music and discordant voices of the party. One voice, however, stood out—a male voice Beans didn't recognize coming from just outside the bathroom.

Clunk. Clunk. Clunk.

"I said I'll be right out!"

He lifted the latch and the door swung open, forced by the weight of Izzy's girlfriend, half-dazed, who fell backward into Beans.

"Hiya, Ange," Beans said. "How you doin'?"

Angie Ianetto—big-boned, muscular, and very pretty—sagged

in his arms. She shook her head to clear the fog as Izzy appeared in the doorway, dressed as a woman from the fifties.

Beans contemplated his friend's short dark wig, poodle skirt, cardigan sweater, and high-heeled pumps. "Interesting choice of costume, Iz."

With a grunt, Beans pushed Angie's limp body into the waiting arms of his friend, realizing that what he thought was someone knocking was actually Izzy banging Angie's head against the door. It had taken some time for Beans and the others to appreciate the nature of Izzy and Angie's love life; Angie had to get roughed up in order to get turned on, and Izzy was just the guy to do it for her.

Beans slipped out with a nod as Izzy dragged Angie, fittingly dressed as an Amazon warrior, into the bedroom.

Gugootz, behind the bar, was wearing a rubber Frankenstein mask pulled up off of his face so that the neck electrodes were at his temples and the green face rested atop his head like a lumpy tam.

Beans motioned the kid for a drink, then turned to survey his options. As usual, swarms of suburban girls had shown up to the party, all hoping to date a guy from Taylor Street. Beans smiled. Life was good. He had his pick of girls, had two amazing partners and best friends, and he was making more money than he could spend.

He turned back to Gugootz. "Nice costume."

"I don't know how guys wear these masks on a score," he said, stirring a drink with a butter knife. "I can't even see through the slits enough to make a fuckin' drink."

"You gotta cut the eyeholes bigger."

Gugootz pushed the tumbler toward Beans. "VO and water, right?"

"Yeah, thanks. How's it going back there? Making any money?"

"Yep. Just like you said I would."

It was his idea to have Gugootz run the bar for the party. Although drinks were always free during parties, tips were customary. Part of Beans's appeal was that everyone close to him made money. The more he liked you, the more you made.

A pair of hands, soft and warm, slipped under the back folds of his toga. "Happy Halloween, Beansie. Nice boxers." She ran her hands up his torso. "Mm, rippled abdomen, firm pecs—me likey."

Laura was his steadiest girl. They had been dating about a year. Beans wasn't ready to commit, and while Laura knew he fooled around, she remained persistent. She pulled her arms back, and he turned to face her. He looked her up and down. On her feet were a pair of brown suede moccasins. Her matching miniskirt was cut in a jagged line at the hem and topped with a fringed jacket. Fire-red braids hung down on either side of her head, at the back of which stood a tall white feather held in place by a beaded headband.

Beans lost himself for a moment. *God, she is gorgeous.* "Let me guess . . ." Beans put a finger to his chin. "You're a nurse, right?"

"Ha-ha. Very funny. I'm an Indian princess." She spun slowly. "You like?"

"Yeah. It's real cute. You want a drink?"

He asked this as if it would be a chore. Truth was, he wasn't thrilled Laura had shown up. How was he supposed to mingle with the other girls? Now, if he did, he'd have to be careful about it. Beans called to Gugootz, who was talking to a girl at the other end of the bar. He had to yell over the music to be heard.

Gugootz hurried over. "What's up?"

"Do you know how to make a slow southern screw?"

Laura's eyes widened. "How did you know?"

"It's your drink, isn't it?"

She smiled broadly. "Yep."

"I know how to make it," Gugootz said. "But we don't have all the ingredients. It'll have to be a plain southern screw."

Laura dug into her fringed handbag and came up with a baggie full of purple grapes.

"Lookie what I brought, Beansie." She shook the bag provocatively.

"What's that for?"

"I heard you were going as Julius Caesar tonight. You go lie on the bed, and I'll feed them to you." She plucked a grape from its stem, put it to Beans's lips, and pushed it into his mouth. She let her finger hang on his lip for a moment, then replaced it with her lips. Her hands slid behind his ears, plunged into his hair, and pulled him close. Beans swallowed down the grape as they kissed, and his hands slid around her waist.

"Sorry, Laur'. Izzy and Ange just went into the bedroom. They might be in there a while."

Laura crossed her arms in a huff.

"It's no big deal." Beans gave a shrug. "Have a drink. Go dance with your friends. We got all night."

"I can't stay. I was supposed to be at my brother's party in Elmwood Park an hour ago. I told him I'd help out. Fuckin' Angie. Sick bitch. Who knows how long she'll take to get warmed up. I've got half a mind to go in there and slap her around myself just to hurry things along."

Beans loved Laura's sudden shift in attitude when she didn't get what she wanted. Sweet and demure one minute, feisty and blunt the next. But at this moment, he loved even more that she had to leave soon. It was a win-win. He could have her, then mingle.

"We can't go to my place," Beans said. "I told Debbie she could use it tonight to have some friends over. And I don't have my car here. Who drove here tonight—you or one of your girlfriends?"

"Me. Why?"

"Well, we could go for a little ride. Tell your friends you'll be right back."

After Laura disappeared into the crowd, Beans stepped behind the bar, filled two glasses halfway with Southern Comfort, and plunged two ice cubes into each. Laura returned with a wide smile, jingling a set of car keys.

Beans handed her one of the glasses. "Here, chug this and let's go."

They clinked glasses and slugged down the whiskey.

Laura finished hers first, then chased it with the southern screw. "Okay, now we can go."

That was another thing Beans loved about her. She could drink any guy he knew under the table.

A minute or so later, as they were walking down the street, she handed him her car keys. Beans never felt comfortable in a car unless he was doing the driving. He headed west on Taylor Street to Laflin and turned right, all the while fiddling with the dial on the radio. He stopped at the sound of Dick Biondi's voice.

"Thanks for joining us tonight for our special All-Request-Oldies Halloween Show. This next song was requested by so many people I can't begin to name them all. This one goes out to you, Chicago." Dick Biondi commenced with, "On Top of a Pizza" to the tune of "On Top of Old Smokey."

Beans drove down Laflin and turned left where Flournoy Street ended in a cul-de-sac encircled by trees and thick hedges. It was a renowned neighborhood make-out spot they called Ankle Lake.

The curbs around the cul-de-sac were nearly a foot tall. On hot summer days, the neighborhood kids would cover the sewer grates with garbage can lids and open the pump—code for turning on the fire hydrant—and flood the thing, creating a "lake" to cool off in. At night, the place was prized for the privacy provided by the surrounding shrubbery. Beans parked at the far end and slid across the bench seat of Laura's old Pontiac.

"Smoke Gets in Your Eyes" by the Platters played on the radio.

By the time the song was over, they were locked in a passionate embrace. Laura's skirt was hiked up over her hips, revealing that she wasn't wearing underwear. Beans had worked loose the last button on her jacket to discover she was also bare under that.

"What a great, great oldie," came Dick Biondi's cheerful baritone. "Boy, that one really brings me back. This next song goes out to Beans on Taylor Street from Maria in Cicero. Here are the Del Vikings with "Come Go with Me.""

Laura went rigid. She set her hands on Beans's forehead and stiff-armed him away. "Who the fuck is Maria?" She kept him at bay with the one arm while using the other to hold closed the lapel of her jacket.

"That?" He reached an arm toward her waist. "It's nothing."

"Don't you fuckin' touch me." Her lips quivered as she bordered on tears.

Beans, initially amused, was beginning to feel sorry. Very sorry. He had to think fast. "Are you really getting mad at me over something on the radio? I don't know no fuckin' Maria. How is it my fault that some random girl has a crush on me?"

"Bullshit!" she snarled. "You're a pig! I shkeeve you. Get out of my car!"

"Don't say stuff like that." Beans was genuinely hurt. "You don't mean it. You assume it's me. But plenty a guys with last names like mine are called Beans in this neighborhood."

"Right," she said, folding her arms across her chest. "How many could there be?"

"Gotta be a dozen, at least. I got two cousins and an uncle called Beans. Trom*bino*, Beeno, Beans. Get it? Trombino's a common name, y'know."

"Yeah," she said. "And I reeely believe you 'cause I'm reeely that stupid."

"I give up." He threw up his hands. "You win. I don't know what else to say."

"Wait." She turned an ear toward him. "What'd you say?"

"I said I don't know what else to say."

"No, no. The first part."

Beans looked at her. "I said I give up. You wi—"

"That's the part," she said, pointing a finger in his face. "That's what I wanted to hear again. I win." She smiled. "Come here, you jerk."

She pulled his head to her chest, and they picked up right where they left off.

• • •

Beans parked Laura's car on Loomis Street, and together they walked back to the club. The only evidence of activity from out on the street was the faint rhythmic thumping of bass escaping through the walls. As Beans turned the knob and the door broke its plane, a gush of noise and energy engulfed them like the hot gale of a tropical storm.

The place was packed with partygoers—some dancing, some drinking, some doing both—as Steve "Silk" Hurley's "Jack Your

Body" flooded the space from four strategically placed four-foot speakers, each of their woofers shaking visibly. The booming bass vibrated Beans's chest, and he felt sure his heart was changing pace to keep time with the music. The main lights had been turned off and replaced with spotlights of various colors aimed at the mirrored disco ball spinning at the center of the ceiling and spewing an ever-changing multicolored confetti of light while a strobe light pulsating from some unseen location flashed kaleidoscopic images onto the crowd in millisecond intervals.

Beans wended his way artfully through the chaos and made it to the bar. Laura wasn't as successful, having gotten separated from him and swallowed up by the sea of bopping, swaying, gyrating vampires, ghosts, and sexy nurses. A search of the place wielded him only quick, occasional glimpses of suede fringe.

He slid onto an empty stool and was immediately accosted by the ugly girl sitting next to him. He strained to hear her words over the music. "What was that?" he asked, cupping a hand behind his ear.

"I said, 'Can I buy you a drink, handsome?'"

Her garishly painted lips seemed to move in slow motion under the effect of the strobe. Then he noticed the razor stubble on her face. When she laid a heavy, hairy-knuckled hand on Beans's thigh, he was momentarily repulsed. Until he realized he was talking to Cosh, wearing a sandy-blond wig, pleated skirt, and a green cardigan with the letter *L* embroidered above his fake left breast. Beans recalled his earlier interaction with Izzy and Angie in the back and put two and two together.

His partners had come dressed as Laverne and Shirley.

"No, thanks," Beans said. "I'm here with someone."

Cosh peeled opened his sweater, proudly revealing an enormous tissue-stuffed bra. "I bet she ain't got what I got."

"Maybe not." Beans laughed. "But I bet you got something she doesn't."

They swiveled, backs to the bar, and studied the girls on the dance floor, where Izzy was currently cavorting with three different partners.

"That son of a bitch sure can dance," Beans said.

Izzy was the center of attention, bopping and bouncing to the beat while using one of his hands to hold Shirley Feeney's hair to his head.

"Yeah, he's gotta have some shine blood in him somewhere."

They stood and Cosh took Beans by the elbow and led him into the kitchen, where Capo was splayed across his leather jacket—dragged out of the bedroom for the occasion. Capo didn't bother to lift his head, just followed Beans around the room with a pair of heavy-lidded eyes.

"What's wrong with him?" Beans sat in one of two available chairs, the rest having been dragged out front for the party.

"He's fuckin' drunk," Cosh said, claiming the other chair. "People been giving him beer all night."

Beans shook his head. "Man, I hope it was imported. Domestic brew gives him the shits."

Cosh adjusted his bra and tugged at the sleeves of the cardigan where it stretched tight over his biceps. "Did you see the Imp-Gay yet?" he asked, just loud enough for Beans to hear over the music. "Imp-Gay" was Pig Latin for "Gimp," which was their nickname for "Step," whose real name was Vinnie.

"No, why?"

"He's all fuckin' oobatz. Says he's got something. Wants a sit-down."

"He's got something, all right—the fuckin' ap-clay."

64

Cosh chuckled. "Yeah, all that burning and itching." He obscured his mouth by pretending to scratch his nose. "He says it's more ort-zay than he's ever seen."

Zort was Taylor Street Italian for *soldi*—money.

"What the fuck is it?" Beans asked.

Cosh shrugged.

"Probably some old lady's life savings under the mattress," Beans said with a roll of his eyes. "He knows we don't do that kinda shit. The fuckin' guy gives me the creeps."

Contempt for Step and his ilk was common among the "honorable" thieves. Beans was proud of his standards, considered theirs victimless crimes, or at least that the victim had it coming. Or was wealthy enough to afford taking the hit.

"Hey, Beano." Step hobbled into the back and extended a hand to Beans. "How you doin'?"

Beans hesitated. To him, Step's hand might as well be fungus. He forced himself to shake it, then made a note to wash up after their conversation.

Izzy clattered in, struggling in his navy-blue pumps. "This is the last time I buy shoes at Penney's," he uttered in a husky falsetto. "I mean, there is just no substitute for quality." He was eating from a bag of grapes, having obviously bumped into Laura.

"Could you guys sit down for a minute?" Step said. "I need to talk to you. You ain't gonna believe this!"

Izzy, seeing there were no other chairs, plopped down sideways on Beans's lap and threw an arm around him.

Beans grunted from the force of his partner's weight. "Fat fucker."

"That's no way to speak to a lady." Izzy kissed Beans on the cheek, leaving a lipstick smear.

"Come on, guys. This is serious." Step stood, hands on his

hips, looking like a frustrated substitute teacher at the head of an unruly class.

To this, Izzy snatched the laurel from Beans's head, tossed it aside, and ran his fingers through Beans's hair. He then drew open the bag of grapes and proceeded to feed them, one at a time, to Beans—not unlike, Beans realized, a Roman slave girl would to an emperor.

"You won't believe what I unloaded at work today," Step said.

Now he had their attention. In the years before they became aware of Step's more distasteful practices, they would occasionally collaborate with him on certain, more palatable, ventures. Most involved Step's position as a freight handler for American Airlines. Anytime he would come across an interesting piece of cargo, Step would divert it to some out-of-the-way area of the airport, for example, behind a dumpster at the back of food services or under the stairs of the employees' entrance to the terminal. Beans, having access to city vehicles, would then "borrow" a truck or van, and he, Cosh, and Izzy would drive it out to O'Hare, where city of Chicago vehicles were routinely waved past security posts. They would then drive onto the field, nonchalantly load the ill-gotten goods onto the truck, and leave the premises raising nary a suspicion. Once back in the neighborhood, they would unload into a garage, and Beans would return the city vehicle before anyone even knew it was gone.

After Beans swallowed the last grape, Izzy lumbered off his lap and said to Step, "Okay, whattaya got?"

"The airline just got a government contract," Step said, glancing around the room. "So this plane arrives from DC, and I get the call to unload it. When I get there, there's a conveyor set up, running from the cargo pit down to an armored car."

"Oh, fuck," Cosh said.

"So they put me in the pit, and I unload these bundles down the belt." Step paused for effect.

Cosh, clearly growing impatient, got to his feet. "Are you gonna tell us what the fuck was in them, or not?"

"You're gonna want to sit back down, Cheese," Step said.

By now, Beans and his partners were all ears, hanging on Step's every word.

"I unloaded thirty-six . . . forty-pound bundles of . . . twenties . . . fifties . . . and hundreds."

"As in . . . dollar bills?" Cosh asked.

"Yes, bills!" Step said. "What the fuck else?"

Beans shot his partners a skeptical look. "No way."

Step threw up three fingers. "Scout's honor."

"Holy fuck!" exclaimed Izzy, tearing off his wig.

Beans joined in with an, "Oh my God."

Cosh tucked his chin and narrowed his eyes on Step. "How many did you get?"

"None."

They grunted in unison and stared at Step, their enthusiasm extinguished.

"I couldn't! There was an armed guard in the pit with me," Step explained, shifting his weight to favor his good leg. "And one at the other end of the conveyor. That's not the point. They got the contract, see? This is gonna happen every month from now 'til whenever."

The wheels in Beans's head spun and whirred like a sewing machine, weaving together Step's scant swaths of information into a tapestry of possible scenarios. This could be the one he had been waiting for. The score to end all scores. The only thing he knew for sure right now was that his gut wouldn't rest until he got this money. But he needed to know more. Every minute detail. More, certainly, than Step could tell him.

Step. Beans was being handed the biggest score of his life—maybe the biggest score in history. But the plan was already flawed before it could be put into motion. *Fucking Step!* Beans would have to tread carefully.

He locked onto Step's eyes. "Who else have you told about this?"

Izzy and Cosh, familiar with his *look*, refrained from comment.

Step cowered under Beans's scrutiny and shoved his trembling hands into his pockets.

"I didn't tell no one," Step replied, holding his ground. "I swear to God. This is too important. I keep my mouth shut. You guys know that."

For reasons unclear to him, Beans believed the guy. "Good." He surveyed the faces in the room. "Let's keep it that way. None of us talks to anyone about this. In fact, this is the last time we talk about it here at the club. Too risky." He returned his steely gaze to Step. "Even the guys at work. I'm sure this'll be the big buzz around there. If they talk about it around you, act disinterested, like it's no big deal." He relaxed and stood back. "I'll be gone all day tomorrow. We'll meet at my house on Sunday and get all the details. Got it?"

They all nodded in agreement, after which, Step limped out of the back and vanished amid the throng of partygoers.

Beans returned to the bar, where Laura was standing on her own beside a group of giggling girls. *She's still here?* "Yo, Gugootz!" Beans made a gesture with his thumb and pinkie—a signal for another drink—then turned to Laura. "I thought you'd be gone by now."

She pursed her lips and looked away.

The opening beat of Divine's "Native Love" shook the woofers, and Beans watched as the girls at the bar waded onto the dance floor, along with just about everyone else in the place. Beans couldn't help notice, given the conversation that had just taken place, the oddly appropriately lyrics. "Step by step, come on!"

He gave Laura a wink. "You wanna boogie with me?"

She crossed her arms and stared him down.

The volume of the music soared, and suddenly the strobe light seemed to flash at quicker intervals, and the disco ball seemed to spin faster.

"What did I do now?" he asked.

She said something he couldn't make out over the blaring music while jutting her chin toward the dance floor.

He pulled her into the kitchen. "Say again?"

"Do you know those girls who were standing next to me?"

"Not well. I've seen them around. Why?"

"You wanna know what they were saying?"

Not particularly. Well, maybe. "What? What were they saying?"

"Well, let's see. Disco Duck was flapping her wings and gums, gushing about Cosh's big muscles. And then there was the hobo. 'Ooh, Izzy's so tall. And have you ever seen him with his shirt off? Ooh.' And then there was Lily Munster, who says you remind her of Dean Martin. Also, she wants to do you."

Dean Martin, huh? I'll take it. "That's it?" Beans said, stifling a smile. "That's what you're pissed about?"

"Oh, and Frito Bandito with the sombrero and giant boobs said she's had all three of you."

Beans searched his memory. It was possible. He filed away the information, along with images of the girls, in his mental file cabinet.

"They were just talkin'." He took Laura's hand. "It doesn't mean anything."

"Were any of them Maria from Cicero?"

Beans rolled his eyes. "I wouldn't know. Because I don't know their names, and I don't know any Maria from Cicero." He led her out of the back and onto the dance floor, where she danced the remainder of the song with her back to him.

CHAPTER 7

A FRITAD' FOR FOUR

ON SUNDAY MORNING, Beans awoke at sunrise.

Despite two nights of consecutive partying, he felt fresh and alert. He had slept well, lulled by swirling visions of airplanes, armored cars, and sacks full of cash.

He walked through the apartment in his boxers, stopping to switch on the coffeemaker on his way to the bathroom, where he relieved himself with the door wide open—one of the perks of living alone. Well, sort of alone. His apartment was in the basement of a three-flat greystone owned by his parents. In the apartment directly above him lived his grandmother, and above that, his mom, dad, and Debbie.

It was common in the neighborhood for an entire apartment building to be occupied by members of the same family. For Beans, it was an ideal situation. He could have his privacy while also enjoying the benefits of living close to his folks, sister, and his gram. There was often a gourmet meal to be had, prepared either by his grandmother or mother, and his younger sister doted on him.

After filling his mug, he grabbed the remote, plopped down into the recliner, and flipped through the channels. Stations lately had taken to replaying Saturday cartoons on Sunday. He stopped when he spotted Bugs Bunny. At the sound of "The Merry-Go-Round Broke Down," he closed his eyes. It was comfort food for his ears, bringing back childhood memories of him and Debbie before school each morning, eating breakfast on TV trays while watching the Ray Rayner show.

The thought of Step snapped him back to the present.

The guys weren't set to arrive until ten o'clock, so he had plenty of time to sweep the place. He drained his coffee and returned to the bedroom, where he kneeled beside the bed, reached under, and pulled out a black Samsonite suitcase. He removed from it a bulletproof vest that rested atop a menagerie of electronic gadgets—police scanners, walkie-talkies, headband flashlights. There were also eavesdropping devices, such as telephone taps, wireless microphones, and miniature cameras. He fished around until he found two rectangular black boxes, each the size of a pocket transistor radio. One—with dials, LEDs, and an antenna—was a bug detector. The other, with just a single knob, was a bug smasher. Or at least that's what he called it.

He carried them to the kitchen, replaced their old batteries with fresh ones from the refrigerator, then extended the bug detector's antenna, turned on the device, and slowly moved around the apartment while swinging the unit back and forth, careful to pause near the telephone, lamps, and wall sockets. He probed under tables and other furniture. It took three trips around the apartment to satisfy him that the space was clear.

He then turned on the smasher and set it on the kitchen windowsill behind his boombox. The smasher emitted waves of varying frequencies designed to disable the signal transmissions of any eavesdropping devices the detector might have missed—or that might be brought into the meeting. This was probably overkill at this early stage, but Beans couldn't take any chances. Their steady stream of successes, which Cosh and Izzy attributed to supernatural luck, he knew was more likely due to exercising extreme caution. He switched on the boombox.

"Just because you're paranoid doesn't mean nobody's watching you," he said aloud to himself.

Lastly, he pulled down all the window shades.

• • •

The boys arrived just as Beans was dividing a fritad' of chopped Italian sausage and eggs into four servings. He set a plateful in front of each of the four chairs at the table, where he had already set out cutlery and napkins.

Izzy and Cosh, as usual, made themselves at home, with Izzy going straight to the fridge for the gallon of orange juice Beans kept there just for him.

"Hey, Iz," Cosh said, grabbing glasses and mugs from the cupboard. "Grab the milk too." He put them on the table and turned to Step. "Whattaya want to drink?"

"Coffee's fine." Step pointed at the table. "What's all this?"

"Sit," Cosh said. "Try it."

Step lowered himself into one of the chairs and put his nose close to the spicy aroma of the sausage. He looked up quizzically at Beans, who was pouring the coffee.

"Never plan a score when you're hungry," Beans explained.

"And never negotiate when you're not." Cosh bobbed his head from side to side with each word—a mocking reminder that he'd heard Beans's sayings a thousand times over.

"Make fun all you want," Beans said. "But you know all the shit I say is true."

Izzy and Cosh sat across from each other on the long sides of the table, and Beans and Step sat at each end.

"Okay, Step. We need every single detail, even the little ones you might think aren't important."

Izzy held up an index finger. "Whoa. Hold on a sec, Beans."

"Whatsa matter?"

"You got any bread?"

Beans stood and passed over the two-pound loaf of Italian bread from the counter, then opened a drawer, drew out a long, serrated knife, and set it on the table in front of Izzy.

"Taylor and Western?" Izzy was inquiring as to the bakery of origin.

"Where else?" Beans said, turning back to Step. "Okay, Step. First of all, where does all this zort come from?"

Izzy coyishly held up a finger. "Um . . . Beansie?"

"Yes, Izzy?" Beans was growing annoyed.

"Got any butter?"

"In the fridge," he said, pointing with his thumb. "Get it yourself."

"Jeez," Izzy said, pushing to his feet. "No need to get obstreperous."

"While you're up, get yourself a butter knife too."

Step waited for Izzy to sit before answering Beans's question. "I guess it comes from a mint in DC. I don't know for sure."

"Okay. Well, how does it *feel*?"

Step scrunched up his nose. "Feel?"

"Yeah. Is it all neat and packed real tight, like new, or . . ."

"So far as I could tell, it was stacked in square bundles and wrapped in blue plastic."

This was not how Beans imagined it in his dreams. "Whattaya mean—blue plastic?"

"You know, like fuckin' Saran Wrap, only blue."

"So you could see through it?"

"Yeah. Like the shit they use to wrap a kid's Easter basket. Comes in pink and green and whatever other color. The blue color made the color of the money look different."

"Weird. I wonder why they do that?" Beans adjusted his mental image of the cash to include blue plastic and continued, "So how are the bundles loaded—in one of those cargo containers, or loose?"

"Loose."

"And it's right in there with the rest of the luggage and freight?"

"Yep. 'Cept it's separated by a net."

Beans sipped his coffee. Neither he nor Step had yet to touch their plates.

"This fuckin' zort might be useless if it's brand new with sequential serial numbers." Cosh picked out a piece of sausage and popped it into his mouth.

Meanwhile, Izzy was fully invested in his meal. Having cut two slices of bread, buttered them, and stuffed his entire portion of fritad' between the two, he now ate it like a sandwich. "Ott ufelef; eecud aunder ik," he mumbled through a mouthful. He tried to push the half-chewed bread and fritad' to one side of his mouth, but his cheeks were at full capacity; there was nowhere for it to go. He tilted his head to one side as if doing so would widen his throat, and managed, slowly, to swallow one cheekful, wincing as it went down.

Step's eyes bounced from Cosh to Beans, then back to Cosh. "What the fuck did he say?"

"He said, 'Not useless; we could launder it.'" Cosh was fluent in Izzy. "Hot as it might be, though, we wouldn't get much for it."

Beans looked at Izzy's plate, now empty, and said, "If you ever quit working out, you're gonna be a fat fuckin' dirigible."

Izzy washed down the remaining food in his mouth with orange juice. "What the fuck is a dirigible?"

"It's a fuckin' blimp," Cosh said. "And he's right, you're gonna have to change your name to Goodyear. Seriously, Iz, can't be healthy, eatin' like that. You look like one of them snakes on Mutual of Omaha after they swallow a whole pig."

Izzy ignored the insults. "Or, we could sit on it for five years and let it cool off."

"I've got some ideas about that," Beans said. "But we need to get our hands on it first." He turned his head to Step. "So, the guard was in the plane with you the whole time?"

"Yeah. One in the pit and one at the bottom of the conveyer with one of those clicker things in his hand counting the bundles as they came down."

"Were they G-men or private guards, like Brinks or Purolator?"

"The guy in the pit with me was Brinks. Not sure about the other. He was wearing a suit. G-man maybe?"

"Do you know where they take the loot?"

"Nope."

"What kind of plane?"

"Seven-twenty-seven."

"Flight number?"

"Three-eleven."

Beans committed those numbers to memory. "Is there any way, like a schedule or written arrangement, that we could find out in advance when they're gonna make the shipments?"

"Probably in the office somewhere, but I don't find out until the plane lands."

Cosh broke off a piece of fritad' with his fork, speared it, and aimed it at Step. "You said you could see through the plastic. Did the zort have bands around it, like at the bank?"

"Yeah, Cheese," Step said. "It did. Banded into stacks about this big." He held his thumb and forefinger about two inches apart. "And all those little stacks were stacked up together."

Cosh swallowed down the bite. "Was there any writing on the bands? Could you read them?"

"There was a logo. A circle with points all around it, y'know, like a sprocket. There was writing around the circle, but I couldn't read it. And it had one big letter in the center. I don't remember what it was."

Izzy dug into his pocket and pulled out a wad of bills folded around his driver's license and held in place with a wide rubber band. He peeled off some twenties and examined them.

Beans was trying to picture the scene in his head. Something wasn't adding up. "Okay, Step. You're in the pit with one guard, and the G-man is at the other end of the conveyor with a counter, right?"

"Right."

"What happens to the bundles when they fall into the truck?"

"What do you mean?"

"Well, do they just flop into a big pile or what?"

"I don't know."

"No, it can't be," Beans said. "There's gotta be another guard inside the truck, receiving the bundles off the conveyor and stacking them up so they're nice and neat."

"I never thought about that, Beans." Step's face flushed. "You gotta be right. Sorry."

The presence of a third man was no minor detail.

"That's okay. That's why we're here today, to figure this all out." Beans spoke to Step as if he were speaking to a child. Comparatively, in terms of expertise, Step *was* a child. "We gotta find out if the guy in the suit rides in the truck with the other two."

Izzy looked up from the money in his hand. "Step, that letter in the circle—was it a *G*?"

Step's face looked as if he'd just stepped on a nail. "Holy fuck, Iz! It *was* a *G*!"

"I know where they take the money," Izzy said.

"Where?" Beans, Cosh, and Step asked in unison.

"Downtown. LaSalle and Jackson."

"How the fuck do you know that?" Step asked.

"Look." Izzy used his forearm to brush aside his empty plate and glass and laid out four twenties faceup on the table. He pointed to the logo on the left side of each. "Is this the logo you saw, Step?"

Step craned his neck. "Uh-huh."

"That's the logo for the Federal Reserve bank." Izzy stood and pointed to the first bill. "You see this one with the *J* in the middle? It's from Kansas City."

"How do you know?" Step asked.

"Because it says so right underneath. And this one, with a *B*, is from New York. The *F* is from Atlanta, Georgia." He pointed to the bills in succession. "And this one, with the *G*?" He smiled wryly. "It's for the Federal Reserve bank in Chicago, which I happen to know is located on the corner of LaSalle and Jackson."

"So they print the zort in DC," Cosh said, nodding, "and ship it out from there to all the main banks in the country, Chicago being one of 'em."

Step's jaw hung open in awe. "You know what? Grand Avenue, fuckin' Green Gang, the Jew, all of 'em—they're fuckin' amateurs. You guys are the best!"

Beans studied Step with a critical eye. Was he just flattering them or was he really so dense that this little bit of common sense astonished him? Did he not plan before his own scores? Was the rest of his crew as stupid as Step?

"Holy fuck," Step continued, "am I glad I hooked up with you guys. We're gonna knock these fuckin' guards over so hard, they won't know what hit 'em."

"Listen," Izzy said, "I don't want to bust your bubble, but a score like this is a pipe dream. I mean, you're talking about robbing the Federal Reserve. Millions of dollars, armed guards, fuckin' G-men, treasury . . ."

Step's face reddened. "What, you're fuckin' chickening out?"

"No," Izzy said. "I'm just telling you, it might never happen. You say we're the best. You know *why* we're the best? Because nobody's ever heard of us. You understand?"

"No, I don't fuckin' understand."

"We don't draw attention to ourselves. We don't pull no flashy cowboy shit. If a job's too risky, we take a pass. And we don't do stickups." Izzy looked at Beans.

"Look, I'm a burglar," Beans said. "Not a killer. There's a big difference between burglary and armed robbery. About ten years, in fact. Not to mention, armed robberies have a habit of turning into murder. I don't kill people for money."

"Then what the fuck am I doing here?" Step was on his feet. "If you guys weren't interested, you should have told me that off the bat. Now I told you my score." He slammed an open palm down on the table, the dishes and cutlery jumping and clanging from the force. "You're tryin' to fuck me! You think you're gonna cut me out of my own score?"

Beans, staring up at Step, remained calm in his seat. It was clear a switch had been flipped in the guy's brain.

"You don't know who you're fuckin' with!" Step continued, spittle balling up in the corners of his mouth. "You don't fuck me. I fuck you!" He pointed a finger at Beans. "I'll fuckin' kill you! I'll kill every one of you!"

Izzy and Cosh sprang to their feet, each grabbing an arm. Then Izzy slid behind Step and thrust a knee into his spine while applying a choke hold.

Step struggled but was held immobilized.

Beans, still seated, picked up the bread knife. "You stupid motherfucker." He spoke with the throaty calm of a man who had acquiesced to the beast within. "You come into my home, eat at my table, and then threaten to kill me?"

Step went limp. He attempted to speak against Izzy's choke hold. "I mnfth . . . I thmfk."

Beans stood, relaxed except for the fingers of his right hand, which were locked around the knife's handle. "And you think I'm gonna give you the *chance* to kill me?" He moved slowly toward Step as he spoke. "You're gonna leave here in a dozen different bags."

Step thrashed his head from side to side, causing Izzy's grip to loosen just enough for him to get words out. "I'm sorry! I'm sorry! I didn't mean it!"

Beans pushed the point of the knife against Step's sternum.

"You can't take me serious," Step rambled on. "When I get upset I say stupid things, but I don't mean 'em. I don't even know what I'm saying. I'm an idiot. You can't take me serious."

He swallowed hard, looking down at the knife. "You said you're not a killer."

"I'm not a killer," Beans said. "But I never said I wouldn't defend myself. When someone threatens to kill me, I take it serious." He put pressure on the knife. Not enough to plunge it in, just enough to pierce the thin skin over his breastplate and draw blood, which seeped through Step's heavy cable-knit sweater.

"You're right! I'm sorry! It was a stupid thing to say, but really, I didn't mean it."

There was a knock at the door.

Keeping the knife to Step's chest, Beans called over his shoulder, "Who is it?"

"It's me, Beans. Can I come in?"

Debbie. Beans, hearing the familiar jingle of keys in his sister's hand, backed up a pace and held the knife to Step's face. "Don't ever threaten us again."

"I-I won't," Step stammered. "I promise."

"Sit back down," Beans ordered. "And don't say a fuckin' word."

Izzy and Cosh released him and Step, trembling, sank into his chair.

"Come on in, Deb," Beans called out.

Debbie turned the key in the lock, stepped inside, and glanced around the room, clearly aware that she had interrupted something. "Hey, guys." She was dressed down today, but nonetheless managed to look attractive in her light-gray sweatsuit.

Step's eyes darted to Debbie and then away. He put a finger to his chest and pushed on the knife's point of entry.

Debbie looked at Beans. "Ma's making gravy. We're eating at three. She wants to know if you'll be there."

"Since when have I ever missed a Sunday?"

Debbie breezed past Beans to Izzy and kissed him on the cheek. "Hi, Iz."

"Hi, hon. How you doin'?"

"Good." Debbie then looked to Step, who was staring down at his hands. "Hello, Vinnie."

Step looked up, forced a smile, and returned his gaze downward.

She turned her attention to Cosh. "Hello, Nicholas." Her tone was provocative, yet reproving, with a side of sisterly.

"Hello, Deborah." His tone mocked hers.

She let down her guard, approached, and slunk into his lap. Gazing into his eyes, she said, "You know, my birthday is coming up. I'll be eighteen soon. You know what that means?"

"You'll be able to vote?"

"It means . . . I'll be a grown woman, and Beans won't be able to stop me from running away with you."

Beans, still holding the knife, pointed it in their direction. "I don't care if you're eighteen or a hundred and eighteen, the only thing running away with you is your imagination." He set down the knife and cleared his throat. "There's plenty of other chairs here, by the way."

Debbie stuck out her tongue at Beans. "Blah, blah, blah. Don't worry, Nicholas. He can't wait to have you for a brother-in-law. You know, we should name our firstborn after him."

Izzy chuckled. "Cheesy Beans. Sounds like something from Taco Bell."

Step let out a nervous snicker, cut it short, then looked to Beans for a reaction.

Despite himself, Beans cracked a smile, trying to hold back his own laughter.

Debbie was on her feet and headed for the door. "I'll tell Ma you'll be there." She whipped her long dark hair behind her. "If you want to come, Nicholas, I'll set up a table on the veranda just for the two of us." She motioned in the direction of their dilapidated back porch.

"Sounds romantic," Cosh said. "But I'm dining at casa Geraldi today."

Beans caught Step eyeing his sister's ass as she walked out the door. He cleared his throat again to break the spell, then reclaimed his seat at the end of the table. "Listen, Step," he said, "we're not going to steal your score. You came to us because you trust us, right?"

"Of course, Beans. I got carried away. Again, I'm sorry. It's just that I'm used to working with guys who are always trying to fuck each other. That's why I work alone whenever I can. I know you guys ain't like that. Y'know what my crew does after every job?"

"What's that?"

"We go to Phil's garage and strip naked so we can all check each other's clothes to make sure no one's holding out."

"Fuck," Beans said. "I couldn't operate like that. I trust these two motherfuckers with my life."

"I know. You guys been together since kiddy-garden. I don't have that luxury. But I gotta work. I gotta make money. The best I can do is to try to find guys who are at least standup enough not to rat me out. My guys would never rat, but they can't be trusted with money."

"That's a fuckin' shame," Beans said.

Cosh drained his coffee and brought the cup back down. "All we're trying to say is we're gonna look at all the possible ways to make this happen. If we can't find a way to do it our way, without whacking the guards, or whatever, we reserve the right to back out."

"That don't mean you can't do it on your own," Izzy said. "If we say no, which we're not saying so far, you could still do this thing yourself. Just use your own guys or put together whoever you want and do it without us. I think I can speak for all of us when I say that we give you our word. If we back out, we'll never mention it to anyone else. This is your score. You do what you want with it."

Cosh and Beans nodded in agreement.

"Or," Beans said, "if you still think we're trying to fuck you, you can walk right now. Either way, you have our word. No hard feelings—from either side, right?"

"No, guys. I wanna work with you. I know you ain't gonna pass on it. It's too fuckin' big."

Beans clenched his jaw. "Let me explain something to you, Step. I see armored cars all day long. Banks, jewelry stores. I wanna grab everything I see. But I don't. You gotta pick your spots, balance the risk against the reward. *Gabeesh*?"

"Yeah, I guess."

"It's not like we're starvin'. We got plenty of irons in the fire right now. I'm sure you do too. Do I want more? You bet. You gotta keep the ball moving 'til you get to the end zone. But"—Beans held up a finger—"we're not gonna jeopardize everything by being stupid. There's no reward big enough to balance the risk of a murder rap. Or worse, getting into a shootout with G-men."

Step had been nodding to all of this, but Beans worried he hadn't really heard a word. *Guy's got a damn short attention span.*

"So what's our next move?" Step asked.

"We need more information. I want you to nose around at work and figure out how we can get some advance notice of these shipments. That's important. See if there's a contract on file in the office, or a schedule, anything. But be careful not to arouse suspicion. Also, get me the names of everyone who works in that office."

"Got it."

Beans got up and pulled open his junk drawer. He shuffled through paper, pens, safety pins, and other random objects until he found what he was looking for. "Here, take this." He handed Step a ring made from a wide aluminum band with a curved razor blade set into it perpendicular, so that it protruded from the wearer's finger.

"Fuck!" Step said. "You could do a lotta damage with this thing. What the fuck is it?"

"Paperboys use 'em to cut the strings on the newspaper bundles."

"What am I supposed to do with it?"

"Keep it at work with you. Next time you get called to unload the zort, put it on backward with the blade inside your palm. It'll look like a regular ring. I want you to cut me off some of that blue plastic wrapping. I wanna check it out. Just a little piece, so no one will notice. Can you do that?"

"Yeah, okay. Sure."

"There's not much else we can do right now. I'll run the route from the airport to the bank on LaSalle. Check out the building, see where the trucks pull in." He looked from Cosh to Izzy. "Can you guys think of anything else?"

They all looked at each other and shrugged.

"Then we're done here," Beans said. "Just go about business as usual. But be careful. We don't want to get picked up for something else before we get a chance to do this one."

Step stood to leave.

"By the way, Step," Beans said. "How's your sheet?"

"Whattaya mean?"

"You ever been convicted of anything? If this goes down, the first place they'll look is at the employees' records."

"Nah, I'm clean," he said. "I been picked up for stupid little shit, y'know, when we were kids. But nothin' serious."

"Good," Beans said. "That's good."

Step shook Izzy's hand, then Cosh's. He approached Beans and threw his arms around him, squeezing hard and slapping his back with both hands. "Thanks for not killing me, Beans."

Beans stiffened in his grip and pushed away, giving his wounded chest a pat. "Let's just forget all about that."

After Step walked out, Beans poured Cosh and himself more coffee.

"Well," Beans said. "Whattaya think?"

Izzy refilled his glass with orange juice. "You know what I think."

"The motherfucker's got a loose wire in his circuit board." Cosh dumped three tablespoons of sugar into his mug and stirred.

"And he's about as sharp as a doorknob," Beans added. "Crazy and stupid—a dangerous combination." He drew a deep breath and let it go. "I don't know how yet, but we're gonna get that money."

"Damn right, we are." Izzy glanced left, grabbed Step's untouched plate, and transferred its contents onto his own.

CHAPTER 8

TOMATO PUREE

ON MONDAY, BEANS met Pat Gibbons as usual at the Lucky Star, where they made small talk after lunch over a cup of oolong tea.

"Did you hear about that girl from your neighborhood?" Pat asked.

"What girl?"

"Emma Pisa. Frankie Pisa's wife."

"What about her?"

Beans had dated Emma a few years back—the only time he'd broken his rule about going with married women. She hated her husband so much that she gave Beans the combination to his safe. But Beans never acted on the intel because he didn't trust her.

"Found dead with a needle in her arm."

Beans's stomach dropped. "Holy shit."

"Fucking drug dealer husband of hers got her hooked. What do you guys call him, Frankie Piece-a-Pizza? Should be Frankie Piece-a-Shit. I hear he used to smack her around pretty good too."

"I knew her pretty well, actually. She was a good kid 'til she got mixed up with that asshole. Thanks for letting me know."

The gears were grinding in Beans's brain. What were the odds, he wondered, Emma's husband had changed the combination on that safe?

"Yeah, the narcs are all talking about it," Pat continued. "They've been trying to nail the husband for a long time."

Beans slid his clipboard across the table. On it were his completed tow reports and under them a fifty-dollar bill—the agreed-upon amount. Another fifty for his Arizona fund, Beans presumed.

Pat passed Beans a short stack of tow orders, along with one blank one. Pat never asked what the blanks were for.

Along with the blank orders, it was understood that Pat would do whatever he could to protect Beans if any trouble popped up—if he wanted the fifties to keep coming, that was. He could tip him off if the heat was on, or help him finagle his way out of a pinch with other cops. As far as Beans was concerned, it was just the cost of doing business, an insurance policy. Well worth 10 percent of the five hundred the chop shop paid him for each car he brought in.

The waiter brought their checks. The Lucky Star had a strict policy of issuing separate checks to each customer, no matter how large the party. Beans assumed this was to prevent arguments among the cheapskate cops who made up the majority of their patronage.

Pat snatched up both checks, reached across the table, and set a hand on Beans's wrist. "I got a little problem. Maybe you can help me out?"

"Hit me," Beans said. "You know I'll do whatever I can."

"My car—the fuckin' gas tank leaks like a sieve."

"Fuck. That's dangerous. You could blow up. Don't drive it."

"I'm not." Pat held the checks at a distance and squinted to see the totals. "But I need a new gas tank. So if you should happen to come across one in your travels . . ."

"Gotcha covered. Might take a few days, though." The chop shop he brought the cars to used a junkyard as a front. They'd probably give Beans a gas tank for free. "What kind of car?"

"Buick wagon. I really appreciate this, Beans."

"No problem. What year?"

"Seventy-eight."

"I'm on it."

A few minutes later, Beans sat in his truck outside the Lucky Star and flipped through the latest round of orders. It looked to be an easy day. The vehicles were all nearby, and from what he could tell, there were no floats—cars without wheels.

He started out toward the address of the first tow while keeping an eye out for a 1980 Olds Cutlass. That was the car de jour, the one Louie at the chop shop needed him to bring in. The main challenge with this hustle was that he couldn't just bring in any old car and get the five hundred. He had to fill specific requests, and there was a new one each time.

• • •

"Did you notice their giardiniera shelf?" Izzy asked.

"No, what about it?" Cosh downshifted into a turn.

As the truck slowed and the engine revved, Izzy's body was pulled forward by its own momentum, then pressed against the door as Cosh rounded the corner.

"He had about twenty jars of Battaglia's brand," Izzy said, referring to their last stop. "He hasn't ordered a case from us in over a month." He rested his feet on the dashboard and scooched his rump down in the seat.

Cosh chuckled to himself. His friend looked like a half-open pocketknife.

"I guess we're just gonna have to remind him that people like ours better."

"Yeah." Izzy reached into the cooler between them and retrieved his orange juice and a stick of pepperoni. "And we might have to pay a visit to that Battaglia salesman again too."

They were headed back to Geraldi's, a deli business that had been in Cosh's family for generations. Cosh had been working there for his dad, Sam, since the day his age reached double digits. Izzy, meanwhile, had gotten his job there at twelve, in part because he'd been friends with Cosh since kindergarten, in part because he was practically a member of the family anyway, and in part because his father, Dickie, had gotten himself thrown into prison. Dickie had been a childhood friend of Sam's, who didn't hesitate to take Izzy under his wing.

When Izzy had first started working at Geraldi's, it was just a little neighborhood deli. Over the years, he and Cosh had grown into skilled salesmen, and the business had blossomed into a citywide wholesaler.

"What do you think about the thing with the Imp-Gay?" Cosh asked, keeping his eyes fixed on the road ahead.

"I like the zort."

"Yeah . . ."

"The motherfucker's a wild card, though." Izzy bit off a piece of pepperoni. "Gives me the willies. I think we should do it ourselves."

"I hear you, brother," Cosh said. "But I don't like cuttin' a guy outta his own score. Besides, he's on the inside. We need him for info."

"Let's see what Beans comes up with. Maybe he can figure a way to keep ol' Gimpy involved without giving him too much responsibility."

Cosh glanced to Izzy with a nod. "If Beans can't come up with something, no one can."

"I don't know," Izzy said. "I think maybe this one's got him stumped."

"Stumped? Beans? Are you kiddin' me? Remember that time with the shotgun?"

"Yeah." Izzy smiled. "He does seem to have an angel on his shoulder."

"This could make us for the rest of our lives, y'know. How many bills you think are in forty pounds?"

"Fuck if I know." Izzy shoved the remainder of the pepperoni in his mouth, chewed twice, and swallowed with a thud. "We gotta make sure we don't grab bags full of one-dollar bills. And how we even gonna know what they're shipping—ones, fives, or hundreds?"

"Thirty forty-pound bags of ones is still a lotta zort," Cosh said.

They grew quiet for a time, and Cosh—and he suspected Izzy as well—mused about a future with all that money.

"Say we get a few million each," Izzy asked, breaking the silence. "What would you do with it?"

"I'd buy a fuckin' yacht and hire a crew of naked broads to sail me to Bimini." It was against Cosh's nature to lie, but there was no way in hell he could tell Izzy what he was really thinking—modest house, bunch of kids . . . Cosh and Debbie, happily ever after. Maybe, if Cosh had all that money, Beans wouldn't consider him just another bum from the neighborhood. He would finally feel comfortable telling his best friend that he was in love with his sister.

Izzy reached back into the cooler. "Lookie what I brought." He held up a gourd-shaped ball of cheese wrapped in netting. "Coshcaval, your fave. Hanker for a hunka? Slab or slice or chunka?"

"You're worried about our giardiniera sales," Cosh said. "The problem is you eatin' all the fuckin' profits."

"Speaking of which, whattaya wanna do for lunch?"

"Lunch?" Cosh said with a laugh. "What do you call a pound of cheese and a stick of pepperoni?"

"An appetizer," Izzy replied. "Seriously, I need a meal. I was thinking Greektown. Whattaya say?"

Cosh turned down Taylor Street and passed by the Jane Addams housing project. Built in the thirties, the public housing development had changed in demographics over the years, from Italian to Black, when the Italians moved out into the surrounding neighborhood. Now, the Blacks and Italians coexisted peacefully by means of an unspoken, mutually agreed upon, voluntary segregation. Taylor Street itself, because of its concentration of stores and businesses, had become a neutral zone. It was understood, however, that the neighborhood's side streets were off-limits to Blacks, while the inner maze of the projects was off-limits to Italians.

"I thought we were gonna spar today." Cosh wasn't as skilled or as fast, and definitely not as tall as Izzy. But at five feet eight and 230 pounds, he could pretty much take whatever Izzy dished out. His mother used to joke that he was built like a fireplug and just as immovable. According to Izzy himself, Cosh's punches were like mule kicks.

"Yeah, so?" Izzy said.

"How you gonna spar on a full stomach?"

"My body's like a Ferrari. It needs fuel in order to run. The good

stuff—high octane. None of that faggy hippie health food shit."
Izzy lifted his shirt to reveal his sculpted abdomen. "See this fuel
tank? Made from steel girders."

"Yeah, right," Cosh said, giving Izzy's middle a whack. "That's
why the last time I hit you with a body shot you almost shit your
pants."

"You mean that one time you connected with a lucky punch?"
Izzy sniffed. "I must've had a little flu bug that day." He set the
cheese back in the cooler. "What the fuck is a Bimini, anyway?"

"It's an island in the Bahamas."

"And how do you know about it?"

"Remember that Jew broad I was seeing, from Lake Shore
Drive? Her father has a sailboat, and that's where he goes."

"Bimini . . . Bimini. The name does ring a bell." Izzy sat quietly
for a moment, then clapped his hands. "I remember! I saw it on
In Search Of . . . You know that place is in the Bermuda Triangle,
right?"

"Get the fuck outta here!"

"Serious. They went scuba diving and found these ancient
ruins. They said that's why the place is cursed, because so many
people died there in some earthquake or tidal wave, or something.
There's like a hundred thousand ghosts floatin' around that whole
area, and all those lost souls created some kind of magnetic field
that makes planes crash and boats sink."

He suspected Izzy was embellishing the story—anything
to exploit Cosh's belief in the supernatural. Nonetheless, Cosh
brought his left hand to his mouth and kissed the gold cross ring
on his pinkie finger. Then he switched hands on the steering wheel
and brought his right hand to his mouth. On this pinkie, he wore
a gold ring bearing the image of Saint Dismas, the Penitent Thief,

who hung bare-chested and lashed to a cross, enhaloed by a background of tiny diamond chips. Anyone who cared to count them would find there were thirteen chips in all.

He made a fist, brought the ring to his lips, then made the sign of the cross. "Fuck Bimini," he said. "I'll go to Mexico."

He turned left on Loomis and into the rut-worn cobblestone alley behind Taylor Street. The physical structures and features of the neighborhood hadn't changed much since the thirties, and nowhere was this more obvious than in the alleyways. The truck hobbled and lurched over the uneven stone path while, inside the cab, he and Izzy bounced like popcorn cooking in a lidded, oiled pan. Cosh threaded the hulking truck down the narrow canyon formed by brick garages and fences on either side. Fifty-five-gallon steel drum garbage cans stood in staggered huddles of three and four in the gaps created where one garage ended and the next began. Cosh navigated between them, often coming within inches of knocking them over as they bobbed and weaved toward the garage that served as Geraldi's warehouse.

As they neared the door, Cosh spotted a young Black man lurking behind a neighboring telephone pole. When Cosh made eye contact, the man pivoted and began riffling through a nearby garbage can.

"This motherfucker's up to something." Cosh sped up briefly and stopped beside the guy. He and Izzy got out of the truck and approached, while the man, whistling loudly, continued to pick through the trash.

"What the fuck you doin' back here, man?" Cosh asked.

"Just lookin' for some 'luminum cans, that's all."

"Bullshit," Cosh said.

The small inset door cut into the overhead garage door swung open, and two more young Black men emerged, arms laden with boxes full of merchandise.

"This who you were whistling for, motherfucker?" Cosh asked.

The two men dropped their boxes.

"Leave him alone!" One of them, wearing a blue knit cap, pulled a knife from the front pocket of his jeans.

Izzy ran at the two, while Cosh blasted the lookout by the garbage can with his right fist. The guy's lower jaw separated sideways from the upper, and he fell forward, his face smacking the stones below.

Cosh turned to help Izzy, who stood over the unconscious bodies of the other two.

"I'm gettin' really sick of this shit," Izzy said. "This is what—the third time in six months?"

"You'd think these junkies would talk to each other, tell the others what they'll get if they rob us."

The kid with the knife, still clutched in his hand, began to come to. "Motherfuckers." He pushed himself to a knee and pointed the knife at Izzy.

Cosh lifted one of the steel drums and dropped it on the guy. The can drove his head into the cobblestone and bounced off, clanking loudly as it rolled away.

"Man, you hit like a girl." Cosh threw Izzy a smirk. "Can't even knock out a fuckin' junkie."

"I knocked out two," Izzy huffed. "You only got one."

"We'll call it even at one and a half each." Cosh pointed to Izzy's chest. "Got a little rip there."

Izzy looked down. "Shit." He unzipped and opened his jacket. "That cocksucker cut me!" The front of his white T-shirt was slit and soaked with a blackish-burgundy stain that grew larger as they looked at it.

"Let me see." Cosh helped Izzy out of his jacket, then gingerly lifted his shirt. "Arms up." He pulled it up off Izzy's head, rolled it into a ball, and used the torn fabric to swab around the area around the wound. "Does it hurt?"

"Don't let any blood get on the ivory. It's hard to get the stains out." Izzy snagged the ivory-handled Colt 1911 out of his waistband and repositioned it to the small of his back.

"Does it hurt?" Cosh asked again.

"Nah, I didn't even feel it at first. Now there's just a little sting."

Cosh cleared away as much blood as he could, revealing a four-inch slash across Izzy's left pec. He put a fingertip on each side of the wound and separated the skin to see how deep it was. "Not bad at all. Just skin. He didn't even get down to the meat. You're one lucky motherfucker. This thing's right over your heart. The guy was ready to kill for a case of tomato puree." He straightened and smiled, relieved his friend wasn't too hurt, and also to reassure Izzy. But where he expected to see fear in his friend's eyes—or at least concern for being cut—he saw only fury.

"Tomato puree?" Izzy marched over to the knife wielder, who now lay on his side, unconscious, in a fetal position. "Tomato puree?" He kicked the kid in the gut. "Tomato puree!" Another kick, this time with more force. Repeating the words, Izzy rammed his size-thirteen foot into the guy again and again, each kick harder than the last. "Tomato—" Something caught Izzy's eye. He crouched down on the junkie's right and pried his fingers away from the knife, which then fell to the ground. He then secured the knife under his foot and held the guy's hand in his two and spread out the fingers.

Cosh watched, his body growing tense, as Izzy slid the man's index finger into his mouth up to the second knuckle and bit down with all his might. There was a crunching sound, then a fountain of red as blood spewed from the stub and coated Izzy's face—the face of his best friend, who now knelt on the ground, wearing the vacant stare of a rabid animal.

Had Izzy gone mad? A sane Izzy would never do this.

Cosh stood, frozen in place, as Izzy whipped his head toward him and spit. The finger sailed out on a mist of blood and saliva, falling at Cosh's feet like the gift of a dead bird from a prodigal tomcat to its loving owner.

"Richie!" Cosh screamed, hoping the use of Izzy's given name, the name they had called him back in the early days of grammar school, might jar his friend back to sanity.

He stared in horror as Izzy took the man's middle finger between his teeth.

Cosh jumped into action, moving behind Izzy and cradling his head in his arms, careful not to get bitten himself. "Stop," he pleaded, shaking Izzy's head. "You have to stop."

There was another crunch before Cosh could wrestle Izzy away. They toppled over together, and as Izzy's body hit the ground, the second finger launched from his mouth with the sound of a cork being popped from a bottle.

"What the fuck is wrong with you?" Cosh said. "Are you fuckin' nuts? You don't know where those fingers have been!"

Izzy, eyes crazed, stared up him and smiled.

• • •

Beans had completed three tows, his daily quota, without having come across the Cutlass Louie was looking for.

Most drivers were expected to complete at least six tows per day, but the Abandoned Vehicle Unit was a new pilot program. One driver in each district was "on loan" to towing for half the day. The other half was scheduled to work at the sanitation yard, assisting the foreman. Beans "assisted" by buying lunch every day, in return for the freedom of staying out on the street. Just another small cost of doing business.

He cruised around the district for the remainder of the afternoon, but no luck.

It was getting close to quitting time, so he headed for the yard. The chop shop, or junkyard as it were, was on the way in, so he decided to stop in to let Louie know of his unsuccessful day and, hopefully, get a gas tank for Pat.

While cruising along just before the bridge on Thirty-Ninth Street, in front of the Vienna Beef packing plant, he spotted what he had been looking for. About one hundred feet ahead, parked half on the street and half on the sidewalk, was a chocolate-brown 1980 Olds Cutlass.

Bingo!

The shop was just over the bridge, and the city yard just beyond that. As a bonus, the Cutlass was illegally parked, giving him an excuse to tow it. He passed by slowly, checking the expiration date on the plate.

Expired! It was meant to be.

He backed up close to the front bumper and hastily filled out the blank tow report with the vehicle's information. He slipped on his brown jersey gloves, snatched up his tool kit, and hopped out of the truck, scanning the area. No one on the street and hardly any traffic.

It's almost too easy.

He pressed his hand down on the hood of the car, feeling the cold steel even through the glove. It had been sitting a while. He set the tool kit on the roof, unzipped it, and slid out the slim-jim and a pair of long-nosed pliers.

A sudden chill raised the hair on the back of his neck.

It was a crisp autumn day. But that wasn't it.

He was excited, as usual, to be stealing. But that wasn't it.

Cautiously, he scanned the area again, looking as far as he could in every direction while slowly turning his body 360 degrees. All clear. He shoved the pliers in his back pocket and worked the slim-jim down between the window and the rubber molding along the doorframe, dragging and jiggling, back and forth, up and down, until he felt it snag the lock mechanism.

A short tug upward and the door was unlocked.

He checked the interior for valuables. Louie was getting the car, so Beans felt more or less entitled to its contents. Alas, nothing. Just a factory stock radio and some random papers in the glove box. He'd pop the trunk later, after he pulled away from the scene.

He reached under the dashboard and pulled the latch to open the hood. He'd have to get the rear wheels to roll freely in order to tow the car from the front. He could tow it from behind, of course, but the prep was more time consuming. In a matter of seconds, he had the transmission linkage disconnected at the steering column. He then manually shifted the car into neutral by pushing down on the linkage bar until he felt the car roll forward a bit. His head and half his body were still under the hood when he heard footsteps nearing hard and fast, loose gravel skittling with each footfall.

"Whoa, whoa, whoa!"

Beans eased out from under the hood, the cotter pin from the linkage still clenched in the pliers in his hand.

A rotund Mexican man, wearing a hairnet and a bloody apron, huffed and puffed and wheezed his way toward him. He was only able to get a few words out between gasps.

"Whuzzup, bro?"

When he reached the car, the man hunched over, knees bent, forearms resting on his thighs. A bloody meat cleaver, speckled with bits of flesh, sinew, and bone, dangled loosely in his right hand.

Beans hopped inside his cab and grabbed the clipboard. "I got orders to tow this car," he said matter-of-factly. The presence of the cleaver warranted caution, but Beans wasn't too concerned. He could handle this out-of-shape fatso, with or without the big knife.

The man straightened some. "Why?"

"I don't know. The cops write 'em up, I just follow the orders. Let's see . . ." Beans stood alongside the man so they could read the order together. "See here?" Beans pointed. "Parked illegally, expired plates." He glanced downward. "Whattaya plannin' to do with that knife? Do I gotta call for a squad car?"

The man held up the cleaver as if he'd never seen it before. "Oh, shit, bro. No, no. I'm sorry." He slid the thing into the apron's giant front pocket. As the blade scraped against the top hem, some grisly bits broke free and dropped into the apron's creases. "I didn't mean to freak you out." He was getting his wind back. "I ran out so fast when I saw you, I forgot to put it down. I work right there." He pointed to the Vienna Beef packing plant.

Beans walked casually to the rear of the tow truck and rested a hand on the boom lever. "Good corned beef," he said as he worked the lever to lower the tow bar. The truck engine revved, and the hydraulics groaned and creaked as the bar came down.

The Mexican hurried over to him. "Can't you give me a break, bro?"

"Well, I'm not supposed to." He glanced down at the man's now-empty hands. "I could get in a lot of trouble."

He gave Beans a look of comprehension, then dug under his apron and into his pants pocket. "This is all I got, bro," he said, coming up with two twenties, a five, and some singles. "Why don't you just take this and have a nice dinner tonight, on me?" He fanned the money like a deck of cards.

This guy catches on quick. Beans remembered what Pat Gibbons told him, about never leaving a guy broke. Beans plucked the two twenties from the man's chubby fingers and left the rest. "I'll just say the car was gone when I got here."

"I really appreciate this, bro. I won't forget it. Thanks."

"Don't mention it," Beans said. "A little advice, though. Renew your plates and don't park on the sidewalk."

"For sure."

The man slow-jogged back to the plant, leaving Beans alone on the street.

As he worked the lever to raise the tow bar, Beans, for a moment, considered becoming a cop. He could get used to people gladly handing over their money to him, instead of him having to steal it. "Nah," he said aloud. "Can't be a hypocrite. Gotta pick a side. Besides, the money ain't as good." He crumpled up the fake tow order. "Well, that was a waste." He'd paid Pat fifty for the blank and only took forty from the Mexican, which left him ten bucks to the bad. It did serve its purpose as an insurance policy, though. The Mexican never questioned it.

CHAPTER 9

A DIME A WEEK

BEANS DOUBLE-PARKED ON May Street, in front of the Survivors Club. Uncle Skinny didn't like to talk on the phone.

He tapped on the door before opening it.

Skinny, facing the door, sat at a card table with a solitaire layout in front of him.

"Hey, Unc. How's it going?" Beans closed the door behind him.

There was a stark contrast between the Survivors Club and the Nailati Club. Whereas the latter was set up like a lounge and so obviously designed for parties, the only decor here came in the form of old fight cards—posters promoting local boxing matches, scattered haphazardly along the walls and windows. The only furniture, card tables and folding chairs. No couch. No television. No bar.

"Hey, Ralphie. What's up?"

"One of the machines got some coins jammed up in the slot. It's been happening a lot. Think we could get it fixed or maybe swap it out for a new one?"

"Yeah, sure," Skinny said with a wave of his hand. "I'll have Frankie come by and take a look."

"Y'know," Beans said, "guys are standing in line, waiting to drop their zort. I think we could use a third machine."

The door opened and in walked Willy the Wiz.

Skinny shot Beans a look over the rim of his glasses and motioned with his eyes to the left toward the kitchen. Beans took the hint and left the room, but his curious nature got the best of him. He closed the door most of the way and stood, peering through the crack.

"Where the fuck you been?" Skinny asked.

"Black Beauty needed a bath."

Willy was referring to his pristine 1984 Lincoln Town Car. He was a fanatic about the thing, which was why he hardly ever left the neighborhood. He arranged his affairs so that pretty much anywhere he needed to go was within walking distance of his apartment on the corner of Taylor and Loomis, above Mama Sue's Restaurant, where he ate lunch and dinner almost every day. Black Beauty, meanwhile, spent most of her time under a tarp. If she had five thousand miles on her, Beans would be amazed.

"So, what's his total figure now?" Skinny thumbed three cards from the top of a deck of red Bicycles and flipped them over to show the bottom card, the queen of diamonds. He snapped it down, half covering the king of spades in the third row of his game.

Willy the Wiz sat across from him and lit a cigarette. "Row five," he said, a short burst of white smoke escaping his lips. "Black six on the red seven."

Skinny shot Willy an annoyed look. "The name of the game is solitaire. You know what that means?"

Willy rested his cigarette in the ashtray to his right, then set a foot up on the empty chair next to him like he was going to tie his shoe—a black Stacy Adams wingtip. He hiked up the leg of his gray Sansabelts and slid his hand into his over-the-calf black silk dress sock, fishing out a long, slender strip of paper. "I got it right here." He patted the breast pocket of his Member's Only jacket. "Fuck. I left my glasses at the kids' club." He held the paper at arm's length and squinted. "It's eighty-six something."

"Jeez. You're blind as a bat." Skinny snatched the slip from Willy's hand and laid it on the table. "Which one is him?"

"Two-oh-six."

Skinny ran a finger down the paper and stopped near the bottom. "Eighty-six, two-fifty? Are you fuckin' serious? Is that his figure or his fuckin' license plate number?" He pushed the paper away as if repulsed by it. "This is your fault. How the fuck could you let this kid get in so deep?"

"That's the way he bets, Skin. He's a fuckin' maniac. Going into Sunday, he was killing us. We owed *him* thirty dimes."

"He lost a hundred and twenty grand in two days?"

"I'm telling you, he bets the whole fuckin' board—three, four dimes a game. Football, basketball, hockey. He don't give a fuck. Then he wraps them up in parlays and robins. It's nothing for him to have a running figure of thirty or forty dimes either way, up or down. He'd never had a problem paying, so I let him go. Usually he'll win some and lose some and only end up owing a few dimes."

"What'd he do, lose every fuckin' game?"

"I think he had two winners and a push on the whole sheet."

One of the Wiz's players lost eighty-six dimes? Beans hadn't realized Willy was even doing that kind of volume.

"Okay." Skinny shook his head. "So out of eighty-six two-fifty, how much did he pay?"

"He came up with twenty-five, and he's askin' for some time. He says he can pay it off in a month or two. Until then, he wants to pay us a dime a week for waiting."

"Where the fuck is he gonna get sixty grand in two months?"

"I don't know, the guy's a fuckin' thief. Maybe he's got something planned."

Skinny thumbed off three more cards and flipped them over without looking. "A dime a week on sixty grand. That's a hell of a break he's asking for. What is that, like, one-and-a-half percent?"

Willy pointed to the cards. "Black jack on the red queen."

"Here, you wanna play so bad, you play." Skinny slammed down the deck. "Why should we give him such a good deal?"

"He's our best customer. The way I see it, it don't hurt us to wait. Let him pay it off, clear his name, and start betting again. It's like he's working for us. He goes out doin' stickups, or whatever the fuck he does, then gives the money to us."

"Where you supposed to meet him?"

"He wants to come here and talk to you today."

"What the fuck's he wanna talk to *me* for?"

"I guess to show you he's sincere. I don't know."

"No, no. I don't want to talk to him. Something ain't right about that kid. He gives me the creeps. You meet him. Make the deal."

"All right. So you're okay with a dime a week?"

"Yeah, but make sure you let that motherfucker know he's getting a sweet deal. A stranger would be paying three dimes a week. Even a friend would be paying two. He better not miss a single payment."

Willy ground out his cigarette and walked out.

"Ralphie!" Skinny called out.

Beans slipped back into the main room. "Yeah, Unc?"

"I'll have Frankie bring you two new machines and take the broken one away."

CHAPTER 10

TOO MUCH WINE

IT WAS ONE of those rare evenings when Beans was in a cheerless mood. He had failed to snag a Cutlass, none of the cars he'd towed that day had any goodies in them, and he wasn't able to get a gas tank for Pat—not a single Buick wagon in Louie's yard.

Beans was getting itchy.

Sure, he had his steady income from the *Playboy* books and his other little schemes. Gugootz had been collecting from Rooster regularly. But they hadn't made a decent score in months. And then there were the nagging images that popped up anytime his mind went still—beautiful blue bundles of cash rolling down a conveyor belt out of the belly of a 727.

He sat alone in his apartment in front of a blank TV, chugging his third glass of Sam Geraldi's homemade dago red. He had yet to figure a way to get the Federal Reserve money without going cowboy, nor had he figured a way to launder the money, should they manage to get their hands on it.

His feelings about Step were still mixed.

With such a fantastic amount of money at stake, he might consider a crude armed robbery. If it were only him, Cosh, and Izzy. They had enough experience to do the job without getting carried away—without unnecessarily hurting the guards. Step, on the other hand, if his reputation accurately preceded him, would just as soon shoot them just for fun. He considered for a fleeting moment, for who knew how many millions there were to be had, if it might be worth committing murder. People had killed for much less.

He swept the idea from his mind. Beans wasn't that guy.

He could see himself losing control in a fit of passion, over something personal or in self-defense, but he could never commit murder just for money, much less plan for it. There were too many safer, easier ways to make money. Maybe he'd never get an all-at-once shot like this again, but there was still plenty out there to be had. This score would have to be his way or not at all.

Pigs get fed, hogs get slaughtered.

He knew himself well enough to know that if he failed to figure out a plan, those roving blue images in his mind would haunt him the rest of his life. He decided to stay home for the night and work on a solution. After he drained the wine in his glass, his face flushed and he began to sweat.

He pitched forward, peeled off his T-shirt, and leaned back in the recliner.

Back to business. To what could he attribute his amazing rate of success so far? His zeal for caution? The ability to pick and choose the best jobs? Hours of research and acute attention to detail? The precision execution of a plan combined with the working relationship between him and his partners?

It was all of this, of course. But what single characteristic did he possess that made all this possible? He lit a cigarette and took a long, deep drag, letting his thoughts swirl like the wisps of smoke dancing toward the ceiling.

Then he sat forward with an epiphany.

Call it intuition, or a kind of empathy, Beans had the ability to detect the thoughts and emotions of other people. This enabled him to predict a person's actions and reactions. His partners, their victims, the police, certainly. But more than that—people in the news, famous figures, even fictional characters.

This was his magic.

He stood and walked to the "library"—aka, the spare bedroom—and glided his fingertips along the top of the door trim until they met with the key. For years, he had kept this room locked up. Not even Cosh and Izzy knew what was in there. Beans had a reputation to protect, and "bookworm," or worse, "nerd," were not part of it.

He slipped the key into the lock and envisioned its teeth raising and letting fall the tumblers as it slid. It was habit. This cheap lock would be a snap to pick if ever he lost the key. He enjoyed the sound of the lock giving way and the door creaking open.

The walls were lined with handcrafted shelves made from pine and filled with books neatly divided into sections by category. One entire wall was dedicated to crime, historical and fictional, as well as underground manuals on safecracking, lockpicking, gunsmithing, explosives, surveillance, disguise, and identity change. There were further sections—military strategy, politics, philosophy, religion. There was also a collection of classic fiction and an entire shelf dedicated to Shakespeare. He'd saved his old schoolbooks, referring to them periodically to brush up on mathematics, history, and science. There was even a section for the paranormal—UFOs, psychic phenomena, reincarnation.

He knew he had the blueprint for this latest maze somewhere in his head. But presently it was in scattered, jagged fragments, like a torn-up road map tossed to the wind. He had only to gather up the pieces and put them in order. He moved directly to the crime section and pulled several books from the shelves. When his arms were full, he carried them into the kitchen, set them on the table, then returned to the room and locked the door.

It was going to be a long night.

He staggered on his way to the coffee table, where he'd left his cigarettes by the ashtray next to the jug of wine and his empty glass. At the sight of the jug, he smacked his tongue against the roof of his mouth. The faint taste still lingered there, and he wanted more. "Eh, what the hell." He picked up his glass, hooked the pinkie of the same hand through the loop handle of the jug, and carried them into the kitchen, his cigarettes and ashtray in the other hand.

•••

After forty or so minutes of reading, drinking, and smoking, Beans roused to a knock at the door. He quietly stacked the books on a chair at the far side of the table and pushed it in.

The room spun as he slipped his shirt back on. "Who is it?"

"It's me, Step."

Beans cursed under his breath. He staggered to the door and opened it.

"Sorry to bother you, Beans. Can I talk to you a minute?"

Beans stepped back and swung an arm in the direction of the kitchen. "Yeah, sure. Come on in."

Step limped past him into the apartment.

"Have a seat." Beans gestured to the table. "Want some wine?"

Step eyed the jug. "Is that homemade?"

"Yep. Cosh's dad makes it." He grabbed a glass from the cupboard and brought it to the table. "Siddown. You hungry?"

"No, thanks. Just a taste of wine."

Beans filled both glasses and slid one over to Step. The wine sloshed in its glass, and a bit spilled onto the table. "I've been racking my brain over this job of yours. Got any more info for me?"

"Not much." Step pulled a folded sheet of loose-leaf paper from his pocket. "I got the list of names of people who work in the office, though."

Beans took the list and raised his glass. "Drink your wine."

Step followed suit. "Salute."

Beans studied the list.

"Fuck," Step said, licking his lips. "This stuff's good."

"Best in the city. Cosh says it's his great-grandfather's recipe, from Italy."

Step finished off his glass. "Do you think he'd sell me some?"

"Sure. But this is last year's batch. I don't think there's any left. This year's won't be ready 'til Christmastime." Beans pointed to a name. "Who's this?"

Step craned his neck to see. "That's some radar you got. Fifteen names on the list and you pick the one good-looking broad on it."

"It's a talent, I guess. She's cute, huh?"

"Gina Vitti? She's fuckin' gorgeous. Every guy at American tries to hit on her. She won't give any of 'em the time of day, though."

"How old?"

"Twenty-one, twenty-two."

"Interesting." If Beans could get close to this girl, he might be able to glean the inside info they needed. He drained his glass and

113

pondered. It helped that she was Italian. Gave them some common ground. It would make it easy to break the ice. He refilled their glasses. "We're making progress, Step, but it's gonna be a slow process. This ain't no smash-and-grab."

"I realize that, Beans. That's kinda why I came here tonight. I gotta make some zort in the meantime."

"Well, if something comes up, I'll let you know."

"I already got something. I just need some help."

"Whattaya got?"

"There's this guy, Carl, I see every morning at the Steak and Egger in Cicero. I eat breakfast there before work, y'know, and we've gotten kinda friendly. He's a truck driver, pulls them piggyback loads from the railroad. Tells me he's got a load of cigarettes he's trying to get rid of."

"Define 'load' and 'got.' How many cigarettes we talkin', and where are they?"

"A whole semitrailer full." Step wiped his mouth with the back of his hand. "He says there was a mix-up at the yard. He was supposed to be picking up an empty, and they gave him this one by mistake. Some fuckup with the paperwork. He drove it a couple blocks to some side street, dropped it, then went back for the empty." Step reached for the jug. "You mind?"

"Not at all. Hit me too." Beans's head was spinning. His inner voice was telling him not to do business while drunk, but the wine overrode his better senses. Booze had a strange effect on Beans. It went straight to his balls. If he was with a girl right now, that wouldn't be a problem. In doing business, however, the effect made him rash and overly bold. "So, where's the trailer now?"

"Just sittin' on the street, waiting for someone to hook up to it. It's only a matter of time before someone finds it."

"So what does he want us to do?"

"Here's the deal. He wants twenty grand for the load. I already got it sold for forty. Once I give him the money, he'll give me the address where he dropped it. I got a driver with a tractor who'll go get it and pull it to wherever I want. He can take it right to the buyer."

"So what's the problem?"

"I don't have twenty grand. All I could scrape up was ten."

"You wanna borrow ten grand?"

"No, that wouldn't be right. I want to go partners with you. You give me ten grand tonight, and I'll give you twenty tomorrow when I sell the load. Fifty-fifty. And I'll take care of the driver out of my end."

"Let me think about it a minute while I take a leak." But Beans had already made up his mind. He stood and staggered into the bathroom.

After relieving himself, he flushed the toilet and turned on the faucet, using the sound for cover. He positioned himself on the edge of the tub, slipping in the effort, and grasped the shower curtain rod to steady himself. If he hadn't caught his balance somewhat beforehand, his weight would have surely brought the thing crashing down. Once he was sure-footed, he reached up and lifted one of the fiberboard panels of the dropped ceiling. Resting atop the adjacent panel were stacks of hundred-dollar bills, rubber banded in bundles of five thousand dollars each. He plucked three stacks from the nearest pile, let the ceiling tile drop back into place, then stepped carefully down from the tub's edge, stuffing the money into his waistband. He turned off the water and walked out.

"You all right?" Step asked.

"Yeah, why?"

"You were in there a while. Sounded like you fell or something."

"Fuckin' tripped, man. Too much wine." Beans dropped down into a chair. "Okay. Whattaya think about this? I'll go in with you, but instead of ten, I wanna give you fifteen. Five each from me, Cosh, and Izzy. Instead of a two-way split, we make it a four-way. We'll only make five grand each instead of ten, but I think it'll go a long way toward making everyone more comfortable about working together. How's that sound?"

Step stared past Beans for a moment and came back. "What the hell? Why not? Can you get a hold of Cosh and Izzy? I need the money tonight."

"No problem. I'll just put in their ends. We'll surprise 'em tomorrow." Beans pulled the money out of his waistband and held it up. "There's fifteen grand here. Count it." He dropped the bills on the table.

Step looked down at the money, then back up at Beans. "I don't need to count it. I trust you."

"Oh, it's not that. I prefer you count it." Beans corked the wine jug. "I'm only human. I could've made a mistake."

CHAPTER 11

BEHIND THE STEAK AND EGGER

STEP'S FEET GREW wetter and wetter as he paced in the alley behind the Steak and Egger. What had started out as a light drizzle late that afternoon had turned into a full-on storm.

Why the fuck had he told Carl to meet him here?

A flash of lightning arched overhead, and Step searched for cover, finding only the fire escape of a skinny apartment building, where he stood, hunched, as the rain sieved through the metal grate above. He flipped up his collar to keep icy droplets from slipping down his neck and jammed his hands in his coat pockets. Reflexively, he patted the envelope tucked behind his belt buckle.

A roll of thunder rumbled in the distance.

He chewed his bottom lip and stared across the alley to the vacant lot, overgrown with bushes and weeds. Had he been cool enough with Beans earlier? Step had become overly wary of seeming too desperate. Eh, even if he had been this time around, Beans probably wouldn't have noticed. That jug of homemade vino was over half-empty by the time he showed up.

117

He wiped at his face and slicked the excess water from his soaked hair. It nagged at him how, even when scores were scarce, a guy like Beans never seemed to hurt for much of anything. Maybe it was all well and good for Beans to change the deal, make only five grand, but Step needed every damn dollar he could get his hands on right now. He was also growing tired of Beans always treatin' him like he was some stupid little shit kid. "I think it'll go a long way in making everyone more comfortable," Step mimicked snidely. For crying out loud, had he not just delivered Beans and his boys the mother of all potential scores?

Step smirked. Ain't it curious how Beans suddenly produced the fifteen grand after a visit to the little boys' room? Not that he would risk crossing the guy. Step hated that he needed Beans to pull off this job. Hated it, but accepted the futility.

If Beans found out he was being hounded by the cops and Skinny's collectors, he was toast. He figured then it was just as well he'd agreed to take five thousand. He was still kicking himself about Sunday—knew he hadn't exactly instilled confidence in them. All those fuckin' questions.

Technically, he hadn't lied. Beans asked if he had ever been *convicted*—not if he was under suspicion—for anything.

His eyes darted left, then right.

Headlights lit up the dark alley before the car appeared. Sheets of sideways rain caught in the beams sparkled like falling shards of glass. Step moved behind a telephone pole until he was sure it was Carl's LTD, then stepped out into the alley and waved. Carl rolled the car slowly along the shiny, blackened pavement until the passenger door came even with Step.

He climbed inside and slapped Carl's knee with the fat, damp envelope. "What's up, buddy? This is for you."

Carl took the envelope and placed it on his lap. He reached into his breast pocket and produced a small piece of paper torn from a notepad. "This is where it is. Truckers use it for a kind of a staging area, for when they have to drop trailers temporarily. There's trailers there all the time, so no one will be suspicious."

"What's this number?" Step asked, pointing to the paper.

"That's the trailer number. In case there's other trailers there, you'll need to know which one it is." He clutched the envelope in his hand and sighed. "Look, Step. I really want to thank you. I told you about my thirteen-year-old daughter, Vicky? Well, she just finished her last round of chemo, and she's in remission. With this money, we can have a future."

"Yeah, sure." Step eyed him absently. He remembered the guy going on and on over successive breakfasts about his kid having some kind of cancer, but he hadn't really paid much attention. "You wanna count that?"

"Nah, I trust you, man. Gotta hurry on home. I've got a pizza date with my Vicky. Told her to order whatever she wants, which means I'll have to choke down some anchovies, but that's a small price to pay to see her smiling again." He held up the envelope. "You have no idea how this is gonna change our lives."

A flash from a bolt of lightning illuminated the trucker's face, and Step's heart jumped in his chest. He was looking at Carl, but he was seeing his father. That nasty, cutting scowl Step could never quite banish from his mind.

"Oh, I bet I do."

A thunderclap directly above rattled the car's windows.

Step slipped a hand into his jacket pocket, gripped his stiletto switchblade, and withdrew it while pressing the button on the handle.

The blade emerged with a snap and a click.

Carl's mouth dropped open and his eyes went wide as Step plunged the weapon into the side of his neck. Halfway in, the blade hit bone. Step wiggled and pushed until it sunk a few more inches, then pulled the thing out. Carl slumped onto the steering wheel.

Step snatched up the envelope as it slid toward the floor and wiped the blade on Carl's pant leg before climbing out of the car.

Back in the alley, he ducked behind a dumpster and grabbed the milk jug full of gasoline and flare he had stashed there earlier that evening. He returned to the Ford, rolled down its windows, and doused the interior and Carl's body with gasoline.

The rain let up, and Step looked to the sky, where a break in the high, hazy clouds revealed a distant three-quarter moon.

"What the hell." He squatted beside the car and dropped his pants.

When he finished, Step lit the flare, tossed it into the car, and walked out of the alley.

CHAPTER 12

EGGS BENEDICT

THE FIRST RAYS of morning sun, like a floodlight through the living room window, bathed Bean's face, and the peaceful blackness of sleep erupted into a wall of fire behind his eyelids. He threw an arm over his eyes and rolled the opposite way with a jerk that nearly toppled the leather recliner. The sudden movement sent a shock wave of pain up his neck that triggered a throb in his head like the thumping of a bass drum.

He let out a low groan. What time was it? Was Step still here?

Beans struggled to his feet and surveyed the room for clues. The drum in his head echoed to the cadence of each footfall made toward the kitchen. The clock on the wall read *5:47*. Step must have let himself out.

Or maybe he was never there at all.

The empty jug and pair of dirty wine glasses assured Beans that this was not the case. How much money did he give him? Ten thousand? No, he had taken down three stacks.

"Fuck!"

He hated this feeling. How could he let his guard down like that? He snatched a clean glass from the cupboard and trudged into the bathroom for some aspirin.

When he opened the mirrored door of the medicine chest, he caught the reflection of the ceiling tiles above the shower. He remembered almost falling off the edge of the tub. He tried to shake two aspirin out of the bottle, but four came out.

"If two are good, four are better."

He popped them all into his mouth and let them sit on the back of his tongue while he filled the glass with water. Then he threw his head back and gulped some down, but not before the chalky pills had already started to dissolve, and a bitter taste like corroded copper wire burned his tongue and palette. He welcomed it. The headache too.

He deserved as much for being so stupid.

He planted his foot on the tub's edge and hoisted himself up. Everything was just as he had left it: five stacks of bills, each divided into five rubber-banded packets of five thousand each. Except for the closest stack, which had only two packets.

Was he at least careful enough last night to make sure Step couldn't tell where he'd gotten the money? He couldn't be sure.

"You stupid motherfucker!"

He grabbed three packets and lobbed them into the tub. Then he reached back in, grabbed three more, and did the same. He repeated the process until all the money lay in the tub, then let the ceiling panel fall back into place.

"Better safe than sorry." He hopped down.

The phone rang as he was walking around the apartment looking for a new hiding place.

Who the fuck calls at six in the morning?

He snatched up the receiver. "Yeah?"

"Hi, Beansie. I didn't wake you up, did I?"

The sound of Laura's voice made him forget all about his headache. Or maybe the aspirin had kicked in.

"No, no. I'm getting ready for work."

"That's what I figured."

"Whatsa matter? You okay?"

"Oh, yeah, I'm fine. I was just thinkin' . . ."

"You were just thinking what?"

"Did you eat yet?"

"No, why?"

"Why don't you play hooky today?" she said. "I'll come over and make you breakfast, and then we can hang out."

Beans had already considered calling in sick, but had decided he shouldn't. Louie would be expecting that Cutlass today, and Pat needed a gas tank.

"Nah, I feel like shit. I was drinking last night."

"We don't have to go anywhere. We can just lay around and watch TV."

Beans knew what that meant: food, sex, and sleep. His three favorite things.

How could he say no?

"What're you gonna cook for me?" he asked.

"It's a surprise. So, you wanna?"

"Okay. But give me a couple hours. How's eight?"

"Eight's perfect. See you then." She hung up.

Beans pulled the phone away from his ear and stared at it. "Why does she never say goodbye?"

After calling in sick to work, he continued searching the apartment. He considered unscrewing the back of the television and stashing his money there, but if some junkie burglar broke in, the television would be the first thing he'd take. Library? No. A locked room would be sure to arouse interest. He opened the kitchen pantry and took down a half-full box of Frosted Flakes. He pulled out the plastic bag, rolled up the top, tossed it onto the table, and carried the empty box into the bathroom, where he knelt by the tub, filled the box partway, then set the bag of cereal on top.

That took care of thirty thousand.

He went back to the pantry, retrieved two more boxes and repeated the procedure. Still, he had five rubber-banded packets, twenty-five thousand, left to hide. He wrapped two of them in tinfoil and put them in the freezer, tossed two out of sight on top of the kitchen cabinets, and put one in his middle dresser drawer. He'd been thinking of taking a vacation. This could be his mad money.

He had just gotten out of the shower when there was a knock at the door. He answered, wearing his navy-blue terrycloth robe and a pair of black leather slippers.

"Mornin', Beansie. Hope you're hungry." Laura was clutching a brown paper grocery sack in each arm.

Beans lingered in the doorway. Laura always looked better in person than he pictured her in his mind. The natural waves of her auburn hair undulated down to the middle of her back. Her complexion was flawless and, unlike most redheads, golden bronze like a Polynesian. She was wearing a white Guess jean jacket with blue denim trim, and a tight white Dago T-shirt, revealing every detail of her breasts. Her jeans, also Guess, conformed to her curves as if painted on.

She cleared her throat. "You wanna help me with these?"

"Nah, I think I'll just stand here and look at you for a while."

With a blush and a smile, Laura thrust one of the bags into his chest. "I got a lotta work to do. Now, bring that in and stay outta my way." She pushed past him and strode into the kitchen.

Beans followed, gawking at her ass.

Once the groceries were safely on the counter, Laura threw her arms around him and kissed him hard on the lips. Then she reached down and squeezed the bulge under his robe. "I'll take care of *him* later," she said. "First, breakfast."

"You're awfully pushy today."

"Yeah, I am. I decided that today is my day."

"You decided, huh? And what does that mean, *your* day?"

"I see the way people are around you." She pulled a skillet from the drawer below the oven and set it on the stove. "The guys at the club, the girls in the neighborhood, even your own family. Everybody does whatever you say."

"That's not true. You act like I go bossing people around all day. Did you come here to pick a fight with me? Because I'm not in the mood." He sunk into a chair at the table and rubbed his temples. "I got a fuckin' hangover."

"I didn't mean it like that," she said. "It's just that you always get your way. I don't know what it is about you, but people just seem to want to please you."

"And you don't?"

"Of course, I do—probably more than anyone."

"So, what's the problem?"

"There is no problem. I was just thinking that it must be boring to always get your way. So, today, I'm gonna please myself, by pleasing you. But you're gonna do what *I* want. Get it?"

"Are you premenstrual?"

She narrowed her eyes, and with the spatula in her hand, pointed to the living room. "Just go watch TV while I make us some food."

"Fine."

Beans flipped through the channels from his recliner while things crashed, clanged, and sizzled in the other room. A smoky, greasy aroma wafted its way through the apartment. It wasn't bacon. Sausage maybe? No.

He stood and peered into the kitchen. "What're you makin'?"

Laura blocked the view of the stove with her body. "Don't come in here! I said it's a surprise. I'll call you when it's ready."

Beans sat back down. "All right. Relax. Jeez." He went back to flipping channels and stopped on the news to catch the weather report. A female reporter was describing a body found in an alley in Cicero.

". . . appears to be the victim of a grisly murder."

Beans, distracted by Laura's strange mood, was only half-listening. "Fuckin' psycho broad," he mumbled under his breath.

". . . what could be determined from the charred remains . . ."

"Okay!" Laura called from the kitchen. "It's ready! You can come in now."

"It's about time," Beans huffed. "I'm starving."

". . . fire right here behind the Steak and Egger restaurant."

The reporter's voice faded as Beans walked into the kitchen.

Beans sat at the table and Laura set a plate in front of him.

He looked down, genuinely—and pleasantly—surprised. "I didn't know you knew how to make eggs Benedict."

"There's a lot that I know that you don't know I know."

"Is that right?"

"Yep."

"Like what?"

"That you like eggs Benedict, for one."

Beans dug into the eggs. "And how'd you know that?"

"It's not important. How is it?"

"Fuckin' delicious," he said. "Aren't you gonna eat yours?"

Laura smiled over him. "I will. I just like to watch you eat."

By the time Laura sat down, Beans was finishing up the last bits on his plate. He chugged his coffee and set down the mug. "Babe, that was really good. Like, *really* good."

"Thanks," she said, looking self-satisfied. "I bet you never had eggs Benedict at home before, have you?"

"Come to think of it, no."

"Haven't you ever heard the old saying?" she asked slyly.

"What old saying?"

"There's two things you can't get at home. Eggs Benedict and…"

"And?"

Laura disappeared under the table, and her head came up between his legs.

She opened his robe. "A blow job."

•••

By noon they had finished their second round of lovemaking. They lay in Beans's bed, Laura's head burrowed into his chest.

"Y'know," she said, "you're a pretty tough guy to get close to."

"What are you talkin' about? If we got any closer, we'd be joined at the hip."

She bit his chest.

"Ow! That fuckin' hurt!"

"You know what I mean," she said. "You never tell me anything. Everything I know about you I had to learn from other people."

"All lies, I assure you."

"What about the good stuff?"

"Oh, well that's all true. So there, now you know everything."

She went to bite him again, but he held her head at bay while squirming out from under her body so they lay side by side, facing each other.

He cradled her face in his hands and looked into her hazel eyes. "Okay," he said. "Let's talk. What do you want to know?"

"I want to know all about you."

"You know I ain't gonna tell you everything."

"I know. There are things you do that I'm sure I don't *want* to know about. I don't need to know all about what you do. What I want to know is who you are. Tell me about you."

"You're going to have to be more specific."

"Okay. What's your favorite color?"

"Orange."

"Orange?" She wrinkled her nose. "Whose favorite color is orange?"

"What the fuck? You asked me my favorite color, I told you, and now you're makin' fun? Fuckin' orange, okay? It also happens to be my favorite flavor."

"Huh. Weird."

"Well, that's what it is. Put a box of oranges in front of me, I'll eat the whole fuckin' thing. You never had roast duck with orange sauce? Fuckin' delicious. Orange marmalade on top of vanilla ice cream? Try it, and you'll see."

"Yuck."

"All right, forget it." He rolled away onto his back and stared at the crack in the ceiling. "You say you want to know about me, then everything I tell you, you think is crazy or weird, or something."

"No, no. C'mon. I'm sorry. Keep going."

"That's all there is. I like orange, so if that makes me weird, so be it. Wait . . ." A curious thought occurred to him. "Wanna know something even weirder?"

She pitched herself up on an elbow and smiled down at him. "Yeah, I do."

"I don't like orange juice."

She lifted an eyebrow. "I'm not even going to touch that one."

"What's going on with you, anyway?" he said. "I thought we had a good thing going. Why you trying to spoil it by getting all mental?"

"Mental? I just wanna know you better. Get an idea of what our future might be."

"Whoa." He sat up. "That's a little too deep. And not like you. Something happened. What happened? Did you meet someone?"

"No!" Her eyes welled. "Fuckin' jerk! You have no idea . . ."

Beans sighed and pulled her close. He kissed her cheeks as the tears began to fall. "Okay, babe. Your turn. Talk to me. Tell me what's going on."

She buried her head in the crook of his neck. "Forget it. It's stupid."

"Babe, I know you too well. Whatever it is, I'm sure it's not stupid. Just tell me." Beans tried to be as reassuring as possible.

"Okay." She cleared her throat and wiped her nose with her wrist. "I'm not pregnant."

What the . . . His head twitched. "I'm sorry, what? You're *not* pregnant?"

"Uh-huh. I missed my period last month, and I thought I was. So I went to the drugstore yesterday and got one of those tests, but it was negative. I wanted to make sure, so I went back this morning and got another one, but it was negative too. That's when I called you." The words fell out of her as if pushed off the edge of a cliff. She wiped her nose again, and continued, "Don't get me wrong. I'm glad I'm not pregnant, but it made me think—what if I was? What would you do? What if you leave me stranded, and there I am trying to raise a baby by myself, and then I thought what if you decided to marry me and you regretted it and wound up hating me and wanting a divorce? That would be even worse 'cause I could never leave you 'cause you're the only man I've ever been with and you're the only man I ever want to be with and I love you."

"You know what?" he said. "I was wrong."

"What do you mean?"

"That *is* fuckin' stupid."

She buried her face with her hands. "See, I told you!"

Beans flipped her onto her back. He straddled her body, pinned her arms down, and brought his face close to hers.

"Listen to me," he said, looking into her eyes. "I would never leave you stranded. I would take care of you and our baby."

Tears streamed down Laura's face, darkening the sheets.

"That doesn't mean I want a baby right now. I'm not ready to get married. But if I was, you wouldn't have to be pregnant for me to marry you." He kissed her eyes, brushing her tears with his lips. The briny moisture seemed to carry her emotion into the pores of his skin. He swallowed down the lump in his throat.

Laura sniffed three choppy breaths into her lungs. "Beans?"

"Yeah, babe?"

"Do you love me?"

Beans hesitated. Not because he had to think about the answer. But because he had never thought about it before. "You know what? Yeah, I fuckin' love you."

He lay down next to her, and they fell asleep.

• • •

They were awakened by a knock at the door.

Beans checked the clock on the nightstand—*4:04*. He rolled out of bed and threw on his robe. "Might be my sister," he said, running a hand through his mussed hair. "Stay here and be quiet."

He opened the door to find Step on the other side, wearing a broad grin.

"Hey, Beans. Can I come in?"

Beans's eyes darted toward the bedroom. "I kinda got company right now."

"Oh, sorry." Step produced an envelope from his jacket pocket and thrust it at Beans. "I came by to give you this."

"What is it?"

"Thirty dimes. Your original fifteen, plus five each for you, Cosh, and Izzy."

"Holy fuck. That was fast."

"I said one day, didn't I? I took care of it last night."

Beans detected the faint smell of gasoline hovering in the narrow stairwell outside his apartment. He sniffed the air between them. "You smell that?"

"Smell what?"

"Never mind." Beans held up the envelope. "Everything went okay? No problems?"

"One-two-three, man. Thanks for helping me out." Step looked behind Beans into the apartment and then waggled his brow. "I'll let you get back to business."

"Thanks." Beans started to close the door, then paused. "Hey, I haven't told the boys about this yet. Haven't had the chance. If you see 'em, don't say anything. We'll make it a surprise."

Halfway up the short cement staircase, Step called over his shoulder, "Okay, yeah. That's cool."

"Who was it?" Laura asked when Beans returned to the bedroom.

He tossed the envelope on the dresser. "Just a friend."

"Is he gone?"

Beans flung himself onto the bed next to her. "Yep."

"How's your hangover?"

"Hangover?" he said. "How could I have a hangover if I'm still drunk?"

"Whattaya mean?"

"I'm drunk, babe. Can't remember a thing we talked about. How'd you get in here? What're you doing in my bed?"

She grabbed a pillow and smacked him with it. "Nice try, mister. You said you loved me, and you don't get to take it back."

"That was the booze talking."

"Very funny. You said it. And do you know what that means?"

Beans snatched the pillow from her hands and held it over his ears. "I'm afraid to ask."

"It means you have to stop treating me like one of your lay-broads."

"Here we go. You sure are in a ball-bustin' mood today, huh?"

"I'm serious. You gotta give me more respect. Not just sex. Take me out to dinner and the movies more often. And except for the whole orange thing, you still haven't told me much about yourself."

"Jeez, gimme a chance. I don't need to be told how to treat my girlfriend."

She regarded him with a skeptical eye.

"You'll see. But as far as getting to know me better, I can't just sit here all day and tell you things. That's not how it works. You'll just have to find out over time."

"Fine. Just one thing, then. Tell me one thing that no one else knows about you."

Beans thought about it. What secret would be significant enough to satisfy her, but not get him into trouble? Finally, he said, "Come with me."

He stood and offered his hand. She pulled the sheet around her, and together they made their way down the hall to the spare bedroom. He snagged the key from the trim and held it up between them.

"I've always wondered what's in there," she said.

"Gotta promise never to tell anyone."

She held a hand to her heart. "Promise."

"I mean it. Even if we break up."

"Just open it," she said.

When the door swung open, Laura stood, transfixed, scanning the room from one end to the other. She glanced up at Beans, amusement dancing in her eyes. "What's all this?"

"I like to read," he said with a shrug. "A lot."

Laura stepped inside and stood amid the high pine shelves. She spun slowly, reading various titles aloud, then stopped. "You've read all these?"

"More or less. I've read all of most of them and most of each of them. Some I've read over and over."

"What's your favorite?"

"Tough question. Anything by Mark Twain. And Alexandre Dumas—*The Man in the Iron Mask*, *The Count of Monte Cristo*. Shakespeare's great . . ."

"Shakespeare? You read Shakespeare?" She stared at him,

incredulous. "God, we had to read that in high school. I hated it. So boring."

"Boring? *Macbeth* has more gore in it than *Friday the 13th*. *The Merchant of Venice* could be about guys from this neighborhood."

"Well, I didn't understand much of it. Any of it. What's one book in here you've read again and again?"

He moved to the section with Eastern religion and philosophy and slid a thin paperback from the stack and handed it to her.

Her brow shot up. "You can read Chinese?"

"No, silly. It's a translation."

"Tao Te Ching? What is it?"

"It's pronounced dow-day-ching. And people have been trying to figure that out for thousands of years."

"What's it about?"

"Depends on who you ask. Most people think it's about religion, or politics. Kinda like a Chinese bible, telling you how to live."

"What do *you* think it's about?"

"I think it's a lot deeper than any of that."

"Why do you read it over and over?"

"Because every time I read it, I understand a little bit more. It's like a puzzle." He reshelved the book. "I gotta go. I got things to do. You can stay here if you want, but I don't know when I'll be back."

"Actually, I gotta get going too," she said. "But I have one more question."

He rolled his eyes playfully. "What now?"

"You *are* Catholic, right?"

Beans chuckled. "Yeah. I was even an altar boy."

She smiled in reply. "Mind if I take a quick shower before I go?"

"I was gonna suggest it, but I didn't know how to tell you." He pinched his nostrils closed with his thumb and forefinger.

She punched his arm. "Very funny."

While Laura showered, Beans counted the money from Step.

It was all there. He took out his share and put the rest back in the envelope for Cosh and Izzy.

He found the bathroom door unlocked, which he took as an invitation. He slipped in quietly, let his robe drop to the floor, and flung open the shower curtain, hoping to surprise Laura.

She was standing there smiling, waiting for him. "What took you so long?"

They made love under the flowing water. She was more relaxed, less inhibited, and more passionate than ever.

"I should have showed you my library a long time ago," he said, stepping out of the stall. He dried off with a large white towel and wrapped it around his waist.

A minute or so later, Laura emerged, dripping wet. "Can you get me a towel?"

He leaned against the sink and folded his arms across his chest. "Nope," he said, admiring her naked body.

"C'mon!" she said. "I'm cold!"

"I wanna look at you."

"You're embarrassing me!"

"Believe me, babe. You've got nothing to be embarrassed about."

She yanked the towel from his waist and wrapped it around herself.

"Yeah," she said, giving him a long, slow once-over. "Neither do you."

While Laura dressed in the bedroom, Beans, still sporting his birthday suit, made himself a ham sandwich and sat down at the kitchen table. Laura appeared from the bedroom looking as fresh as she had when she'd arrived that morning.

"I thought you had things to do?" she said.

"I do, but I'm hungry. Want one?"

"No. Traffic's probably brutal on the Eisenhower by now. I'd better go. Call me later?"

"If I get home early enough. If not, I'll call you tomorrow, okay?"

"Okay." She kissed him goodbye and walked out.

CHAPTER 13

PAVLOV'S BELL

BEANS GOT TO the club around six that evening. The usual after-work crowd was scattered about, sitting or standing at the bar or playing cards at the tables. A small group was gathered around the television, where a bootleg porno played to fill in the dead air before the Bulls game. Save for a few misfits, most were in their twenties, and decidedly blue collar. Lots of reinforced denim, work boots, and flannel. The majority were city workers—truck drivers, equipment operators, general laborers. There were a few who worked on the presses at the *Chicago Tribune* and others who worked at McCormick Place, setting up booths for the trade shows. Some of the better dressed guys were traders at the Merc—Chicago Mercantile Exchange. Each one had some kind of clout, a connection, be it to an alderman, a union boss, or an Outfit guy.

Beans paused just inside the doorway, waiting for his usual greeting from Capo, but the dog was nowhere in sight.

"Yo, Beans! What's up?" one of the guys called from the couch.

"Where's Capo?"

The guy shrugged.

Beans strode into the kitchen to find Capo, drool hanging from his jowls, staring up at Pete the Bum.

Peter Catanzaro was just that—a bum. A bona fide hobo. The guys felt sorry for him and let him hang around the club so he had someplace warm to go to. He grew up in the neighborhood, and his reputation as one of the toughest streetfighters of his day, was legendary. All the guys in the neighborhood had grown up hearing stories about Pete's exploits. Beans's favorite was the one where Pete jumped from the roof of a three-story building onto a cop who was clubbing his friend. Not only did Pete emerge unscathed from the venture, he beat the cop to a bloody pulp.

Presently, Pete sat at the kitchen table gumming a meatball sandwich, red gravy dripping into the tattered cuff of his tattered tweed sportscoat.

"Capo!" Beans called. "Don't you say hello anymore?"

At the sound of Beans's voice, Capo's tail beat wildly against a chair leg, but his gaze remained fixed on Pete and the sandwich.

"Hey, lil' Trombino," Pete rasped. "Take this mongrel for a canter, y'dig? He won' lemme eat in peace. Ah'm gon' bite him on his ass he don' lee me 'lone."

Pete called all the guys by their last names with lil' in front. He was in his midfifties and had grown up with most of their fathers. He'd spent his latest fourteen years in a Louisiana prison and, while there, his manner of speaking had picked up a New Orleans-Beatnik flavor.

"How are you going to bite him with no teeth, Pete?" Beans teased. "You can't even bite that sandwich. I gotta talk to Doc about making you a set of new choppers."

Pete dropped the sandwich and banged the table with both fists. "Oh no you doesn't!" He stared at Beans with the eyes of a lunatic.

Doc, a forty-year-old dentist from Indiana who had recently moved his practice to Chicago, was the other club misfit. He had an apartment in Little Italy and had become enamored with the neighborhood culture. Most of the guys were suspicious of him, thinking he was either a faggot who liked to hang around young men, or a government plant, a snitch. To be on the safe side, Beans had him checked out and followed for a while. While he couldn't be sure whether the guy was a fag or not, it was doubtful he was a snitch. The only thing Beans knew for sure was that Doc was a degenerate gambler. Beans let him join the club because he was the biggest contributor on craps night.

As for Pete, Beans wasn't sure how to react. Was this sudden rage going to send the guy into one of his fits or was he merely being comical?

Pete brushed a hand through his gray crew cut and rubbed his scalp as if recalling an old injury. "Ah passed enough days in the bastille to 'cipher what's on that sissy's brain when he sees my purdy, jibless kisser. You keep that sugar plum fairy 'way from me, dig?"

Beans set a finger to his lips. "Shh. Be quiet." He glanced over his shoulder and came back. "The guy's in the next room. He might hear you."

"I don't give a flyin' rat's ass," Pete returned. "Don't like sissies. Never did. Diced up a few um'm in the joint."

"Well, that sissy out there drops about a nickel a week in here, so just leave him alone." Beans took a short breath and exhaled. "Have you seen Cosh or Izzy around?"

"What chu speakin'? Timbuktu? What the fuck is gosharizzi?"

"I *said* Cosh or Izzy."

Beans took it slow, but Pete just stared at him.

He tried another route. "Geraldi and Tonsi?"

"Oh, yeah. Now them's good kids. Brung me this." Pete picked up the sandwich with both hands. "Dirty shame 'bout Dickie Boy. I wish I run into that trigger-happy screw in a dark alley . . ."

"Yo, Pete." Beans said, trying to bring the guy back to reality. "Where are they?"

"Who?"

"Cosh. And Izzy."

"Fuck do I know? Am I my brother's keeper?"

"All right. I gotta go. Take it easy."

Pete touched his fingertips to his forehead. "Salamalakem."

Beans started out of the back, then stopped, glancing over his shoulder at Capo. "You comin'?"

His eyes found Beans, bounced back to the sandwich, then back to Beans.

"I know, boy," Beans said. "Decisions, decisions." Beans walked out into the main room and toward the front. "Any you guys see Cosh or Izzy?"

"They were just here looking for you," a husky voice boomed from behind the bar. "Said to tell you they'd be at the cheese store."

"Thanks."

• • •

The cool evening air of autumn filled his lungs as he made the short walk from the club to Geraldi's. He thrust his hands into the pockets of his leather jacket and, through the lining, fondled the handle of his revolver.

Beans and the boys were strictly against using guns when

committing their burglaries—the mere presence of a gun compounded the charge, if caught—but they all carried them religiously during the course of a regular day. He patted the thick envelope in his breast pocket, holding five thousand each for Cosh and Izzy.

As he strolled down Taylor Street, observing people going about their business, he couldn't help the top-of-the-world feeling that came over him. *How many of these people have ever even seen ten thousand dollars all at once?* he thought.

Geraldi's was a small, unassuming storefront. The only sign was painted on the window. With a sense of anticipation, Beans gripped the latch and pushed open the door, triggering the bell mounted on a spring above. The bell may as well have been rung by Pavlov himself; he stepped in, immediately engulfed by an array of spicy, mouthwatering aromas. He eyed hungrily the cheeses and dried sausages hanging in their nettings all around the store. Shelves were stacked with jars of homemade roasted red peppers, olives, and giardiniera. Inside the counter's deli case were fresh pasta salads and lunchmeats.

"We're in the back, Beans!" Cosh called out.

Beans made his way to the kitchen in the back, where he found Cosh standing over the stove and Izzy sitting at the table behind a plate of ravioli.

"Where've you been, Beans?" Izzy asked. "We been looking for you."

"Yeah, where you been, buddy?" Cosh asked.

"I've been looking for you guys too." Beans sensed something amiss. He looked from one to the other. "What's up?"

Izzy and Cosh exchanged a look that raised the hair on Bean's neck.

"Tell him," Cosh said to Izzy.

"You tell him. I'm eating." Izzy forked up three raviolis and shoved them into his mouth.

"One of you better tell me something."

Cosh let out a sigh. "The cops were here a little while ago."

"And?"

"They found some project junkies all beat-up in the alley behind our garage."

"And?"

"And nothing." Cosh reached into a cabinet and took down two plates. "They came in, asked a few questions, and left." He filled the plates with ravioli from a huge stockpot on the stove. "Sit down. What do you want to drink?"

Beans sat, but didn't answer. He considered pushing the issue, then decided against it. He wasn't even sure why.

Cosh ladled thick red gravy from another large simmering pot onto the pasta. He set the plates on the table. "How 'bout a Coke?"

When Beans looked up at him, Cosh averted his eyes.

"Sure," Beans said. "Coke's fine. Oh . . ." He reached into his breast pocket. "I almost forgot." He tossed the envelope on the table.

"What's that?" Izzy asked.

"Open it."

Izzy ripped off the top of the envelope and plucked out a rubber-banded brick of hundreds.

"What's this for?"

"The Gimp had a load of cigarettes. Made us partners."

"No shit!" Izzy exclaimed.

Cosh eyed the bundle. "How much is there?"

"Ten dimes," Beans said. "We got five grand each. I took mine out already."

"I don't get it," Izzy said. "Partners? Just like that? What's the catch?"

"We financed it. It was a last-minute thing, and I didn't have time to talk to you guys about it. I put in your ends. Didn't think you'd mind. Pass the cheese, will you?"

"Beautiful." Cosh handed Beans a swirled-glass shaker of grated Pecorino. "So maybe this guy ain't so bad after all?"

"I still don't trust him." Izzy snapped off the rubber bands and counted the money. "Do you, Beans?"

"The only guys I trust are in this room right now. But I'll tell you this: we're gonna get that airplane money. I don't know how yet, but it's all I can think about. So, for now at least, we gotta make him *think* we trust him. We need him." Beans looked at Izzy, then to Cosh—this time able to catch his friends' eye. "Agreed?"

"You really think we got a shot?" Cosh asked.

"I do."

"Do you think this guy will stand up if it goes bad?" Izzy asked.

Beans contemplated. "I gotta figure a way so that's not a factor. Leave it to me. We're gonna do this."

CHAPTER 14

A FREE NEWSPAPER

STEP WAS STUCK in the limbo space between sleeping and waking.

This was when his worst memories surfaced. He wanted to escape his own mind, to fully wake up, to stop the rush of distressing images and dismal scenes—as well the squalid second-floor apartment on Taylor Street above Blind Dan's Barbershop where he lived with his mother, Nancy.

His father, a raging alcoholic, had lived on the streets since his mother had kicked him out when Step, then still known only as Vinnie, was nine years old. He didn't see his father again until five years later, on his fourteenth birthday. That was the last time anybody saw him. Step had run to him and hugged him, thinking it was the best birthday present ever. But the son of a bitch didn't even know it was his birthday. He just needed money.

Step had thrown up his arms to stop the blow, but a swinging backhand sent the spindly, crippled teen tumbling across the room. This gave his father just enough time to punch his mother's face before Step could jump onto his back and snake his scrawny arms around his neck. But Step was no match for his father, who effortlessly flipped Step over his head onto the glass coffee table.

A thud, a crash of shattering glass, then nothing.

He came to just in time to see his father reach under his mother's mattress and take their life savings. Step moved to stop him, but his body was trapped inside the coffee table's mangled brass frame. The son of a bitch laughed as he sidestepped between Step and his mother, who was sitting on the floor cupping a hand over her bloodied nose and mouth.

After he had managed to disentangle himself, Step left the apartment and went looking for his father, who wasn't hard to find. There, in the alley behind VB's liquor store, Step got the money back. Turned out that was easy too. His father lay on the cobblestone, barely conscious, a nearly empty pint of Jim Beam in his hand.

When he returned home, Step handed his mother the money— most of it was still there, at least—and checked her wounds. Her nose wasn't broken, but she might have needed a stitch in her lip if the bleeding hadn't stopped a little while later. He'd gone to the kitchen sink then and, glancing over his shoulder to make sure his mother wasn't watching, drew the bloody steak knife from his sleeve. He slathered it in dish soap, scrubbed it with a paper towel until it was clean, then replaced it in the drying rack.

His mother had somehow eked out a living for the two of them, waitressing at Lou Mitchell's. You'd think after thirteen years they'd give her a damn raise. They were the busiest breakfast joint in Chicago, for crying out loud. Six days a week, she started work at 6:00 a.m. From the fourth grade on, every weekday morning, Step was left to get to school on his own. His mother called it the honor system—a system Step violated so brazenly that the nuns at

Pompeii School had given up on him before he had even reached fifth grade. After that, his mother—she was more stubborn, God bless her—enrolled him in four different schools in three years. Until she, too, gave up.

Step spent his youth learning to scam. He would ride the "L" trains around Chicago, duping passengers with three-card monte, or wander around the Loop selling knockoff Rolexes to unaware tourists and businessmen—always giving his mother half of what he made.

In his mind, that made it okay to do just about anything.

He had joined the club when Beans, Cosh, and Izzy first started it. He wasn't in school and had no job, so he had plenty of leisure time to loll about. The other members treated him as if he were different, weird, so he remained steadfastly suspicious of them all, preferring to do business with the fringe element—guys with similar upbringings who he'd worked with on the streets and a few of the functioning neighborhood junkies.

This morning was pretty much like any other day off. He lay on his back in bed, fixated on the zigzags of the damaged, stained plaster above while the nimbus of sleep faded and a more recent memory seized his brain, making his heart thump harder. He rose, hustled to the window, and opened it, nearly knocking over the potted plant on the sill. He thrust his head out, as well as half his body, scanning back and forth, until his eyes located the desired object. On the front stoop of the town house two doors down and across the street lay a copy of the *Chicago Sun Times* that his neighbor had yet to pick up.

He hopped into a pair of blue jeans that lay crumpled on the floor, then squirmed into his gym shoes. He hurried out of the apartment and down the stairs, at the bottom of which, he opened the building's entry door. He paused, poking his head outside. The coast was clear. Down the steps and across the street he ran, bare-chested, shoelaces flopping, out into the autumn chill. After retrieving the paper, he reversed track, crossing the street again, and slipped back into the building.

"Pretty quick for a gimp!" he said aloud to his many mockers, wherever they were, while taking the stairs two at a time. Once back inside the apartment, Step carried the paper into the kitchen, where the smell of coffee tickled his nostrils. His mother had been gone three hours by then, but she always managed to put on a pot for him before she left for work. After pouring himself a cup, he slapped the paper down on the table and sat.

Page after page, Step frantically skimmed over the articles, stopping at the *Metro* section on page 29, where he spotted a three-inch piece with the headline *Cicero Man Set on Fire*. He read it three times, then put his finger to each line, counting as he went down.

"Seventeen," he said. "Not bad."

He pushed away from the table and went into his bedroom, where he shoved a hand under the mattress and pulled out a three-ring binder. After returning to the kitchen, he grabbed the Pritt glue and a pair of scissors from the junk drawer, cut out the article, and then, before gluing in his latest entry, fanned through the pages of the scrapbook, admiring the chronicles of his life's more noteworthy exploits. There, affixed to pages of thick construction paper, were other similar clippings. Page one featured his father's six-line obituary.

No articles about a drunken bum found rolled in an alley.

Next were multiple short blurbs with eye-catching headlines, such as *Family of Four Tortured for Hours* and *Burglary Gone Bad*.

He came to the next blank page, opposite the page with an article headlined, *Girl Found Murdered at Home in Chinatown*, and drew a small rectangle in the center with the glue stick and carefully pressed the new entry on top, smoothing out the wrinkles with the pad of his thumb. He then sat back, drank his coffee, and thought about the day ahead.

One of the benefits of working for the airline was the schedule—rotating days off. Step liked when they fell in the middle of the week, providing the opportunity to commit his capers when most men of the house were at work. On days when he had nothing scheduled, he hung around the club, watching TV and betting on the horses with the Wiz. Today would be one of those days. Except for the betting part. Skinny had ordered him cut off until his debt was paid in full.

Lucky for him he had a bookmaker in Bridgeport.

Step closed the scrapbook, returned to his room, and replaced it. His hand, still sandwiched between the box spring and mattress, slid toward the foot of the bed, and he pulled out the wad of bills hidden there.

He wanted to count them again, just for fun.

He had sold the load of cigarettes for fifty thousand, not forty like he told Beans. He never paid for it. Too bad for his trucker friend from the Steak and Egger. Step had to give Beans and the boys their fifteen thousand back plus fifteen more. That left thirty-five thousand, two of which he used to pay to have the load transported to the buyer. With the remaining thirty-three, he could pay off the twenty-six thousand he owed Linco, set aside four thousand to pay the Wiz for the next four weeks, give his mother fifteen hundred, and still have fifteen hundred left for pocket money.

Back in the kitchen, he tucked fifteen hundred in an envelope, wrote *Mom* on the front, and set it on the table, propped up against the salt shaker.

"I do it all for you, Mom."

CHAPTER 15

CAN'T WAIT FOR CHRISTMAS

BEANS SAT AT the club's kitchen table, facing the doorway into the main room, but only half paying attention to the chatter of the other members. Thanksgiving had come and gone, and the club was abuzz with anticipation for the annual Christmas party.

On this Monday evening, even though most of the guys had money riding on the Bears-Lions game playing on the television, most of the conversation was about the upcoming festivities.

Johnny "the Goose" DiGussa was down on a knee, facing the half dozen or so other members seated in a semicircle around the TV set. "Okay, start over," he said. "We got Cicero, Berwyn, Elmwood Park, Melrose Park. What else?"

"Addison," one called out.

"Schaumburg," came another.

They were running through the cliques of girls, if past performance was any indicator, who could be expected to attend the party.

Johnny pried up the tab of a can of Old Style beer. The familiar

151

pop-and-pfft sound awakened Capo, who had been asleep under a nearby card table. He sprang to his feet, sauntered over to Johnny, and sat beside him, at attention. Johnny poured a small puddle of beer on the floor, and Capo lapped it up readily.

"Man, I can't fuckin' wait," he said. "Broads from five different suburbs."

Louie "the Gawk" stood and smacked Johnny in the head. "No. That's seven, moron. And don't let Beans catch you giving the dog that crap. It upsets his stomach." He grabbed Capo by the collar, pulled him a few feet away, and knelt, emptying the last of his Heineken on the floor.

Capo lapped it up.

Beans changed seats at the table so that his back was now to the group.

He became oblivious to the chatter as he studied the swath of blue cellophane he held between his thumb and forefinger. The information-gathering process was coming along nicely. As requested, Step had deftly used the knife-ring to slice off a piece of the bundle wrapping without the guards noticing. He also discovered that the Federal Reserve always called the office of American Airlines at least three days prior to shipment to confirm. He noted that the money was routinely flown in on a 727, and, although American ran multiple flights a day from DC to O'Hare, only one, arriving at 11:05 a.m., was a 727.

The flight arrival time was ideal, in that Cosh and Izzy finished their daily deliveries by ten. At 10:40 each day, they arrived at the airport and hung by the gate, watching as the planes were unloaded. The last time the money was flown in, Izzy used three rolls of film, snapping pictures of the unloading procedure. They then followed the armored car downtown and into the alley behind the Federal Reserve bank, where the loading docks were located, and made note of the route.

Beans glanced up at the clock. Cosh and Izzy should have been back by now. He got up and slipped behind the bar, poured himself a glass of Fortissimo, then dropped a dollar in the box.

The door of the club opened and Cosh walked in, carrying a paper sack loaded to the brim with sandwiches from Al's Beef. Izzy came in right behind him, holding a smaller bag, and held up the order list.

Cosh grabbed the top sandwich and read the side of the greasy wax-paper wrapping. "Combo, dipped, hot peppers."

Izzy ran his eyes down the list. "That's Puzzom's."

Cosh lobbed the soggy bundle to the slim, dark-haired member sitting on the couch.

Puzzom caught it, gingerly, and held it away from his body to keep the oil from dripping onto his clothes. "Thanks," he said. "Keep the change."

"Fourteen cents," Izzy said. "You're a real humanitarian."

"Beef with sweet," Cosh called out.

"Beef with sweet peppers," Izzy repeated. "Turtle."

They continued until the bag was empty, then walked into the back with the smaller bag, which held sandwiches for Beans and themselves.

"Hey, Beans," Izzy called out. "Hit me with a splash of that ink, will ya'?"

"Make it two," Cosh said.

Beans slipped two more dollars in the box, poured two more glasses of wine, then carried them into the kitchen.

"Put a chair in front of that door so the dog can't get in," Cosh said. "I'd like to eat without sneezing."

Beans did as he asked and sat down in front of the beef sandwich Izzy had set out for him. The other two were already at the table, unwrapping their own sandwiches.

"I think your new best friend got himself into a little pickle," Izzy said.

Beans knew immediately that he was referring to Step. Saying "your new best friend" was Izzy-speak sarcasm meaning, "The guy's a piece of shit."

"Step? What'd he do?"

"Not sure," Izzy said with a mouthful and a shrug. "But Skinny was slapping the fuck out of him."

Beans let out a short chuckle through his nose. Despite the serious bearing this might have on the future of their big score, the image of his uncle slapping the Gimp was such that he couldn't disguise his amusement. "Get the fuck outta here," he said.

Cosh laughed, shaking his head. "We were walking past the Survivors Club, and we were gonna ask the old guys if they wanted a sandwich. But when we went to open the door, it was locked. So, naturally, we looked in through the window. That's when we saw it."

"Tell me exactly what you saw," Beans said, switching his tone to serious. "What was Step doing—just standing there taking it?"

"He didn't have no choice," Izzy said.

"You know those two punks from the Island we see Skinny with sometimes? They had Step by the arms. I never seen Skinny so out of his head. His face was beet red. He was really winding up on the kid." Cosh sipped his wine.

Beans zeroed in on Izzy. "And the rest of the club was empty?"

"The Wiz was there and that cockeyed BM from Bridgeport— what do they call him? Clorox, or Lysol, or something?"

"You mean Linco?"

"Yeah."

"And what were they doing during all this?"

"Just sitting there, looking stupid," Izzy said. "Other than them, we didn't see anyone else in the place."

Beans stared down at his sandwich. This wasn't good. Skinny and the Wiz, a bookmaker from Bridgeport, and two guys from the Island. If Step managed to piss these guys off, he was not long for this world. Good thing was they were just smacking him around. He couldn't have fucked up too bad, or they would have just whacked him without warning.

"That motherfucker better not get himself popped. Not yet, anyway. We still need him." Beans chugged his wine, stood, and left the room.

"Hey!" Izzy called as Beans made his way toward the front. "You gonna eat this sandwich?"

Beans walked out of the club, slamming the door behind him.

• • •

Beans wished he had a different kind of relationship with his uncle Skinny. Then he could just ask him. The way things stood between them now, discussing business was out of the question. They each pretended that they didn't know what the other was up to. By not speaking of their respective exploits, Skinny was giving Beans his tacit blessing. And Beans, though he would never flaunt it, was secure in knowing that Uncle Skinny had his back.

A couple of blocks from the Survivors Club, Beans spotted a dim pair of headlights approaching from the east. Out of sheer habit, he began trying to identify the car. He made a practice of being familiar with every car in the neighborhood, and was ever on the alert for a strange car hanging around, as had been his practice for years. Being familiar with every car in the neighborhood made it easier to recognize any that looked out of place. He had trained himself to recognize the make, model, and year of a car by the slightest bit of detail—an outline, or a headlight or tail-light configuration. This also came in handy when following someone at a distance or watching in his own rear-view mirror to assess whether or not he was being followed.

For the moment, all he could discern was that the car was either a Ford or a Lincoln. He started running down a list in his head of neighborhood guys who drove those makes. Way too many. As the vehicle drew nearer, he could see it was either gray or white.

The car caught the red light at Taylor and Racine.

Granada. Definitely a Ford Granada.

Puzzom drove a light-blue Granada that might appear gray or white from a distance, but he was still on the couch at the club when Beans had walked out. Maybe he had loaned the car to someone else? Beans continued down the sidewalk. Definitely white. No one he knew drove a white Granada. Another car came up behind at the light and stopped, its headlights shining through the rear window of the Ford and illuminating its interior. Beans could see the silhouette of big hair. It was a girl.

Beans stepped off the curb and stood between two parked cars. When the light changed, he moved into the street, timing it so that by the time she arrived at his position, he was standing at the center between the east and westbound lanes.

The woman stopped to let him cross, but he waved her past. When she rolled by, slowly, they made eye contact. Beans checked her out as thoroughly as possible from this vantage point. Perfectly manicured red fingernails rested atop the steering wheel. And on her fingers, an array of twinkling gold and diamond rings, sparkling like Christmas against her brown spa-tanned skin. Her face, too, was tanned, and Beans could tell by the way it stretched taut over her delicate bone structure that she was a slender girl. A bit heavier on the makeup than to his liking, perhaps, but she was definitely good-looking.

"Yo, Mare," he called, acting as if she were someone he knew. "Hold up!"

She stopped and rolled down the window.

"Oh, sorry." Beans threw up a hand. "I thought you were someone else."

Mascara streaked down her face, dragged by a torrent of ongoing tears.

"Hey," he said, stepping closer. "Are you okay?"

"Not really." An open bottle of red wine was wedged between her thighs. "I just caught my asshole boyfriend in bed with another girl."

"Wow," Beans said. "He sounds like a real jagoff. We should go get even with him."

She hesitated, looking Beans up and down. She started to say something, then cut herself off. "I'm sick of men. I'm gonna go join a convent."

Beans smiled. "Don't let one monkey stop your whole show."

She looked up, making eye contact.

Beans took full advantage of the opportunity, peering deeply into her eyes—his Jedi-mind-control-pickup stare.

Her expression softened. "Get in. I can use some help with this bottle."

Beans walked around to the other side of the car and slid into the passenger seat. "You ever been to Ankle Lake?"

• • •

An hour later, she was dropping him off at the Survivors Club.

"You better not lose my number," she warned. "If you don't call, I *will* come looking for you."

"I believe you would," he said with a laugh. "Hey, I never asked. What's your boyfriend's name?"

"Ex-boyfriend, you mean." She snorted. "Pete Mariani. You know him?"

"Petey Slugs? Known him my whole life. Always with a beautiful girl. I never did understand what they see in him."

"Looking back, I'll never understand it myself," she said. "But thanks for the compliment. And for cheering me up."

"My pleasure."

Beans climbed out of the Granada, and she drove away.

He stood on the sidewalk at the corner of Taylor and May, in front of the Survivors Club. Streetlights out a block in each direction. Not a soul in sight. He savored the dark, the quiet stillness, while staring at the club's large storefront windows that, while painted over in black and gold, shone enough to let him know the lights were still on inside. He studied the script lettering, *Survivors S.A.C.*—Social Athletic Club. Beans snickered. The most athletic thing these guys did was shuffle cards.

And social? More like sociopathic.

Beans pondered how to broach the subject of Step with Skinny. His uncle would not appreciate any perceived attempt by Beans to meddle in his affairs. And how could he ask questions without revealing the reason for his interest? If Skinny so much as suspected the potential magnitude of Beans's impending score, he would surely try to muscle his way into it—put his own guys on it, maybe even take over the whole plan. Family or not, that was just the way these Outfit guys were.

"Fuck it."

He decided not to talk to Skinny. The job was too important to risk it getting poisoned. He could try pumping the Wiz for information. Plus, by tomorrow, there would be whispers all over the neighborhood. Beans would just have to sift out the truth from the bullshit.

A door slammed in the distance. "I'm gonna kill that motherfucker!"

Beans peered down Taylor to Aberdeen, where a hulking figure was kicking and pounding on the door of the "Nut House."

Beans trotted down the block to investigate, the racket growing louder and clearer as he neared the local tavern.

"You can't stay in there forever!" Another kick at the door shook the frame and echoed off the surrounding buildings. "Don't make me break your fuckin' door, Vito!"

Beans picked up the pace. Someone was going to kill Vito, and he didn't want to miss it.

Charlie Carlucci's foot connected again with the still-closed door. "I'll twist your fuckin' head off, you motherfucker!"

And he probably could too.

Charlie was one of three brothers, all built like oak trees, and with nicknames like Panzer, Creeper, and Bunyan. All three worked the docks at the South Water Market.

Nobody fucked with them.

Charlie stood on the tavern's iron stoop, hammering away with his bare fists. The entire door was obscured by his massive frame.

"I got all night," he shouted. "You gotta come out sometime!"

Beans approached cautiously, making sure to keep a safe distance. "Hey, Charlie. Everything okay?"

159

Charlie spun with the agility of an alley cat, and squinted into the dark. "Beans!" He loped off the stoop.

Beans was smothered in a bear hug before he could react.

Charlie kissed the top of his head. "I never got the chance to thank you for helping out my father."

"Don't mention it," Beans mumbled against Charlie's armpit. He managed to push away. "That guy ain't fuckin' with him anymore?"

"Are you kiddin'? Dad says the guy won't even look at him."

Beans pointed to the tavern. "Everything okay in there?"

"Oh, yeah." He nodded and glanced back. "I'm just gonna kill that fuckin' little punk."

"Vito?" This didn't make sense to Beans. Vito was an asshole, but he didn't fit the description "little punk."

"Nah, man. Petey Slugs. Vito's got him locked up in there so I can't get at him."

Must be some kinda karma. "Petey Slugs, huh? Anything I can do to help?"

"Nah. I appreciate the offer, but this is personal." Charlie turned and started back to the door of the tavern.

"Listen," Beans said. "Don't say anything, but if it makes you feel any better, I just fucked Petey's girlfriend."

Once again, Beans found himself engulfed by Charlie's considerable girth.

Again he kissed the top of Beans's head, then held him at arm's length by the shoulders. "You gotta love this guy!"

Charlie let go and Beans stumbled backward.

• • •

Beans lit a cigarette and started back toward the Nailati Club, strolling down Taylor Street past the projects. When he got to

160

Loomis, he changed his mind and turned right toward home. After passing by Peanut Park, he heard a rustling in the bushes behind him.

He spun and reached for his gun.

"That you, Beans?" One of the neighborhood kids, about twelve, stepped clear of the thicket.

"What the fuck's wrong with you, kid? You could get shot sneakin' up on a guy like that. What were you doin' back there?"

"Sorry, Beans," the kid said. "Mind if I walk with you for a little?"

The kid smelled like a sewer.

"Sure," Beans said. "What's up?"

"Nuthin'. But if the cops come, I was with you all night, okay?"

Beans chuckled. "Are you guys throwin' eggs at the buses again? Halloween was almost two months ago."

"Yeah," he said with a shrug. "But we found a dozen we'd stashed that we forgot about. Man, do they stink."

Beans turned to flick his cigarette. When he turned back, the kid was gone.

A blue-and-white patrol car rolled by.

"Nice reflexes," he said to the kid who wasn't there.

A minute or so later, he was descending the stairs to his apartment while digging the key out of his pocket. As he attempted to put it in the lock, the door creaked open. No way had Beans forgotten to lock up when he left earlier.

His hand went for his gun.

He glanced back up the stairwell behind him, then peered through the cracked door. No lights on inside. With his free hand, he reached inside to the left and flicked the switch. He pushed open the door just wide enough to slip through.

Her body lay facedown about five feet beyond the threshold. A saucer-sized pool of blood had formed on the floor to the right of her head—a result of the dripping gash in her scalp.

"Debbie!"

Beans dropped to his knees, set a hand under her neck, and turned over her listless body.

Her eyes fluttered open, and she groaned. "What the fuck hit me?"

Beans planted a loud smacking kiss on her forehead and gently laid her back down. "You're gonna be okay," he said. "Just hold on." Back on his feet, pistol in hand, Beans darted into and around each room of the apartment. After making sure the place was clear, he picked up the phone and dialed 911, then returned to his sister, who was trying to sit up. "Deb," he said, swiping a throw pillow from the couch. "Don't try to get up. There's an ambulance on the way."

"It's not that bad, Beans. I don't need an ambulance." She pushed herself up onto one knee, went immediately pale, and wobbled sideways with a dry heave.

"I said, don't try to get up."

He eased her back down and, while slipping the pillow behind her head, noticed for the first time the porcelain lid of the toilet tank lying on the hardwood behind the door. "I guess that's what you got kabonged with. What the fuck happened? Who hit you?"

"I don't know. I opened the door and *wham*! Lights out."

Beans went into the bathroom, took a washcloth from the cabinet, and brought it out to her. "Here. Hold this to your head. You're still bleeding." An unpleasant odor suddenly permeated his senses. Beans sniffed at the air. "What is that?"

"What is what?"

"Debbie, did you . . . do something . . . in your pants?"

"What? No!"

"I'm just saying, sometimes it can happen when you get knocked out. It's nothing to be embarrassed about."

"Seriously, Beans. I think I'd know."

"Then what the fuck is that?" Beans walked through the apartment. As he neared the kitchen, the stench grew stronger. He flipped on the overhead light.

There, next to the kitchen table, was a pile of feces.

"What the . . . did you have a dog in here?" he called to Debbie.

"Are you nuts?" she returned. "Why would I bring a dog into your apartment? Where would I even get a dog?"

He backed up into the living room. "What the fuck is going on in this town?"

Debbie tried again to get to her feet, but crumpled to the floor, unconscious.

Beans repositioned the pillow under her head and called the club for Cosh and Izzy. They arrived before the ambulance.

"What the fuck happened?" Izzy asked.

"I don't know. I got home and she was on the floor."

Cosh, his face gone ashen, knelt beside Debbie and put an ear to her nose. "She's breathing," he said, letting loose an audible sigh of relief. "She's gonna be okay."

Beans stared down at his friend. Was Cosh blinking back tears?

"Where the fuck is the ambulance?" Cosh said. "Izzy, go drive around the neighborhood. See if you see anybody weird."

"That's not a bad idea." Izzy hurried out the door.

"Beans, go see if your parents or your grandmother saw or heard anything. And call 911 again!"

"Nobody's home upstairs," Beans said, lifting the phone. "They went to Zi Bep's house for dinner. Whoever did this was watching the house."

The faint wail of a far-off siren rippled in the background and intensified with each passing second. Beans replaced the handset.

Cosh, meanwhile, returned his attention to Debbie. "Hang in there. You're gonna be okay. Fuck!" he said. "Go get me a glass of water."

"You're thirsty? *Now*?"

"It's not for me! I want to splash her face, see if I can wake her up."

The siren crescendoed with earsplitting force, then went silent. Beans dashed outside and ushered the paramedics into the apartment. Cosh stood and made room for them to do their job.

Together, they watched and listened as the paramedics knelt beside Debbie and rattled off a stream of medical terminology while checking her vitals. They fitted her neck with a brace, lifted her gently onto a stretcher, and strapped her in.

"We're gonna ride with her," Cosh said. It wasn't a request.

"Rules say only one of you can ride."

"I don't give a f—"

"Cosh!" Beans said. "Do me a favor. Go to Zi Bep's house and tell my parents."

Cosh stood down. "Okay." He turned to the paramedics. "Which hospital are you taking her to?"

"Cabrini is the closest."

• • •

Later that night, Beans stood at the foot of Debbie's hospital bed, which was flanked on either side by his parents and his grandmother, who sat clutching her rosary and mumbling some prayer in Italian.

Beans moved in behind her and gave her shoulder a gentle squeeze. "Don't worry, Gram. She's gonna be okay. The doctor said he thinks she'll wake up soon."

A pretty young nurse quietly entered into the room—a familiar face from the neighborhood Beans couldn't quite put a name to. *Lydia? Lenora?*

"I'm sorry, you guys," she said, tucking a lock of bottle-blond hair behind her ear. "But it's way past visiting hours."

Beans began to protest.

"No, problem, Lucy." Cosh left Izzy standing by the window and stepped into the place Beans had just vacated. "Your mom and dad are exhausted, Beans. You should take them home and get some rest yourself." He looked at the nurse. "You'll be here all night, right?"

"Until six." She gave a small smile. "I promise I'll take good care of her."

"You see," Cosh said. "Debbie's in good hands. We can come back bright and early tomorrow."

Beans hung back as Cosh ushered the group out of the room. Izzy was the first out, followed by Beans's father. After his mother and grandmother each kissed Debbie's forehead and walked out, Beans set a hand on Cosh's back.

"You okay?"

Cosh's glistening eyes said it all. He really and truly loved Debbie.

She could do a lot worse. Beans stared down at his sister—her bandaged head and pale face. She looked so tiny and meek, lying there quietly in the bed. But Beans knew she was strong. He set a hand on Cosh's back. "Come on," he said. "Let's get out of here."

They joined the others at the elevator and rode down to the lobby.

As they made their way toward the main doors, Cosh, bringing up the rear, stopped. "I'm parked on the side," he announced to the group. "I'm gonna use the other exit."

Beans eyed him, then nodded. "See you tomorrow, brother."

• • •

Brother. Cosh liked the sound of that.

He watched as the others filed out through the hospital's sliding glass doors and disappeared into the night. Then he reversed course to the elevator and rode it back up to the fifth floor.

Inside Debbie's room, he found Nurse Lucy Russo bent over Debbie, attending to her IV. "Hi," he said.

Lucy jumped. "Oh, hi. You're back."

He approached the bed and slipped a folded hundred-dollar bill into Lucy's palm. "She's gonna wake up soon. And I'm gonna be here when she does."

Lucy glanced down and smiled. "You're sweet. I'll get you a more comfortable chair." A few minutes later, she returned, wheeling an aqua-green vinyl recliner into the room. On it sat a folded blanket and two pillows. She continued to the far wall and used her knee to position the chair into the corner. "The call button is on the bed," she said. "Let me know if you need anything else."

"Thanks. I'm good for now."

"Oh, I almost forgot." She dug into the pocket of her crisp white nursing uniform and handed back the hundred-dollar bill. "We got ice cream and pudding in the fridge at the nurses' station."

Now it was Cosh's turn to smile. "Thanks."

After Lucy left the room, closing the door quietly behind her, Cosh rolled the chair out of the corner and pushed it flush against the bed. He then sat down, reclined, and stretched his hand to Debbie's, nestling it within his own.

•••

Beans arrived at the hospital at eight the next morning, sixty minutes before visiting hours. He breezed casually into the lobby, slipped past the front-desk guard—distracted by a janitor, shlepping by with his bucket on wheels—and rounded the corner to the elevators. A minute later, he stepped onto the fifth floor and proceeded stealthily down the mostly vacant corridor to room 516 on the left. He pushed the door open a crack and poked his head inside. There, at his sister's bedside, slept Cosh, his hand clasped over hers.

Beans eased his head out and pulled the door closed.

Debbie was around thirteen when he first noticed her starry-eyed gaze anytime Cosh came over to the house. It was around the time of Debbie's sixteenth birthday when Beans caught Cosh, while joining the family for Sunday dinner, stealing glances of Debbie from across the table.

To this day, neither had confessed to the fact.

Beans returned to the main lobby and to the bank of pay phones there, dialing the direct number to Debbie's room.

Midway through the third ring, there was a clatter on the other end of the line, then, "Hello?"

"Who's this?" Beans smiled to himself.

"Beans?" His friend suddenly sounded much more alert. "It's me—Cosh."

"What the fuck are you doing there?"

"I got a lot of work to do today. I wanted to come early to see how she's doing."

"And how *is* she doing?"

There was a pause, then, "Holy fuck, Beans! She's waking up! Must have been the sound of the phone ringing."

Beans looked to the heavens and said a silent prayer. "I'll be right there! Call the nurse!"

CHAPTER 16

TRIPLE JEOPARDY

"SO, SHE'S OKAY?" Pat smothered his usual morning eggroll with sweet-and-sour sauce.

"Yeah," Beans said. "She was unconscious for about twelve hours. Then in the hospital four days. They discharged her yesterday afternoon."

"I'm not kiddin', Beans. You don't know how lucky she is. That sick fuck. He's already killed one girl—that we know of. You remember, that Chinese girl a few doors down that I told you about?"

"I remember," Beans said.

"Homicide is looking at him for two others, too, including the charred guy in in Cicero."

Beans remembered that story from somewhere. "Wait," he said. "Didn't they find that guy in a car? I thought the burglar was more the home-invasion type?"

"He was," Pat said, "until one of the cops called to the scene slipped on a heaping pile of shit next to the burned-out vehicle."

"How do you know it wasn't just some stray dog?" Beans asked.

"They test that shit," Pat said, cracking a smile. "No pun intended." He shoveled a forkful of eggroll into his mouth.

"Okay, Pat." Beans dumped an extra sugar into his coffee and stirred. He hadn't been able to eat much the past few days, and he figured he could use the calories. "This is personal. Tell me everything you know."

"Well, obviously, so far, the guy's been hard to pin down. No consistent MO or patterns to the hits. He operates all over the city and the suburbs."

"So why do you think he picked me?"

"Don't know. Do you keep a lot of cash at your place? Maybe someone blabbed."

Beans wondered if Pat was trying to get him to admit to something. "I drive a tow truck, Pat. I'm not exactly rollin' in it."

"Well, then. Maybe it's someone you know."

"Keep going." Beans sipped his coffee.

"The way it looks, the guy was in the bathroom when he heard Debbie put the key in the door. Probably wiping his ass, the disgusting fuck. So he grabs the tank lid—no prints on that, by the way—slides behind the entry door, and when she walks in . . . *powie*."

Picturing the scene made Bean's heart pound against his shirt. He felt heat rising in his face.

"You gotta keep calm, Beans," Pat said. "Main thing is, your sister's okay."

Beans exhaled. "Yeah, I know. What else do we know about this guy?"

"Well, he's a pretty competent burglar, for one. Always wears gloves and a mask. Locks don't seem to slow him down much. And in most cases—aside from yours, apparently, and who knows about the truck driver in Cicero—the guy knows who's got the cash and where it's hidden."

Truck driver in Cicero.

Pat set down his fork and leaned close, his faded blue eyes growing cold. "And then there's the part where he's a sick, twisted fuck—robs old ladies, gets off on torturing people, and likes to leave a nasty steaming dump at every crime scene." Pat sat back hard, the chair legs beneath screeching under his weight. "Oh, and according to the seven-year-old daughter of the family over in Oak Brook, who he tortured for over three hours, guy's tall, skinny, and walks funny." Pat air-quoted the last two words.

Beans's stomach lurched. "Funny?"

"Yeah. She was the only one who got a good look at the guy before they were blindfolded and strapped to the chairs around their own goddamn dining room table. Came wandering out of a nearby bathroom after the fucker had her mom, dad, and eleven-year-old brother at gunpoint, facedown, on the living room floor." Pat gave a shrug. "We can only assume she meant that he walks with some kinda limp."

The blood rushed into Beans's face again, and the room swirled around him. It all made sense now. *Son of a bitch!*

Fuckin' Sam's dago red. If Beans hadn't been so drunk that night, so fucking careless, Step never would have learned where he hid his money.

The assault on Debbie was all his fault. *Fuck!*

"Thanks, Pat. I owe you one." He stood up and walked out of the restaurant as if he were in a trance, whispering to himself, "Remember, Beans, if you lose your head, your ass goes with it. If you lose your head, your ass goes with it."

He got back in his truck, lit a cigarette, and popped a Frankie

Valli tape into the tape player. He had no intention of losing his head. He just had to let the rush of violent, spinning thoughts spin for a while, until they lost momentum. He took a deep drag, closed his eyes, and listened to the music.

For a split second, a dozen images flashed in his mind like a strobe light. He tried to organize and memorize the images, but they were gone as fast as they came. It was the perfect plan. He knew it. But he couldn't make sense of it. He had to find some sanity. He had to talk to Cosh and Izzy.

By the time he'd smoked the cigarette down to the filter, he was pulling into the city yard. He parked the truck, announced to his foreman that he was ill, climbed into his car, and drove straight to Geraldi's.

He double-parked the Ninety-Eight out front and walked inside. The little bell above the door did not, this time, draw out the usual assortment of flavorful thoughts. Thankfully, the store was empty of customers.

He marched through into the back.

"Yo, Beans. What's up?" Cosh was grabbing a Coke from the fridge. "Just rolled in from the route."

"We gotta talk," Beans said. "Who's here?"

"Just me and Izzy." Cosh turned and shrugged. "I just sent our new counter girl to lunch. I don't think she's gonna work out. The girl doesn't know her prosciutt' from her gabagol'."

Beans paced the kitchen. "Lock the front. Flip the sign on the door."

"Okay." Cosh eyed him warily while setting the can of pop on the table. "I'll be right back."

Just as Cosh returned, Izzy appeared from the warehouse.

He looked from Cosh to Beans. "What the fuck's going on?"

Beans sat them both down and rattled off the details Pat Gibbons had given him—everything from the dead Chinese girl, the seared truck driver in Cicero, the tortured family of four . . . to the tall, skinny intruder who "walked funny."

Cosh rose and walked into the pantry. He emerged with a shotgun and lobbed it to Iz, who caught it in one hand. Cosh went in for another and came back. "Sorry, Beans. There's only two. You'll have to use that peashooter you got."

Beans looked from one to the other. "What the fuck are you guys doing?"

Izzy pumped the shotgun to put a shell into the chamber. "We're gonna fuckin' splatter the Gimp all over that shitty apartment he lives in."

"I know he's home," Cosh said, following Izzy's lead. "We just drove by the building. His car's parked out front."

"Now, just hold on a minute." Beans dropped into a chair. "I didn't come here to rile you guys up. I came here because I hoped you guys would be more clear-headed than me."

Cosh lifted his jacket off the chairback. "Only thing clear to me right now is that there's nothing to talk about. He could have killed Debbie." His face went dark. "Fuck that Gimp in his ass. He's done."

"How can I be the calm one here? She's *my* sister!"

Izzy pointed a finger at Beans. "Don't ever insult us like that. She's not just *your* sister. She's *our* sister."

Beans stared back at Izzy. If he weren't so furious with himself right now, he'd be struggling to keep his eyes dry. A quick glance to Cosh was all he could stand. Beans had never seen his friend so agitated. "Okay, guys," Beans said. "We're all on the same page here. I'm not saying we don't do it. I'm just saying not yet.

We gotta be smart. What good does it do anybody if we all wind up in prison? So, let's talk about this for a sec."

Cosh and Izzy rested the shotguns against the wall.

"Okay," Izzy said. "But like Cosh said, there's really nothing to talk about."

"What do you mean?" Beans asked. "We've got at least a few million things to talk about."

Izzy shook his head. "You need to understand one thing, Beans."

"What?"

Izzy made a pistol with his thumb and forefinger. "You know he plans to kill us, right?"

"He's gonna *try* to kill us."

Cosh held up a hand like a traffic cop. "Whoa, what the fuck are you guys talking about?"

"Step," Izzy said. "If he killed that truck driver for twenty grand, whattaya think he'd do for ten million? Do you think he plans on sharing and caring?"

Cosh reclaimed his shotgun. "What the fuck are we doing just sittin' here, then? Are we just gonna sit around and wait for him take potshots at us? Let's get him first."

"Relax," Beans said. "Remember, we still need Step to pull off this job. More importantly, he needs us. I'm sure he has some devious plan to take us out, but he won't execute that until *after* we get him the money. We just gotta get to him first, after *we* get the money."

Izzy covered Beans's hand with his. "You're not thinking this through. Step won't have to wait 'til after we get the money. He only needs you to figure out *how* to get it and then tell him the plan. Once he's knows that, he doesn't need us anymore. That's when he'll make his move. Get what I'm saying?"

Beans's heart slowed some. "You're saying that whatever plan I come up with, Step ain't gonna learn about it 'til the last minute."

"Exactly." Izzy snagged Cosh's Coke from the table and took a swig. "Bluh," he said, tongue wagging out of his mouth. "Where's my orange juice?"

CHAPTER 17

THE BACK ROOM

IT WAS A crisp, clear December night.

Beans double-parked on Seventy-Fifth Court, in front of Laura's house in Elmwood Park, then turned up the collar of his leather jacket to brace himself against the early winter chill. As he walked to her door, Beans couldn't help but look back to his 1984 Oldsmobile Ninety-Eight, charcoal gray with a light-gray vinyl top. It was sporting a fresh wash and wax, and the street lights reflecting off its finish made it glimmer like a gentle breeze on a crystal clear lake.

He climbed the steps to the door and rang the bell.

Laura's older brother opened it and let him in.

"Hey, Beans. How's it goin'?"

He held out his hand, and Beans gave it a firm shake.

"I'm good, Tony," he said. "Thanks for askin'."

He remembered Laura telling him that Tony liked him because Beans always looked him in the eye when they spoke—a sign of respect his father had impressed on him through the years and of which Beans had made a habit.

Laura's little ten-year-old brother, Nicky, came sliding into the entryway in his stocking feet and used Beans as a brake, slamming into his legs and wrapping his arms around his waist. "Hi, Beans. Wanna go shoot my new BB gun?"

"Heck yeah," Beans said, always happy to indulge the kid. "But it's nighttime now." He tousled Nicky's hair. "You gotta go to bed pretty soon. Plus, it's your sister's birthday. I'm taking her out to dinner."

"I guess that's okay," Nicky said. "Since it's her birthday." He leaned in and whispered, "But I know you'd rather hang out with me."

"That's true," Beans whispered back. "But don't tell Laura. She'll get jealous."

Laura appeared on the stairs and made her way down. Beans couldn't take his eyes off of her.

She wore a blue satin halter-top jumpsuit, cinched at the waist with a matching belt, white high-heeled pumps, and a white headband that contrasted nicely with her golden complexion and blazing-red hair, which she tossed dramatically. "Like it?" she said. "I had it highlighted."

Beans darted his eyes toward Tony and Nicky. Hopefully they weren't able to read his thoughts. "I don't get it," he said. "You're a hundred percent Italian. Where does the red come from?"

"I don't know," she said with a shrug. "Maybe my great-grand-father? My aunt told me he was a redhead, but I never met him." She gripped his hand. "Where're you taking me tonight?"

"It's a surprise. You like seafood, right?"

"It's my favorite." She lifted a black full-length leather coat with fur collar from the coatrack beside the door. "Hey, we match tonight." She stroked her palm against the lapel of Beans's black leather blazer. Beans stepped aside to let Laura through the door first, ogling her body as she moved down the steps.

"I love this car," Laura said as Beans started the Ninety-Eight and took off down the street. She ran her hand along the plush velour-covered seat, then reached forward to turn on the radio, which was set to the oldies station playing "Betcha by Golly, Wow."

Beans poked at the preset buttons until he found WBMX. Alisha's "All Night Passion" dance-club sounds reverberated through the car.

"I like the other one," Laura said, reaching to change it back.

Beans grabbed her wrist. "Well, I like this one. And I'm the captain of this ship. You are therefore not authorized to operate the control panel."

"You just don't want the oldies station on because you're afraid Maria will dedicate another song to you." She sat back and crossed her arms.

"How many times I gotta tell you?" Beans said. "I don't know no fuckin' Maria. Are you really gonna start a fight with me on your birthday?"

"Not so long as you put the Stylistics back on."

"Fine."

They rode for a while without speaking as Beans took them west down North Avenue.

Laura flipped up the armrest and scooched close. "So, where are we going?"

He put his arm around her. "Slicker Sam's."

"What the fuck is that?" she said, turning her head toward him. "It sounds like a strip joint."

"You never heard of Slicker Sam's? It's in Melrose Park. You like raw clams, right?"

"I love raw clams. Also, baked clams, calamari, pretty much all seafood."

"Then this is the place for you."

After a few more turns, Beans parked on a side street a block down from the restaurant. They hurried through the cold and entered into a corridor lined with signed photographs of singers and movie stars, all dedicated to Sam and extolling his cooking.

A hostess approached. "Hi, hon. Two of you?"

"Yeah," Beans said. "Is it possible to sit in Maria's section?"

"Let me check. She's pretty full." The hostess hurried off.

Laura turned to him, eyes wide, lips pressed thin.

Before she could say anything, the hostess returned. "Okay." She smiled. "Follow me."

They followed her through the crowded dining room, where Dean Martin was playing on the jukebox. The tables were covered in red-and-white checkered tablecloths, and just about all were occupied with patrons talking and laughing as they enjoyed their meals. The ceiling was covered in wooden garden lattice intertwined with plastic vines and white Italian Christmas lights. The walls, like those along the corridor, were speckled with photographs of famous people who had dined there. In the center of the largest wall was a chalkboard with the menu scrawled on it.

"Maria will be right with you."

They removed their coats and draped them on the backs of their chairs. Beans waited for Laura to sit, then took a seat across from her. "You want a drink?"

"Sure."

A middle-aged, roly-poly spitfire with curly brown hair sauntered up to the table. "Hey, Beanth. Howth it goin?" she lisped through the gap in her two front teeth.

"I'm good, Maria. And you?"

"You know me—workin' hard for the money."

"Don't I know it. Maria, this is Laura." He gestured between them, palm up, to Laura. "Laura, Maria."

"Nice to meet you." Laura grinned, throwing a glance to Beans. "You look familiar. Are you from Cicero, by any chance?"

Damn. Girl's gotta memory on her.

"Nope, right here in Melrosthe Park." She set a pair of chubby fists on her hips. "You guyths want drinkths?"

Laura's smile faded.

"A slow southern screw and a VO and water," Beans answered.

"Sthome people call it a sthlow *comfortable* sthcrew." Maria winked.

"Yeah, well, I'm from the south side of Taylor Street, which ain't so comfortable, y'know?"

Maria laughed. "I'll be right back, hon," she called over her shoulder.

When Maria was out of earshot, Beans leaned toward Laura. "I can't believe you interrogated the waitress."

"It was just a question. Besides, I had to know."

"C'mon. She's a sweetheart, but she's like fifty years old."

"Hey, I don't know what kind of kinky shit you're into."

Maria returned and set their drinks on the table. Beans and Laura caught each other's eye and laughed.

"You're fuckin' nuts; you know that?" Beans said to her.

"Yeah, and don't you forget it."

"I don't want to interrupt," Maria said. "Any appetizers for you?"

"Mind if I order for both of us?" Beans asked.

Laura shrugged and nodded.

He looked up at Maria. "Can I give you the whole order now?"

"Fire away." Maria put a pen to her pad.

"We'll have half a dozen raw, half a dozen baked, and two orders of king crab legs. Oh, and a bottle of Santa Margherita Pinot Grigio."

"You got it, hon." Maria turned and hustled away.

Beans reached into his jacket pocket for his Winstons and Zippo, his knuckles bumping the small, square jewelry box beside the cigarettes.

Laura, meanwhile, opened her purse, drew out her Virginia Slims, and plucked one from the pack.

Beans put a cigarette between his lips, snapped open the Zippo, and rolled the flint wheel. He reached across the table, held it to Laura's cigarette, then lit his own.

He picked up his drink. "Happy birthday."

Laura clinked her drink to his. "Thank you."

"Do you want your present now, or later?" Beans asked.

"I thought this was my present."

"No. There's this, and then we're going somewhere else. Plus there's an actual present. It's going to be a late night."

"Well then, I can't wait. I can't stand suspense."

Beans reached back into his pocket for the box and set it on the table in front of her. It was hinged, the kind that opens like a clamshell, and covered in gray velvet with a brass band around the middle where the two halves came together.

Her eyes widened at the sight of it. "What, no wrapping paper?" she teased.

"I'm not much of a wrapper. Just open it."

"No card?"

"I don't do cards either. If you don't want the fuckin' thing, I'll put it back in my pocket and we can forget about it."

"I'm just playin' with you," she said. "Don't be so sensitive."

Maria swayed up to the table with a tray of raw clams on a bed of shaved ice, her plump hips brushing the tablecloths of the tables she passed on the way. "The baked will be up in a few minuths." She placed the tray in the center of the table. "Nithe boxth. Whath's the occashion?"

Laura giggled. "It's my birthday."

"Happy birthday, thweety. What'd you get?"

"I don't know, I haven't opened it yet."

"Mind if I watch you open it?"

"Not at all." Laura opened the box and held it out for the three of them to see. She gasped. "A tennis bracelet! Are those real diamonds?" The stones were a prism of color, sparkling bright and bluish white.

Maria gave a whistle. "Believe me, hon. I know my jewelry, and them are real. And they're thet in platinum. Beautiful."

Laura jumped up and lunged toward Beans, throwing her arms around his neck. "Thank you!"

"Happy Birthday, baby. You like it?"

"It's beautiful." She planted a kiss on his mouth.

"Here, let me see. I'll help you put it on."

Laura handed him the box and held out her left arm. Beans draped the bracelet over her wrist and clasped it.

"Oh my God, I love it." She sat back down.

Beans picked up a lemon wedge. "This okay on the clams?"

"Yep."

"Tabasco?" He grabbed the bottle.

"Yeah, but I'll do that myself. I like just a drop."

After dribbling the spicy pepper sauce over the three raw clams closest to him, he passed the bottle to her. She gently dotted each of her three. They each picked up a shell, put it to their lips, and inhaled their clams with a slurp and a gulp.

"These are really good." She picked up another and tossed it back.

Beans stared at her in amazement. "I've never been with a girl who likes raw clams before. And you really seem to like them. You want more?"

"No. I'm ready to move on to the baked."

As if on cue, Maria appeared again with a tray of baked clams and their wine. "The wine'th on me, by the way. Happy birthday, hon." She opened the wine, poured two glasses, and nestled the bottle in a bucket of ice.

"Maria, no," Beans said. "That's too much."

"I don't want to hear another word about it."

Maria checked her watch, gave Beans a wink, and again walked off.

"What a sweetheart," Laura said.

"Yeah, I'll say. Look." Beans pointed to the jukebox.

Maria dropped in a quarter and pressed some buttons. The room went silent as the patrons noticed, and all turned toward Maria in anticipation.

"Why does everyone seem to know what's going on but me?" Laura asked.

"Just watch."

The strong, raspy voice of Tina Turner singing "Proud Mary," drowned out by Maria belting out every note and putting her own lilt to every syllable, took over the dining room, underscored by Ike's deep bass. She stood, back to the jukebox, hands resting on the machine as if she were holding it back.

A grin grew across Laura's face and turned into a broad, gaping smile that showed off her brilliant white teeth. "No friggin' way! She sings?" She flashed Beans a curious look. "Her lisp is gone! How is that even possible?"

Maria finished the first, slow half of the song, then the horn section kicked in and the tempo picked up. She exploded into the frenetic momentum with a new fervor. She came away from the jukebox, twirling a dish towel in each hand, hanging right in there with Tina. The crowd went wild—cheering, whistling, and clapping—as Maria danced around the room, occasionally bumping her corpulent hips against male diners and drawing roars of laughter from the crowd. When the song was over, she ducked into the kitchen and disappeared.

The entire restaurant was on their feet in applause.

A few minutes later, she reappeared at the table with their crab—the legs so long they hung out and over the oversized serving bowl like a giant thorny desert flower. She then set down pairs of scissors and nutcrackers, as well as another bowl, this one for their empty shells.

Once Maria's hands were free, Laura stood and flung her arms around her. "That was amazing!"

"Thank you, hon. I'm glad you liked it." She turned her head to Beans. "I like thith one. She'th a keeper. I'll be right back with your melted butter."

Laura lifted her wine and sipped. "So, what did she mean just now by '*this* one'? How many girls does she see you with?"

Beans threw up his hands. "Fuckin' unbelievable. The woman gives you a compliment and you gotta twist it all up into something else."

"I was just askin'. Am I just one of many?" She cocked an eyebrow. "Where do I stand with you, Beans?"

Maria came back with a small metal bowl filled with melted butter and seated in a wire stand with a lit candle below.

"Y'know," Beans said after Maria excused herself, "I existed before I met you. Sometimes I come here with the guys, and yeah, I've been here with girls too. And yeah, for a while, you were one of several. But after a year now, it's just you. Okay?"

She smiled slightly and raised her glass. "Okay. I'm sorry. I don't wanna fight. We're having a great night. Let's eat."

Beans brought his glass to hers, then put it to his lips, muttering, "Fuckin' psycho," before taking a drink.

Truth told, he really got a kick out of this woman.

They proceeded to crack and cut their crab and dip the succulent meat into the butter. They were provided seafood forks, but used their fingers instead. Early on, while using the nutcracker, Laura launched an errant shrapnel of shell onto an adjacent table, where an older man, sixtyish, sat alone.

She smiled sheepishly and giggled. "I'm so sorry."

"No problem, honey," he said, raising his two-olive martini.

When they finished, Maria appeared. "How was everything?"

Laura sat back, setting a delicate hand on her middle. "Delicious."

"Perfect, as always," Beans added.

"Any coffee, desert?"

"Not for me." Beans patted his belly and looked to Laura.

"God no," she said. "I'm so full."

"Just the check." Beans said. "Whenever you're ready."

"Check's already been taken care of."

Beans furrowed his brow and glanced around the restaurant. "By who?"

Maria cocked her head, gesturing to a table in the corner to her left, where there sat a party of six business types, all male.

Beans caught the eye of one of the gentlemen and gave a discreet nod. "Well, then." He produced his money, folded around his driver's license and held in place by a wide rubber band.

He snapped off the rubber band and peeled off two hundred-dollar bills. "I'd like to buy that table a round of drinks. Keep the rest for yourself."

"Thanks, Beans." She smiled at Laura. "It was a pleasure to meet you."

"The pleasure was all mine. I can't wait to come back and see you again."

When Maria was gone, Laura pointed discreetly to the table in the corner. "So who is that?"

Beans leaned close. "The mayor of Stone Park."

"Why would the mayor of Stone Park pay our tab?"

"I guess he likes me," Beans said with a shrug. "I help him out sometimes."

• • •

Back in the car, Laura snuggled up close as Beans made his way to First Avenue, turned south toward the Eisenhower Expressway, and headed eastbound toward the city. As a matter of routine, no matter where the date took them, they typically ended up on Taylor Street. But when Beans passed the exit for Ashland Boulevard and Paulina Street, and the next, at Racine, Laura asked, "Now where're we going?"

"It's a surprise," he said. "Don't worry. You're gonna like it."

He took the Kennedy to Ohio Street, then onto Rush Street, heading north. After a few blocks, he pulled into a self-park lot and continued to the far end, where there were three empty spaces, and parked in the center one.

They got out and walked to the booth, where an Arabic man sat watching a small black-and-white TV.

The attendant stood. "Ten bucks, my friend."

"I'd like all three spaces," he said, handing over three tens. He drew a folded twenty from his jacket pocket and held it out between two fingers. "Don't let anyone park on either side of me."

The man pocketed the money. "You're the boss, mister."

As they strolled down Rush Street, Laura's arm threaded through his, they passed a man, visibly drunk, hugging a light pole with one arm. Beans noted the teardrop tattoo on his left cheek and the tattooed knuckles of his opposite hand, which held a nearly empty bottle of Cuervo Silver.

"Hey, you," the man mumbled.

They ignored him and kept on walking. Beans, though prepared as always for an encounter, also made a habit, whenever possible, of avoiding trouble.

"Hey, motherfucker!"

The guy pushed himself away from the pole and stumbled before catching his balance. He repositioned his grip on the tequila bottle, holding it upside down by the neck. He smashed the bottle against the pole, shattering the bottom, and moved into their path, wielding the jagged glass toward Beans. "Gimme your fuckin' money."

Beans waited patiently for the guy to lunge, and when he did, Beans would be ready. Shift left, slap down the arm, and hit the guy with a straight right—an effective and efficient route to a broken nose.

To his surprise, Laura moved between them. "Leave us alone! Just go away!"

In an instant, Beans reassessed the situation, grabbing Laura's coat by its fur collar and jerking her back and to the left. The situation was just too damn sticky to take chances.

Beans pulled his .38 and aimed it at the man's stomach. "You need to get the fuck outta here, motherfucker," he said, cocking the hammer.

"Okay, okay." The guy staggered back. "Take it easy, man."

"Drop the fuckin' bottle!"

Beans took a step toward him, and the drunk took a step back. He bent his knees and laid it on the sidewalk.

"Now," Beans said, taking another step closer, "get the fuck outta here."

The man straightened and bolted into the street, nearly tumbling, then caught himself and kept running.

Beans scanned the area to make sure he was gone, then tucked the .38 back into his waistband.

He turned to Laura. "What the fuck is wrong with you?"

"What?" she said, searching his face.

"What I mean is what the fuck did you think you were doing?"

"I was protecting you. What's wrong with that?"

"Protecting me? And what the fuck were you gonna do if he came at you with that bottle?"

"I dunno."

"You're fuckin' nuts. Don't ever do that again, you hear me?"

"Yeah."

"If there's ever any trouble, you put me between you and the trouble. Not the other way around. Understand? I got a gun. You don't. And if I can't handle a situation with my hands, I'll use the gun. What're you gonna use? You know kung fu and didn't tell me? What?"

"I dunno. It was just my first reaction, you know, to protect you."

"Never again."

"Okay."

Beans held her face in his hands and kissed her forehead, eyes, and then lips. "You fuckin' whacko." Beans had been with lots of girls, but never one willing to die for him.

They crossed the street, and Beans pointed to a black awning. "It's right there."

"The Back Room?" Laura asked. "I never heard of it."

They ducked inside and into a long and narrow exposed-brick corridor where they walked single file to the sound of Lenny Lynn's voice singing, "Teach Me Tonight." At the end of the corridor, they were greeted by an attractive woman, unfamiliar to Beans, wearing a tuxedo.

"Hi, guys," she said. "Just the two of you?"

"Yeah." Beans peered into the room just beyond her and took a look around.

"You know there's a two-drink minimum, right?"

Beans nodded and pressed a twenty into her palm. "Any chance we can get that empty table by the stage?"

"No problem. Follow me."

The room, though dimly lit, was illuminated by random shafts of light cutting beams through a giant hovering cloud of cigarette smoke. Well-dressed patrons sat at tiny two-tops that dotted the room, while some lounged at a red-leather banquette lining one entire wall.

Lenny Lynn had finished the song, and the band was about to take a break. Arthur Porter was on the saxophone. Beans didn't recognize the drummer or the organist. The band threaded their way toward the bar as Beans and Laura followed the hostess in the opposite direction to their table beside the stage.

As they crossed paths, Lenny Lynn held out a hand to Beans. "Good to see you, man."

Beans took his hand between his two. "Good to see you too, man."

The drummer and the organist each gave him a nod as they passed. Arthur Porter trailed, wearing a broad smile. He and Beans threw open their arms and hugged, slapping each other's back. They pushed away and held each other at arm's distance.

"How you doin', my brother?" Arthur asked.

"Can't complain. How 'bout you?"

"Workin' a lot. In other words, life is good. Got a new album coming out and a gig in Japan comin' up."

"Awesome. Good for you." Beans drew Laura to his side. "Laura, this is Art Porter, best saxophone player that ever lived."

"Don't listen to this guy," he said. "It's a pleasure to meet you."

"Nice to meet you."

The hostess, looking annoyed, stood waiting by their table.

Beans and Laura slipped into their chairs.

"The waitress will be right with you." She turned and hurried off.

The stage lights reflected off the thick chrome lining of the bass drum and landed on Laura's bracelet, lighting up its diamonds like fire.

She rested the hand on Beans's wrist. "Got any sunglasses on you?"

He laughed.

"Seriously," she said, leaning in for a kiss, "I love it."

"Hey, guys. What can I get you?" Their waitress—tall, thin,

and sandy-haired, with a perfect set of gleaming white teeth—was nearly the antithesis of Maria. She'd been working at the club about a year now.

"Well, that depends," Beans said, flashing a smile. "Can your bartender make a slow southern screw?"

"I can ask."

"It's just Southern Comfort, sloe gin, and orange juice. If not, then just Southern Comfort and orange juice. And a VO and water for me."

She gave a quick nod and flitted away.

"So," Laura said, "I guess you come here a lot, huh?"

Beans sensed her jealousy rising again.

"I suppose. Mostly when these guys are playing. Lenny's talented, and Art, he's really fuckin' talented. Got a hell of a career ahead of him."

"So you come here with the guys, then?"

Beans set his hand over hers. "Stop," he said firmly. "Please."

"Okay." She scooched her chair closer and draped an arm over his shoulder.

They sat quietly for a time while the rest of the patrons chattered on.

The waitress returned with four drinks, setting two in front of Laura and two in front of Beans. "Here you go." She pointed to the tumblers in front of Laura. "He knew your drink, honey."

"Great, thanks," Laura said. "How come two drinks each?"

The waitress looked at Beans, who fielded the question on her behalf.

"There's a two-drink minimum per person. These are our two drinks."

"But what if I want more?"

The waitress chuckled. "I'll be here all night, hon."

When she turned to leave, Beans tapped her elbow.

"What do you need, hon?"

"Do me a favor—get the band a round on me?"

"You got it."

After the band retook the stage, Lenny crooned and bellowed through his repertoire as Art wailed on the sax. Near the end of the set, when Lenny sang the opening notes to "You'll Never Find Another Love Like Mine," Beans tapped Laura's arm.

"Hear that?" he said. "He sounds just like Lou Rawls."

When the song concluded, Lenny announced another break.

After the other band members left the stage, Art, his alto sax still in hand, moved in front of the center mic. "I'd like to dedicate a little something to a special lady on her special day." Art dropped to a knee on the stage in front of Laura.

As the tune of the birthday song drifted out into the room, Laura covered her face with her hands and squealed. When Art finished, the crowd cheered and applauded.

Laura reached up and grasped Art's hand. "Thank you."

"My pleasure. Happy birthday."

She leaned into Beans. "You're just full of surprises, aren't you?"

Beans merely shrugged.

They ordered two more drinks each and stayed through the band's third set. By the time they stood to leave, Beans's head was spinning. Laura, by contrast, though still giddy, seemed fine.

Later, outside, as they made their way to the parking lot, Beans, still wary of their surroundings, kept his hand on the butt of the .38.

"I had a fantastic time tonight," Laura said. "It's kind of amazing how well we get along."

"Yeah," he said. "It's kind of like fate or something."

"Well, that's just bullshit."

"Why do you say that?" And he thought he was being romantic. Any other girl would have loved to hear those words. "What—you don't believe in fate?"

"If I left things to fate, we probably wouldn't be together. I chose you."

"You chose me, huh?" Though, he supposed, he didn't hate the sound of that. "So what, I didn't get a choice?"

They stepped off the curb to cross the street to the parking lot.

"Of course you did," she said. "I chose you, and you chose me. We're together because of that, not because of some stupid fate. Your actions decide your fate."

The parking lot attendant was long gone, and the booth dark. Beans's Ninety-Eight was the only car left in the lot. They got in and drove down Rush Street to Division, and down Division past his usual haunts—BBC's and P.S. Chicago, where Beans discreetly surveyed any patrons hanging outside, looking for his friends. The last thing he needed was for Laura to learn where he liked to hang out when he wasn't with her. Thankfully, she wasn't into the bar scene and so didn't frequent Division Street, which afforded Beans some natural freedom.

As they sat at the light at Division and Clark, Beans rolled down the window for a cold shot of air.

"Brrr!" Laura said. "It's freezing out."

"Sorry, babe. The booze went to my head. Just gotta wake up a—"

"Hey, handsome." A wrinkled old bag lady had appeared at Beans's window. She flashed a toothless grin. "Gimme a dollar, and I'll show you my tits."

Beans dug in his pocket, came up with a bill, and handed it over. "I'll give you ten to keep 'em covered."

"Thank you, sweety." She snatched the money and disappeared.

Laura's jaw hung open. "What the fuck was that?"

"Mailbox Mary."

"Who the fuck is Mailbox Mary?"

"She goes up and down Division, mooching money."

"Does she really show her boobs to people?"

Beans nodded. "For a buck. Pretty cheap deal, huh?"

Laura scrunched her face, but half-laughed. "Can you close your window now, before any more bums attack us?"

"I need to leave it open so I don't fall asleep."

"Wow. When did you become such a lightweight?"

"Not sure what it is, but the drinks really hit me tonight."

"We should get some food in you."

Beans knew what that meant. Back to his place for pizza, sex, and sleep. He was defenseless.

CHAPTER 18

PIECE-A-PIZZA'S PETE

"**SO, WHAT DID** you want to show me?" Izzy asked.

Beans cruised slowly down Bowler Street and slowed as he passed a dumpster that had been dropped at the curb. "See that two-flat right there?"

"Ain't that where Frankie Piece-a-Pizza lives? I heard his wife OD'd."

"Yeah. He's on the first floor. The second is being gutted and remodeled."

"Okay, so?"

"He's got a pete in his bedroom closet."

"How do you know?"

Beans pointed to his magic eye. "I see things."

"Kinda close to home, ain't it? Don't you always say, 'Don't shit where you eat?'"

"Yeah," Beans said with a shrug. "But I think we should make an exception in this case. I've got ideas in my head about the big thing. We're gonna need financing."

"I hear he's movin' tons of shit," Izzy said.

"Yeah, big numbers. Only deals in kilos."

Izzy scrutinized the building. "The bottom flat is bugged."

"Yeah, and foil tape on the windows."

"I didn't see anything on the top floor."

"Good eye." Beans appreciated Izzy's capacity for observation. "Construction workers comin' and goin' on the second floor. No bug up there."

"What kind of pete? Can you open it?"

"Not sure what kind, exactly. Some big old clunker. Maybe a Baum. I could open it if I had to, but it doesn't matter. I got the combo."

Izzy went momentarily silent. Though they never discussed it, he was aware of Beans's past romance with Emma Pisa.

"I don't really wanna deal with selling that shit," Izzy said.

"Me neither. So, here's the thing: he never keeps the dope at home. Only the zort. Also, he's goin' out of town next week."

As always, Beans had done his homework.

• • •

The blade of the circular saw screamed as Cosh plunged it into the hardwood floor. Beans glanced between the scene outside the window and Cosh's progress as he gently slowed the saw, going inch by inch forward, over the black lines he had drawn—a square, two by two feet.

Beans moved to check on Gugootz, who was staring out the window of the back bedroom, keeping an eye on the alley.

"Hey," he said, giving the kid's shoulder a smack. "Take them fuckin' phones off and pay attention."

Gugootz, looking hangdog, slid the headphones down around his neck.

Beans returned to scouring the scene outside the front window, his gaze sweeping the street below in both directions. No activity, save for the faint flicker of movement inside the getaway car, where Izzy fidgeted behind the wheel.

Is he dancing? Beans rolled his eyes.

The wail of the saw wound down and ceased with a tinny clang as Cosh completed the first cut. He rose from his knees, ran his ham hock of a forearm across his sweaty brow, and drew a long, slow breath in through his nose, setting off a machine gun of snorts in rat-a-tat succession. He fished into his front pants pocket for a Benadryl and popped it in his mouth. Then his hand went to a back pocket, presumably for the requisite handkerchief, but it came up empty. "Fuck," he said. "I must have left it in the car."

"What's wrong with you?" Beans asked.

"What—I can't wipe my forehead now?"

"No. I mean whatever that noise was coming out of your schnozz." Beans attempted to mimic the sound and failed.

"You know I got allergies," Cosh said. "Must be something in the wood."

"Great," Beans muttered. "Now he's allergic to wood."

Cosh finished off the other three lines of the square in short time, snorting occasionally as he went. He set down the saw, stood, and motioned for Beans to bring over the two pry bars leaning against the wall beside the front window.

Beans gripped one five-foot, thirty-pound bar in each hand, then hove them up to rest on either shoulder. He rolled off one to Cosh, and they stood, side by side, each jamming the flat, forked tongue of his pry bar into the slit of the cut in the floor. Each then dropped to a knee, bringing the bars down with them. The patch of wood creaked and splintered as it gave way, then rose about an inch.

Beans and Cosh rotated to the next line and repeated the process. They worked their way around the square, jamming, dropping, and pulling, until Cosh was able to get a good grip on the square wooden divot, which he ripped out with his bare hands, yanking the nails from the joists like clumps of grass from their roots. He tossed it aside, and they stared down into their newly cut doorway.

"Fuck!" they both said at once.

There was a joist dead center of the square.

"You think I can fit through one side?" Beans asked.

"Fuck that. I got it." Cosh went back to work with the pry bar, plunging it down along the inside edges of the square and breaking the laths and plaster from the ceiling of the apartment below. Once there was enough room, he tossed aside the pry bar, picked up the saw, and swiftly cut the joist vertically at each end. The cast-off section of joist plummeted into the darkness, and they listened as it crashed down onto the rubble of plaster and lath below.

Beans slid an aluminum ladder into the hole, stretched on a headlamp, slipped an empty gym bag over his shoulder, then shimmied downward into the blackness.

"You all right?" Cosh said from above.

"I'm good," Beans called up when his feet hit the floor below.

He switched on the headlamp and crept gingerly around Pizza's apartment as if testing the ice on a newly frozen lake. Once in the bedroom, he located the closet and pulled open the door. Into his pocket he went, coming up with a small slip of paper with a series of numbers. Though he had memorized the combination, Beans wanted to be doubly sure.

He found the dial of the antique black steel box, made three full clockwise rotations, then brought it to zero. Holding up the paper in his left hand, he confirmed the combination, replaced it in his pocket, and turned the dial slowly, one hashmark at a time, hitting the first two numbers, then slowly dialing back until he heard the metal clink.

Beans cranked down on the handle and pulled.

• • •

Outside in the driver's seat of the getaway car, Izzy sat, quietly singing and bobbing his head to "Super Freak" by Rick James.

He glanced to the flat, as he had every thirty seconds for the last half hour. *All quiet on the Western Front.*

Another glance toward the building, then one in the rear-view mirror.

Izzy reached forward and killed the radio, watching as a taxi rolled down the street from behind, passed him, and double-parked in front of the building.

The driver got out and opened the trunk. A man emerged from the back seat and met him at the rear of the bright-yellow Caprice.

Frankie Piece-a-Pizza. "Fuck!"

Izzy reached for the door handle, then hesitated, realizing he couldn't let Frankie see his face. He scanned the interior of the car and spotted Cosh's handkerchief beside him on the passenger seat. He held it up by two of its corners, checking for snot. Then, satisfied it was clean, he folded it diagonally and tied it around his face, bandit-style.

He climbed out of the car and followed Frankie at a safe distance as he lifted his suitcase from the cab's trunk and walked toward the door of the two-flat.

Frankie was putting the key in the lock when Izzy approached from behind and tapped his shoulder. "Excuse me, sir."

As Frankie turned, his jaw met with Izzy's enormous fist—

a perfect left hook. Two of Frankie's teeth sailed from his mouth and tinkled down the front stoop. He crumpled to the cement, out cold.

Izzy gripped him by the collar and pushed open the door to the apartment.

"Yo, Freddie," he whispered inside. "It's me!"

•••

Hearing their established code name, Beans backed away from the safe and poked his head out of the bedroom. "Freddie?" he said. "That you?"

He spotted Izzy in the front doorway, dragging a limp body into the apartment.

"Gimme a hand, will ya?" he said.

Beans lowered the bag to the floor below the hole in the ceiling. "Who the fuck is that?"

"It's fuckin' Pizza."

Beans gripped Frankie's collar and helped Izzy pull Frankie over the threshold. "He isn't supposed to be home for three days."

"I guess he didn't get the memo. You all set here?"

"What's going on down there?" Cosh called down the hole.

"It's all fine," Beans answered. "Drop the rope."

A moment later, the rope appeared, dangling out of the hole, stopping about two feet from the floor.

"So we're good to go, then?" Izzy asked.

Beans snatched up the bag. "We're golden."

"You take care of the zort," Izzy said. "I'll take care of him."

While Beans waited, keeping an eye out, Izzy disappeared into the bedroom and returned a few seconds later with a pillowcase. En route back to Frankie, he stopped and eyed a telephone sitting on a small wood table beside a tired pickle-green loveseat. He unplugged the phone and pulled its cord from the wall.

He fitted the pillowcase over Frankie's head, rolled him onto his belly, and used the cord to tie his hands and feet together behind him like a calf being readied for branding.

When he was satisfied that Frankie Piece-a-Pizza had been adequately bound, Izzy stood, waved to Beans, and ducked out the door.

Beans tied the bag to the end of the rope, which Cosh then pulled up through the hole. "Is it any good?" he called down.

"Open it up and check it out."

A beat later, Beans heard, "Fuckin' beautiful, Freddie."

CHAPTER 19

NEED A HAND?

BEANS HAD COMPLETED three tows in two hours, so he was basically done for the day. He sat in his truck, listening to music and going over and over the details. Step and the money were all he could think about. By the time Frankie Valli was on the last "floop-doop-doobie-doop" of "Marlena," Beans had a rough sketch of a plan in his head. He tossed what was left of his cigarette out of the window and released the parking brake.

After fighting traffic for twenty minutes, Beans arrived at Tommy-Gun Tommy's Army Surplus Store on North Lincoln Avenue. He parked the truck in front of a hydrant and strode inside the brightly lit, well-kempt store where, as they say, there was a place for everything and everything was in its place. Carousel racks loaded with uniforms, fatigues, and camouflage clothing. Walls lined with shelves holding sleeping bags, canteens, and other camping gear. There was even a sizable newsstand, with copies of *Soldier of Fortune*, *Gung Ho*, and *Combat Illustrated*, as well as *Penthouse*, *Hustler* and *Playboy*—the *Playboys* supplied by Beans, of course.

Tommy, his back to the door, was stocking the shelves behind the counter. He was always easy to spot with his green army jacket and red ponytail. "Can I help you?" he asked without turning around.

"Yeah," Beans said. "I'd like a hand job, please."

"Fuckin' asshole." Tommy turned around, a bundle of pea-green wool army socks clutched to his chest with a prosthetic hand. "It's not already time for the magazine's new edition, is it?"

"Nah. I need something."

"What's up?"

"Got any C-4?"

"Now, where the fuck do you suppose I would get C-4?"

"I don't know. Maybe in the back room . . . in that wooden crate that says *Comp C-4* on it?"

"You fucker." Tommy dropped the socks onto the counter. "I let you in my back room once for two minutes and you take inventory?"

"Sorry, man. I have a semi-photographic memory." Beans cleared his throat. "I need two stun guns too."

"Two stun guns and some Play-Doh. How much do you need?"

"Enough to obliterate a truck. You figure it out."

"You stay out here from now on," Tommy said, wagging a plastic finger over the counter. "I'll be right back."

"I need eight incendiaries too," Beans called out.

"Motherfucker." Tommy stopped and turned. "Eight? This shit ain't gonna be cheap, you know."

"How much?"

"Well, you're gonna need about a grand's worth of C-4, stun guns are a C-note apiece, and the firebombs are three hundred apiece."

"So, thirty-six hundred. That'll be fine."

"Okay." Tommy went to the front door, locked it, and flipped the sign on the window to *Closed*. Then he stalked into the back room and slammed the door behind him.

Several minutes later, he came out holding a brown paper bag with string handles and placed it on the counter. One at a time, with his good hand, he gently removed eight odd-looking red hand grenades; a stack of rectangular cubes, resembling modeling clay, wrapped in clear plastic; and two stun guns.

He lined the goods on the counter.

Beans studied them. "Okay. What do I need to know about these?"

"The stun guns are pretty self-explanatory. Be very careful with the grenades. You see that it says TH3 on them? That's thermate. Burns *anything*. The shit burns so hot it will melt a Sherman tank. If you give me some more details, I can show you how to make the C-4 do what you need it to do."

"Perfect," Beans said. "So far I owe you thirty-six hundred. Make it four dimes and give me what I need to set it all off remotely."

CHAPTER 20

WHEN DOGS FLY

"**HELLO, AND THANK** you for calling American Airlines. My name is Mary Ann."

The traffic outside nearly drowned out the lady's voice. Beans slid closed the phone booth's bifold door. "Yes, hello, sorry," he said in a lispy, sing-song voice. "I couldn't hear you very well. I have a question."

"Hi. My name is Mary Ann. How can I help you?" Her manner was sweet and professional.

"Well, I'm going to be traveling from DC to Chicago . . ."

"Mm-hmm."

"Well, I'm going to be traveling with my dog . . ."

"No problem, sir. Are you familiar with our policies and procedures when traveling with an animal companion?"

"Yes, yes. I know all that. Here's my concern: my flight shows that the plane I'll be on is a 727."

"Yes. That's very likely."

"Well, he's a large dog, and it's my understanding that he'll have to be crated and travel in the cargo hold. Is that correct?"

"Yes, that's correct."

"Well, my friend Paul has a sister who's a flight attendant, and we were talking at a party the other night, and she said that she wasn't sure if the cargo hold of a 727 is heated and pressurized."

"Sir, I can assure you, if we have a live animal in cargo, the hold will be heated and pressurized."

"You're one hundred percent sure of that?"

"Absolutely. We've never had a problem. I travel with my dog all the time. Your dog will be fine."

"Have you traveled with him on a 727?"

"As a matter of fact, I have."

"Thank you," Beans said. "That's very reassuring."

"Of course. Is there anything else I can help you with today?"

"No, Mary Ann. Thank you, you've been very helpful."

Beans hung up the phone, cranked down on the coin return lever a few times, then poked his finger into the coin return chute and felt around. Nothing.

He shrugged. "Sometimes you get lucky. Sometimes you don't."

CHAPTER 21

BEANS WHO?

JIMMY "GUGOOTZ" POPE lived with his parents in an apartment above DeLeo's Bakery. On this particular day, at this particular moment, Jimmy had no plans. He didn't spend a lot of time at home, but when he did, he usually locked himself in his room and did the same thing he did pretty much everywhere else—listen to music. Jimmy lived practically his whole life to music. He even planned his days to music. Or rather, he planned music to his days. Most mornings, before he left the house, he recorded a mixtape of songs that complemented in some way whatever he had scheduled.

Today, however, he lay in bed, his full-size, cushy headphones clamped over his ears, listening to Earth, Wind, and Fire on his prize possession—a Realistic dual cassette player and recorder.

His room was crowded, even though there wasn't much furniture—just a bed, a dresser, and an old wood chair for a nightstand. Any free space was occupied by stacked leatherette cases packed with cassette tapes. There were thirty-two cases in all, each holding twenty-four cassettes.

The piercing ring of the old rotary phone beside his head penetrated the music like an ice pick. He sprung up and grabbed it before it could ring again, then pulled off the headphones and tossed them aside, making sure they landed safely on the bed.

He put the trimline handset to his ear. It was cool and felt good. "Hello?"

"Hello, Jimmy?"

"Speaking."

"Gugootz, it's Beans. How you doin'?"

"Oh hey, Beans. I'm good. What's up?"

Jimmy was still getting used to his nickname, which everyone else at the club had embraced pretty much straightaway. At first, the suggestion that his head resembled some kind of vegetable squash didn't exactly sit well with him, but when he considered that Cosh was named for cheese and Beans was, well, Beans, it didn't seem so bad. Mostly, he didn't feel worthy of a nickname these days. Other than having him meet with Rooster every two weeks, Beans hadn't given him much to do lately, other than to serve drinks at parties.

"Say, how tall are you?" Beans asked.

"Five feet five."

"And how much do you weigh?"

"I dunno, one-fifteen?"

"So, are you learning any real carpentry on that job of yours, or are you just another wingnut warrior?"

Jimmy had recently joined the carpenters union and, like a few other members of the club, was working at McCormick Place, building booths for trade shows.

"I been doing side jobs with my dad since I was ten," Jimmy told Beans. "What do you need?"

"Does your father still have a little wood shop set up in your garage?"

"Sure."

"I'll be in the alley behind your place in ten minutes. Meet me there."

After Beans hung up, Jimmy replaced the handset and tried to think of the perfect song to pop into his Walkman for the occasion. *Alley . . . garage . . . Beans . . .* "Fuck it."

Every once in a while, the perfect song eluded him. He removed Earth, Wind, and Fire from the tape deck on his dresser, slid it into its slot in the open cassette holder on his bed, and set the case on one of multiple stacks of cases scattered throughout his room.

He slid his feet into a pair of slip-on Keds, shrugged into his wine-red Member's Only jacket, and swiped the key hanging beside the back door on his way out. When he reached the bottom of the porch stairs, Beans was already there.

"Where the hell'd you call from?" Jimmy said. "My basement?"

Beans motioned to the garage. "Can we go inside?"

"Sure."

Jimmy used the key to open the padlock on the garage side door, and he and Beans went inside.

"First of all, kid," Beans said, his expression serious, "not a word of this to anyone, okay?"

"Of course."

"Seriously. No one. Not even Cosh or Izzy. If someone comes up to you and says they saw you talking to Beans, you say, 'Beans who?' Got it?"

"Got it."

"Before I tell you anything more, I gotta know. Are you up for something big?"

"Definitely."

"By big, I mean enormous," Beans continued. "That bullshit at the car wash and Rooster—candy from a baby. This one's dangerous, and what I need from you is a big, big part of it. An even end for you this time. You with me?"

He had been waiting for a chance to really prove himself to Beans, and here Beans was handing it to him on, well, if not a silver, some kind of platter. But the way Beans was talkin' made Jimmy nervous, made his gut churn like that day last summer up at Six Flags in Gurnee while riding the Demon coaster after wolfing down two corn dogs and a funnel cake topped with cinnamon and sugar.

So, yeah. Jimmy was nervous.

Jimmy was nervous. But maybe not Gugootz.

No, Gugootz wouldn't flinch.

"Kid." Beans snapped his fingers in front of Jimmy's face. "I said, are you with me?"

Gugootz came to and looked Beans in the eye. "I'm in. Tell me."

"No. I'm not telling you. Y'know how people joke around, sayin', 'If I tell you, I'll have to kill you?' That's how serious this is. All I need to know is that you're in, and all you need to know is what I tell you."

"Fine, Beans. I'm in. What do you need?"

"Not only do you not know what's going on," Beans said, "you don't even know that there *is* something going on. So, if someone comes to you and says, 'Hey, I heard Beans is up to something,' your answer is . . ."

Gugootz cocked his head and shrugged. "Beans who?"

For the first time since their conversation had started, Beans cracked a smile. Then he proceeded to tell Gugootz as little as possible, after which, he asked, "So, you think you can handle it, kid?"

"I don't think. I know."

"Don't get cocky. Now, what kind of gizmo are you gonna use for the locking mechanism?"

"I haven't figured that out yet, but I will."

"I'm gonna want to know every little detail, so when you know, you tell me."

"Okay."

"And you're sure you're not claustrophobic?"

"Positive. Not a problem."

Beans handed Gugootz a hundred-dollar bill. "A C-note should cover lumber and hardware, right?"

"More than enough, Beans."

"Save the receipts and bring me the change."

"Of course."

"I'm just kidding, kid." He mussed Gugootz's hair. "Keep the change."

CHAPTER 22

STONEY'S ISLAND

IZZY STOOD IN front of the new glass entry door of the old, enormous warehouse.

It looked out of place. The building was being converted into loft office spaces. He held the door for Cosh and Gugootz, then followed them in. The bare brick walls inside had been newly tuck-pointed, and the ceiling was supported by a lattice of massive wooden beams. The exposed heat ducts were new, and the battered hardwood floors had been refurbished and coated with a gloss finish.

"Nice joint," Izzy said. "I guess this is what they call industrial chic."

Cosh nodded. "Yeah, Stoney always did have class."

Izzy pressed the up arrow for the elevator, which dinged and opened almost immediately. "Must have been sitting here waiting for us."

Izzy got on, followed by Cosh and Gugootz.

The walls inside the old freight elevator were covered in cloth padding that reminded Izzy of moving blankets. Like the rest of the building, it had obviously been recently renovated.

Izzy eyed the elevator's control panel. "Beans said the third floor, right?" He pressed the button and turned his head to Cosh. "When's the last time you saw him?"

"Gotta be five years," Cosh said.

Izzy glanced behind them to the kid. "You don't know Stoney too well, do you, Gugootz?"

"I haven't seen him since I was in grammar school."

"He sure got a raw deal last time around," Cosh said.

"Yeah. Of all the shit he's done, to go down for that nonsense is a dirty shame." Izzy briefly drifted off into the memory of him and Stoney stealing cars when they were twelve.

The elevator dinged again, and the door slid open.

There was Stoney, waiting for them. He was bigger than Izzy remembered. But as it had always been, his chubby freckled face and bright eyes made him instantly endearing.

"Welcome to Stoney's Island," he said, flashing a boyish smile that could seduce an alligator.

"Good to see you, kid." Cosh rushed him and attempted a hug, but Stoney was a good head taller than Cosh and twice as wide. Cosh could barely get his arms around the guy's middle.

"Good to see you guys too."

Izzy joined in to make it a group hug. "It's been too long, buddy."

Stoney pushed out of the huddle and looked at Gugootz. "Jimmy Pope! You were just a little kid last time I saw you. You guys are just in time for pizza. Come on in."

"Wait," Izzy said. "Hold on."

He and Cosh dug into their pockets and peeled off a hundred-dollar bill each from their wads of cash. It was tradition. The first time you saw a friend who had just been released, you gave him a C-note to help him get back on his feet. The idea was that you'd get it back when it was your turn. They thrust the money at Stoney.

"No need for that, guys." Stoney said. "I been out almost a year now. Look around. I'm doin' fine."

"Doesn't matter," Cosh said. "You gotta take it or it's bad luck."

"Fine. But I'm just gonna take it off your bill."

Stoney led them into his work space, and Izzy surveyed the room.

"Holy shit!" he exclaimed.

Just one corner of this space could have been the office of a Fortune 500 CEO. There was a huge teak desk with a tufted oxblood leather chair and a matching chesterfield sofa. Rows of antique oak file cabinets and modern art hanging on the exposed brick walls. Plastic folding tables covered with photography equipment and laminating machines—and pizza. There were two photo booths—one with a plain-white background, and the other with an enormous blowup of an Illinois driver's license on a magnetic board, complete with moveable plastic letters and numbers. It was proportioned so that when a person stood in front with his face where the ID photograph was meant to go, and a photo was taken at the exact correct distance, the result was a perfect Illinois driver's license, complete with the necessary information.

"Wow," Izzy said. "You ain't fuckin' around."

Stoney plopped into his office chair. "All top-of-the-line equipment. Some of the same stuff the state uses. So, talk to me. What do you guys need?"

Cosh and Gugootz sat on the oxblood sofa.

"We each need a driver's license," Izzy said, snatching a slice of pepperoni pizza. "They can't be mojo ones. We actually have to use them, and they gotta check out."

"See that?" Stoney pointed to the elaborate background. "I can do one of those in fifteen minutes. But that's only for the college kids. It'll get you past a bouncer, but that's about it. If you need something that'll get you by a cop, you'll need something a little more detailed. I'll also need to build you each an identity. It'll take time, but once you have it, you'll be able to take out a fuckin' mortgage with it."

Izzy put his pizza on a paper plate and set it on the table. "It doesn't have to be that complicated. We just need to use them once or twice. They can be from Maryland, Delaware, or Virginia. Preferably, each one of us from a different state, and then two from Illinois."

"Aw, fuck," Stoney said. "I'm only set up for Illinois. Each state is a little different. If you really need out-of-state, I gotta reach out to a guy. Unless . . ." He tapped his chin with his index finger. "Unless we start with an Illinois license and then you can transfer it anywhere you want."

"That's not ideal," Izzy said. "We really don't want any connection to Chicago. But if that's the best you can do, I guess we can take a shot. Do me a favor, though. Reach out and see. Y'know, about the out-of-state ones. If you gotta duke the guy a little more, no problem. We ain't afraid to pay."

"Okay," Stoney said. "But let's at least get the pictures out of the way. Who wants to go first?"

Gugootz raised a finger. "Hey, Stoney, can you make me one of *those* too?" He pointed to the giant driver's license.

"Sure, kid. I'll throw it in as a freebie. It'll get you into BBC's or any nightclub you want."

CHAPTER 23

GONE IN A FLASH

BEANS WAITED UNTIL twelve forty-five to go to the club.

Willy the Wiz was still there, but most of his customers had gone. Two of the old guys from the Survivors Club were just leaving when Beans walked through the door, and Willy sat alone at one of the card tables, hand resting on the tattered manilla envelope he used to transport the betting slips. Also in front of him were a scratch sheet with the day's schedule, a ceramic coffee mug filled with pens, and a stack of blank slips.

"Hey, Beans," Willy said, glancing over his readers. "How's it goin'?"

"Not bad. How's the action today?"

"Regular."

A man of few words. Beans headed to the back. "Any coffee left?"

"Should probably be about a half a pot," Willy said.

Capo sat, thick tail thumping in anticipation, on the other side of two chairs blocking the doorway between the kitchen and the bar.

"I can't believe the old guys are afraid of Capo," Beans said, pulling the chairs away. "Did mean old Willy put you in jail? I'll bust you out, buddy." He dropped to a knee, and the shepherd licked his face while Beans stroked his silky ears. "Good boy." He turned his head toward Willy. "Can I get you some coffee?"

Willy looked at his watch. "Sure, what the hell."

Beans poured coffee into two Styrofoam cups and returned to the card table, offering one to Willy. "You take it black, right?"

Willy nodded.

"Can I ask you something?" Beans said, taking a seat across from him. "Just between us?"

Another nod.

"That paper you use . . . that's flash paper, right?"

"Mm-hmm."

"Can I try one?"

"Sure. Here." Willy passed the top slip to Beans. "Hold it by a corner."

Beans held the paper between his thumb and forefinger, while Willy reached into his pocket for his Zippo, flipped the lid open, and sparked it.

"Ready?"

"Yep."

Willy held the lighter to the paper. It burst into flames with a flash and a poof, and then disappeared without a trace.

Capo barked.

"Holy fuck!" Beans said.

"Pretty cool, huh?"

"I'll say. Where can I get some?"

"What—you gonna start bookmaking?"

Beans laughed. "No. That's way too much work. I need it for something else."

"I can get you some, but it ain't cheap."

Yeah, I'm hearing that a lot these days. "I need a lot of it."

"Well, costs me a quarter a sheet. How much we talkin'?"

Beans hesitated, then said, "You can't say anything to anyone, okay?"

Willy removed his readers and set them on the table. "This is me you're talking to. How much?"

"Oh, like . . . twenty thousand sheets?"

"Are you fuckin' nuts?" Willy's head pitched forward. "What the fuck are you gonna do with all that? That's five grand. I buy a hundred sheets at a time. I don't even know if my guy can get that much."

Beans knew he would have to appeal to Willy's mercenary nature. "Talk to your guy. Maybe he can go to his supplier. I'll pay you a dollar a sheet, but this has to be strictly on the QT. Seriously, you can make some nice money, but no one can know." No way Willy could resist a 300 percent profit.

"Let me see what I can do."

"Thanks." Beans looked down at Capo, who was lazing at his feet. "I'm gonna take this guy for a walk."

"Goose was here earlier," Willy said, sipping his coffee. "Took him about half an hour ago."

"Yeah, well, he's starting to get a beer belly. He could use the exercise."

• • •

Capo, pulling hard on the leash, led the way in through the back door of Geraldi's Deli. Nose in the air, head swinging side to side, he yanked Beans to a shelving unit stacked with boxes and sat.

A few feet away, adjacent to their parked delivery truck, Izzy and Cosh stood on either side of a large plastic dog crate.

Cosh whistled. "C'mere, boy! C'mon, get in."

Capo didn't budge, his gaze fixed on the boxes full of cured pepperoni and salami.

"The dog's on overload in here," Beans said, unhooking the leash. "Too many fuckin' food smells."

Izzy reached over to an open box on another shelf and came up with a package of biscotti. He tore open the plastic with his teeth, jiggled out a cookie, bit off half, and held the other half out to Capo. "Here, boy." An attempted whistle through his teeth brought only spewed cookie crumbs and a haphazard "pfft."

Nonetheless, Capo went for the cookie, which Izzy pulled up at the last moment and pitched into the crate.

Capo trotted inside and Beans snapped closed the grated door. "Good boy, Capo."

"How's he fit?" Cosh asked.

"Seems okay," Beans said, peering into the crate.

"What about when he lies down?" Izzy asked.

Beans waited for Capo to finish his treat, then snapped his fingers. "Capo! Down!"

Capo obeyed, happily it seemed, assuming a sphinx position, then lowering his head to rest on his forelegs.

CHAPTER 24

STARTING TO GEL

BEANS WALKED AROUND his apartment, implementing his security protocols.

Sweep for bugs—check. Bug smasher on—check. Radio on and shades drawn—check and check.

Izzy, Cosh, and Gugootz were due any minute. He set bottles of VO, Jack Daniels, and Absolut on the table, respectively, in front of where he, Izzy, and Cosh usually sat. For Gugootz, he'd stashed a six-pack of Old Style in the refrigerator.

He heard them arguing outside the door before he even heard a knock.

"It's open. Come on in!"

The argument continued as the three walked inside.

"You're fuckin' nuts!" Izzy said. "Let's ask Beans."

He peeked his head out of the kitchen. "Ask me what?"

"Who's better looking," Cosh said, "Cindy Crawford or Christie Brinkley?"

"Neither," Gugootz cut in. "It's Brooke Shields by a mile."

Izzy set his hands on his hips. "What do you think, Beans?"

"I'm more of a Kelly LeBrock guy myself." He shrugged. "Gugootz, go in the fridge, grab yourself a beer. And grab the club soda too. And the bucket of ice from the freezer. You two make yourselves some drinks. We've got a lot to talk about."

They took their places around the table.

"Okay, Iz," Beans said, pouring the VO over the water in his glass. "How's it going with Stoney?"

Izzy produced a thin stack of IDs from his pocket and slapped it on the table. "Fuckin' beautiful. Cost an extra G-note each to get the ones from the other states. Stoney said he had to take care of another guy."

"Okay. Write that down on the expenses so you can get reimbursed." Beans perused the various driver's licenses, picked one out of the stack, and held it up to Gugootz's face. "Victor Vogelmeyer from Alexandria, Virginia? That's the best name Stoney could come up with?"

Gugootz shrugged. "He says he doesn't make up the names; they're actually real people, y'know, so that they check out if you get stopped. The picture is pretty good, I think. Look at that mustache. Can't even tell it's me."

"Yeah," Izzy said, "it makes you look handsome 'cause it covers up part of your face."

"I hope you bought more than just one of them mustaches," Beans said. "In case you need a backup. How are the crates coming?"

"Just about done," Gugootz said. "They look nailed shut, but the nails are dummies. Four of them open from the outside, with a secret catch. Mine opens from either inside or out, same kind of catch."

Beans nodded. "I've got everything from Tommy ready to go. Capo's all set."

"You really don't have to put Capo in there, Beans." Gugootz snapped the pop-top off his beer can. "I'm sure there'll be oxygen."

"I'm not taking any chances. If there's a dog in there, they gotta have heat and oxygen." Beans got up and went to the closet by the door, out of which he pulled an insulated sleeping bag and an oxygen tank with hose and canula. "I got these for you too. Just in case." He set them on the floor in the entryway and returned to the kitchen. "Cosh, what about you?"

"Now that we got the IDs, I'll be able to rent a house with a garage in DC, and I'll be able to buy one van there and two here."

Beans sipped his drink. "Cosh, you're gonna have to fly to DC alone and rent the house. Then you can buy the van there and register it at that address. Then, drive it back here, get the crates, and drive back to DC." He took another drink and set down his glass. "Meanwhile, you guys gotta help me make the bundles. We need a copy machine to make the fake money—tops and bottoms."

"I saw a copy machine at Cabrini Hospital. It's in a little room next to the cafeteria." Cosh pointed a finger at Gugootz. "Me and the kid can snaggle it."

"Yeah, we can," the kid said with a nod. "No problem."

"We only need about thirty copies," Beans said. "So no need to swipe the machine. Just sneak in there and use it."

"Hey, Beans . . ." Gugootz held up a finger. "How do we know what denomination to make the bundles?"

"Good question. That's the biggest variable. Step says most of the bundles are usually twenties. Plus, he says it looks like they're only counting how many bundles and not really paying attention to the denomination of the bills. So, we'll use twenties. Doesn't really matter, since they're all gonna disintegrate anyways. But don't forget, for the real zort, you need to grab bundles that have twenties. Those will spend the best. People are always suspicious of C-notes and fifties, and it takes too many small bills to buy anything big. Hopefully there will be enough twenties for an even swap-out. If not, go for fifties and tens."

Izzy rested his arms on the table and smiled. "Everything's starting to gel."

"The only problem is that blue fuckin' plastic," Beans said. "I can't find it anywhere."

"It's gotta be out there somewhere." Cosh crossed his fingers. "Once we get everything lined up, you can have Step plant the bug."

"Good. This is good. Okay, let's go over it again—the whole thing."

"Seriously?" Gugootz said. "But I gotta date." He glanced around the table. "We know the plan, right? How many times we gotta go over it?"

"Only about a hundred," Beans scolded. "Stay seated, kid." He took a breath and let it go. "Now, one more time, all the way through, and pay attention."

"Okay," Izzy began. "We use Stoney's IDs to buy two vans here and a van in DC. We rent a house in DC with a garage. We gotta drive the DC van back here, load it with the crates and phony bundles, then drive it back to DC and leave it in the garage until it's time."

"Good, but hold on," Beans said, noticing the puzzled expression on Gugootz's face. "You got a question, kid?"

"A couple, actually. Why are we buying vans? Why don't we just steal 'em?"

"Because," Beans said, "I don't want to get pulled over by some Dudley Do-Right cop for some stupid reason and have the plates come back hot. That reminds me . . ." Beans looked to Izzy. "Once you get the vans, bring them over to Dirty Dave and have him check them out front to back. Mechanical, electrical, everything. I don't want there to be any reason to get pulled over, and I don't want them breaking down right in the middle of everything." He turned back to Gugootz. "What was your other question?"

"Why do we have to buy a van in DC, drive it back here and load it up, then drive it back to DC? Why can't we buy all the vans here and load one up and drive it to DC? We could save a trip."

"Because we're gonna abandon the van at the DC airport," Izzy said. "Sooner or later, they're gonna find it. If it's registered in Chicago, it will raise a flag. If it's registered in DC, they might not connect it to the job. And if they do, they'll be looking for guys in DC."

"Everything we do is for a reason," Beans explained. "That's why we need to stick to every detail of the plan, even if it doesn't seem important. It could be the difference between getting pinched or not. Talk about the crates."

"I built five." Gugootz swigged his beer. "One big, four small. The big one's for me, obviously, with an inside latch, and one on the outside, in case of emergency. I'll show you guys where. The others are for the bundles. We can fit two bundles in each. Once the plane is in the air, I let myself out and find the real bundles that have twenties in them."

Beans held up a finger. "What if there aren't eight bundles of twenties?"

"I take as many twenties as there are, then go for fifties or tens."

"Good. Go on."

"I swap out the bundles, take our fake bundles out of the crates, put the real bundles into the crates, and stack the fake ones back in with the rest of the real ones. Then I get back into my crate before the plane lands."

"Good. Don't forget to check on Capo while you're out of the box. Actually, bring a Heineken with you to make sure he's comfortable. Also, don't forget the blanket and the oxygen, just in case." Beans didn't want him to miss any details. "Cosh, tell us about DC."

Cosh drained his glass of Absolut and soda and set it down. "Once we get the call, me and the kid fly out to DC with Capo. We spend the night in the rented house, and in the morning the kid gets in his crate and the dog gets in his crate. I deliver the crate with the kid and the crates with the phony bundles to the airport. I get Capo checked in, leave the van in the airport parking lot, then get on the plane and fly home. When we land in Chicago, Izzy takes one of the Chicago vans and picks up me and the dog at the terminal at O'Hare. Then we go around to freight and pick up the crates with the kid and the zort. Drive home."

"I still gotta get the air freight paperwork and stickers from Johnny Hot Dogs," Beans said. "You'll need those before you take off. Don't forget to wipe down the van and wear gloves the whole time you're in it." Beans turned to Gugootz. "And you, don't forget to wear gloves in the cargo hold, and when you're handling the bundles."

Gugootz nodded.

Beans looked at Izzy. "Go."

"I wait for the plane to land at O'Hare, pick up Cosh and Capo at the terminal, then we go to freight and pick up the crates.

If Gugootz is still alive, we let him out of his crate. If not, we toss the crate into the river."

"Don't even fuck around about that!" Gugootz said. "I'm nervous enough as it is."

Beans laid a hand down on the table in front of the kid. "Remember what I said about being nervous." He turned his head to Izzy. "Don't fuck with the kid's head. We need him thinking clearly."

CHAPTER 25

A BAD DAY TO BE A GOAT

BEANS SAT WITH his back against the armrest of the couch, one leg extended down the cushions and one on the floor. Capo was curled up on the floor by his foot, back pressed against the bottom edge of the leather upholstery. The club was quiet, for now, until the usual crowd started trickling in to watch the Saturday college football games on the TV, where currently a bowling tournament was unfolding.

Beans stopped stroking Capo's ears to grab the remote control resting on his chest and flipped through the channels. He stopped on a Bugs Bunny cartoon—the one with Babyface Finster, one of his favorites.

The doorknob rattled, and Capo sprang to his feet.

Cosh walked in, and Capo trotted over to him and stuck his nose in his crotch.

"Son of a bitch!" Cosh said, pushing the dog away. "Get the fuck outta here. Great. Now my fuckin' balls are probably gonna swell up." He searched his pockets. "Where's my Benadryl? You"— he pointed to Capo—"go lay down."

Capo sat and stared up at him. "Beans," Cosh said, "tell him."

"Capo, go lie on your jacket." The dog got to his feet and skulked into the back. "Look at him. You hurt his feelings."

"*I* hurt *his* feelings? How's he gonna feel when I start wheezing?" Cosh walked into the kitchen.

A moment later, Beans smiled at the familiar rumble of Milk Bones being jostled in their box.

Cosh walked out, drying his hands on a paper towel. "Babyface Finster!" he exclaimed, catching a glimpse of the TV.

"Have a seat." Beans sat up to make room.

"Watch this!" Cosh said, planting himself on the center cushion. "When Bugs turns off the light . . ."

They sat together, belly-laughing, as Bugs turned out the light and Babyface kabonged him with a baseball bat. Cosh laughed so hard he doubled over and nearly fell off the couch.

He came back up, wiping away tears. "Whoever writes this shit is a fuckin' genius."

"It reminds me of that time—"

"You read my mind, man." Cosh composed himself and cleared his throat. "How're you feeling?"

Beans clicked off the TV. "I feel great."

"You know what I mean. It looks like this thing is really going to happen. You got the most dangerous part. We can scrap the whole plan. We really don't need it."

"No, I need to do it."

"Yeah, I know," Cosh said. "I know you know this, but I gotta say it. If anything happens, I'm gonna take care of your family."

"Debbie too?"

"Debbie?"

"I want you to take care of her too."

"Of course." Cosh went silent a moment, then, "What are you saying, Beans?"

"C'mon. I'm only half-blind. When were you gonna to talk to me about it?"

"Beans, I swear to God. Nothing has ever happened between us."

"What the fuck is wrong with you?" Beans said, growing exasperated. "Why do you think I wouldn't approve?"

"You always said you didn't want her to go with a bum from the neighborhood."

"And since when are you a bum? You and Iz are the best guys I know. You're both fuckin' nuts, but, of the two of you, you're the least nuts. How could I hope for a better guy for my sister?"

Cosh leaned forward and rested his elbows on his knees. He turned his head back to Beans. "Seriously?"

"You're already my brother, man. Might as well make it official."

Cosh came up and leaned back on the couch. "Man, I can't tell you how relieved I am to hear that. It's been drivin' me crazy."

"Plus," Beans said, "you're going to be a millionaire soon."

The door opened, and Pete the Bum trudged into the club. "Hey, lil' Geraldi," he said, "Is 'at yer boat out front?"

"Yeah. Why?"

"Ize hopin' you kin gimme a lift t' the mission on Ashland. They givin' away winter coats."

Cosh looked at Beans. "Feel like taking a ride?"

"Sure. What the hell."

Cosh surveyed Pete's filthy clothes. "Give me five minutes. I just had the interior shampooed. Gotta put the seat covers on."

•••

235

"Where's this mission, Pete?" Cosh asked. "Ashland and what?"

"Eighteenth," Pete said from the back seat. "Right on the corner. R'you a golfer?" He held up the nine iron he found at his feet.

"Nah," Cosh said, giving Beans a wink. "That's just for emergencies."

Cosh drove east to Loomis and turned right. They drove south toward Eighteenth Street, then caught the light at Sixteenth and Loomis, where a street vendor was selling homemade tamales from a two-wheeled cart.

"Son of a bitch," Cosh said, looking out the window. "Is that fuckin' Billy Goat?"

Beans eyed the scruffy, heavyset customer handing over a wad of crumpled bills. "Yep."

Cosh turned to Beans and winked. "Good thing you never told Pete what that piece of shit said about him."

"Yeah, good thing," Beans said.

"Fuck you talkin' 'bout?" Pete said.

"It's nothing, really," Cosh said.

"Yeah, don't worry about it." Beans chuckled to himself; it was the one thing you should never say to an Italian.

"Don't worry about it?" Pete responded, right on cue. "What the fuck did he say?"

"He's a big bullshitter, Pete." Cosh glanced in the rear-view. "Seriously, it's no big deal."

"You don't tell me what he said, ah'm gon' bus this back window with this club."

"Okay, okay. Fine." Cosh snickered quietly. "But it's really no big deal. He said he did time with you in County."

"That kid?" Pete said. "Last time I was in County, he was in fuckin' diapers."

"Yeah, I know." Cosh nodded. "That's why it's no big deal, what he said."

"It's a big deal to me. What else he say?"

"He said he punked you in County."

"Lemme tell you sompin'," Pete said, "any punkin' goin' on, I'se the punk*er*, not the punk*ee*." Pete grabbed the nine iron, opened the car door, and marched over to the tamale cart.

The light turned green, but Cosh hung back long enough for them to watch Pete swing the club, the shaft of which connected with Billy's neck and bent around it. Pete then tossed the mangled weapon aside and used his fists to pummel Billy "the Goat" Godina to the ground.

Cosh hit the gas. "That'll teach that piece of shit to give us a bad tip."

They continued south down Loomis, laughing all the way.

"Sometimes, my friend," Beans said, cradling his ribs, "you are pure genius."

CHAPTER 26

THEY'RE OUT. I'M IN.

BEANS WALKED OUT of the club, his eyes discreetly drawn to the yellow Gran Torino parked across the street. The one that had been there when he'd arrived an hour ago. The car was not familiar to him, and someone was sitting low in the driver's seat so that only his eyes and the top of his head were visible.

He strolled about halfway down the block, resisting the urge to turn around for a second look, and walked into Johnny's Hot Dogs, where he had arranged to meet with Step.

He sat at the counter, studying the massive hammerhead shark hanging on the wall in front of him. Johnny was a fisherman. Written on the wall beside the shark's mouth was a cartoon bubble that read *If I wasn't so hungry, I wouldn't have got caught.*

While he perused the menu board, Beans got a nagging feeling. Again, discreetly, he turned his head, spotting straightaway the Torino, which was now parked directly across from Johnny's. This time, he managed to catch a glimpse of the driver just before he slid down in the seat.

Beans breathed deep. He would have to force himself to

disguise the rage he felt toward Step. Step might be crazy, but he was obviously wary of business partners. Beans needed him at ease and off guard.

Celia, carrying a glass coffee carafe, moved in front of Beans, set a dark brown mug on the counter, and filled it.

"Thanks, Mrs. T," Beans said.

Celia was the mother of Beans's boyhood friend, Johnny Hot Dogs Jr. It occurred to Beans that he still addressed the parents of friends by mister and missus.

"What's Johnny up to these days?"

"Working a weird shift—four a.m. to noon. Then he usually comes here and helps me in the shop. He's such a good boy."

Beans smiled. "Always has been."

She had obviously never found out that Beans and Johnny Jr., at fourteen, used to steal Johnny Sr.'s station wagon and go for joyrides. "Still working at that air freight place?"

"Yeah. The boss likes him. Just gave him a raise."

The door jangled, and Step pushed his way inside. He tottered to the counter and sat beside Beans. "Hiya, Celia."

"Hi, Vin." She poured him some coffee. "What can I get you?"

Step looked at Beans. "You gonna eat?"

"Cheeseburger and fries, I think."

"Sounds good." Step turned his head to Celia. "Make it two."

She moved to the other end of the counter, turned her back, and went to work at the grill.

"So, what's up?" Step asked.

Beans had to be careful, not sound too sugary, lest Step become suspicious. "Well, I got bad news, bad news, good news, and bad news—in that order."

"Okay, let's have it."

"Bad news one: I'm still working on it, but I don't see a way to do this without some rough stuff. Bad news two: if there has to be rough stuff, Cosh and Izzy are out. Good news: I'm still in, rough stuff or not. And, I think I have a plan for how the two of us can do it alone. Bad news three: my plan isn't perfect yet, so I need a little more time to work things out."

"A little more time is okay," Step said. "A lot more time could be bad." Step shifted on his stool, inadvertently brushing Beans's arm with his own.

Beans fought hard the impulse to bristle and draw away. He'd known the guy was shit from the start. Now he knew why, having learned the full complement of Step's business activities—as well, his proclivities.

Not to mention Debbie.

Still, he sensed Step's antennae rising and had to play it cool.

"Couple questions," Step said. "Cosh and Izzy? Do I gotta worry about them talking to anyone?"

"You know them. If they say they're out, they'll never mention it again. Not even to you or me. I vouch for them a hundred percent. I give you my word."

Step sipped his coffee and set down the mug. "Good enough. Another question: Why're you still in? You were the one who made the big deal about going cowboy."

"Yeah, well, I still don't like it. But I think you and I might end up with five or six million apiece. This might be the last thing I ever have to do. Plus, like I said, I'm still working on a way to keep the rough stuff to a minimum."

"So it's just you and me." Step eyed Beans skeptically. "I don't see how we can do this with only two guys, but we'll see what you come up with."

Step was growing annoyed. Beans could feel it.

"Leave it to me," he said. "You'll see."

Step glanced at his watch. "I gotta go."

"Aren't you gonna eat your burger?"

Step tossed ten bucks on the counter. "Nah. Forgot I gotta be somewhere. Give mine to Pete the Bum."

"Will do."

Beans watched him limp out, get into his car, and drive off.

The Torino, he noted, was still parked across the street. Beans turned back around and emptied a sugar packet into his lukewarm coffee.

A minute later, the chimes on the door jangled again.

Beans didn't bother to turn around. "Got a new ride I see."

His stalker slid onto Step's vacated stool. "You know how I love yellow." He tugged at the lapels of his bright gold Latin Kings letterman sweater, with its multitude of patches and black trim.

"I thought you guys only wear those things when you're gonna rumble?"

"We got two. My other one is for war. This one's my party sweater." He flashed Beans a toothy smile.

Beans chuckled. "So, Little Man, what brings you around here?"

"Remember that time you and Iz saved my ass in Cicero?"

"Of course. We don't usually get involved in gang shit, but you looked like you could use a hand."

"Well, I figure I owe you one." He gestured with his head to where Step had just pulled away from the curb. "That squirrelly motherfucker has some mighty bad intentions, my friend."

"I was expecting something," Beans said. "What's he up to?"

"Says he's gonna take care of you himself." Little Man kept his voice low. "Wants me to take care of your boys."

"When?"

"Don't know. He's waiting for something. Told me to wait for a call."

"Did he give you the money yet?"

"I told him the rate is ten grand each. He said if I can wait 'til after it's done, he'd pay double."

"I see." Beans pressed his lips together and nodded. "Sorry to say, you're not gonna be able to collect from that guy." He turned his head to Little Man. "But sit tight. I'll handle it. And then you can collect from me."

"Nah, man." He was back on his feet. "I said I owed you one. Now we're even."

After Little Man walked out, Beans stayed on, ate his burger, had Pete's bagged up, then hailed Celia for more coffee. "You expecting Johnny today?" he asked her.

Celia tipped the carafe over his mug. "Said he'd be here by one."

CHAPTER 27

MORE WINE

BEANS SAT AT his kitchen table, studying multiple swaths of blue plastic cellophane. There were eight in all, seven of which were laid out in a line in front of him, and another in his right hand pinched between his thumb and forefinger. The latter was the one Step had cut from the money bundle with the ring knife. He picked up the first in the line with his left hand and held the two swaths side by side to compare. Not a match.

He set that one down, took a long chug of Sam's homemade wine from a goblet the size of a small fishbowl, then lifted the second swath and held it next to the original. Nope. Another chug of wine. He continued down the line, each comparison topped off with wine. He'd been at it for almost an hour. Every test sample was a little bit different from the original—either by way of shade or texture. This was his sixth time through the line, with the hope that, somehow, one of them would suddenly, magically match up. He had been to every plastic manufacturer in town. He'd even visited at least a dozen gift shops and florists, with no luck.

He refilled his glass, went into the living room, and plopped down in his recliner. Without a match for the plastic, the plan was blown. He dreaded having to tell the boys. Dreaded even more having to go through with the phony plan with Step.

Beans was unaccustomed to failure and hopelessness. He didn't like it.

His scalp felt as if stretched too tight over his skull. He dug a knuckle into each temple, attempting to squeeze out the pain. He drank down half of the glass of wine in one gulp, leaned back, and closed his eyes.

Bang! Bang! Bang!

"Beans! Open up!"

He sat up with a start. "Gugootz?" He shuffled to the door and let the kid in. "You scared the fuck outta me. Whatsa matter?"

"The fuckin' FBI were at Geraldi's. They took Cosh and Izzy."

"What? What for? What happened?"

"No idea. D'you think they're onto our plan?"

"Fuck." Beans ran a hand through his hair. "Everything's turning to shit."

CHAPTER 28

BLUE STRETCH

"OKAY," BEANS SAID. "So what the fuck happened?"

He and Gugootz sat across from Cosh and Izzy in Geraldi's back room.

"You're not gonna believe this," Izzy said, downing two fingers of Jack Daniels. "Remember a while ago we told you the cops were here about them three junkies they found *menza morte* in the alley?"

"Yeah?"

"Turns out one of the three was an FBI informant ratting out his dealer. They needed to investigate to see if it was some kind of retaliation or something."

"So what'd you tell them?"

"We didn't tell 'em shit. Just clammed-up. They were pretty sure it was me and Cosh who did it, but they can't prove anything."

"I don't think they give a fuck about us," Cosh said. "They just want to make sure it wasn't done by the guy he's ratting on."

"So they just let you go?" Gugootz asked.

"Yeah," Izzy said with a shrug. "They gave us the treatment for a while, then they printed us, took our pictures, and let us go."

"Why would they print you if you were just being questioned?" Beans asked.

"Don't know. They said we didn't need a lawyer, but we called Sid anyway. He didn't seem too concerned, though."

Cosh stood and went to the stove, where he dipped a ladle into a large pot of simmering gravy. He looked back at Beans. "You want a meatball sandwich?"

Beans checked his watch. "Actually, I gotta go. The Wiz's guy is supposed to deliver the flash paper today. I don't know what the fuck we're gonna do with twenty thousand sheets of that shit if we don't find the right blue plastic. I already paid him, though, and it's not like he's gonna take a return for store credit."

• • •

Beans paced in the alley between Lexington and Polk Streets, waiting for the truck. Willy said three o'clock, and it was three-fifteen. Beans had given him the twenty thousand in advance. His suspicious nature made him wonder if Willy was pulling a fast one. Just as his mind began generating worst-case scenarios, a truck lumbered into the alley. Beans stood in front of the garage and waved the driver on.

The truck advanced slowly, bouncing over the cobblestones. Then the driver navigated past the garage just far enough to line up the rear end of the truck with the open garage door.

The driver's side door opened, and the driver sprung out without bothering to use the step. "You Beans?"

"Yep."

The driver—short, stocky, and wearing a faded Cubs cap— waddled to the back of the truck and pulled down on the lever to lower the hydraulic tailgate. He then stepped onto the tailgate and worked the lever to raise it. He gripped the rope strapped to the door handle, heaved it up with a clatter, and disappeared into the darkness.

Beans could hear him working the pallet jack.

When the skid of flash paper, twenty thousand sheets' worth, moved onto the tailgate, Beans's jaw dropped. The driver lowered the tailgate to the ground, where Beans stood, stunned, staring at the load.

"What the fuck is that?" he asked the driver.

"Forty cases of paper. That's what you ordered, ain't it?"

"No, I mean . . ." Beans approached the skid and pointed to the cases, each held together with a familiar blue plastic wrap. He produced his pocket knife, sliced off a piece, and held it up. "What's this?"

"That's just the stretch film they use at the warehouse," the driver said with a shrug. "Keeps everything wrapped up nice and tight and in place."

Beans rubbed the plastic between his fingers. A perfect match. "Where can I get some of this?" he asked.

"I don't know—a warehouse supply store, I guess. It comes in rolls, like this." He tapped the top of a roll strapped to the inside of the trailer. "They always give us a roll to keep with us in the trucks."

Beans dug into his pocket and peeled off a hundred-dollar bill from his wad of cash. He held it out to the driver. "Can I buy that from you?"

The driver looked down at the cash and back up at Beans. "Hell, yeah!"

CHAPTER 29

BIG BLUE BUNDLES OF LOVE

THERE WAS A "Shave and a Haircut" knock on the aluminum garage door.

Beans, Izzy, and Cosh stopped their work, while Cosh went to the door.

"Who is it?" he asked.

"It's me. Open up."

Cosh flung open the overhead door with a single-handed upward thrust. The door rattled and shook as it rolled its way up the frame.

Gugootz struggled to carry in the antiquated paper cutter.

"It's about fuckin' time," Cosh said. "We're working with scissors here."

"This fuckin' thing is heavy." The blade swung open as he walked.

Cosh pulled the overhead door closed with another violent thrust, and it rattled its way back down. He took the cutter from Gugootz and plunked it on the table.

"Did you have any trouble?" Beans asked.

"It was right where it always is—in the storeroom with the extra chalkboards and the audio-visual equipment. Good ol' Sister Maybeth, always neat and orderly. There was one thing, though . . ."

Beans didn't like the sound of that. He looked up from his work setting up the incendiary grenades. "What does that mean?"

"John the janitor sort of caught me."

"Define 'sort of.' Did you give him the pint, like I said?"

"Yeah, but he didn't need it. He was already fuckin' plastered, could hardly stand up. But he cracked it open anyway and chugged down half in a single gulp. Then he mumbled something like, 'All the priests at Notre Dame go with whores.' And then he passed out."

Izzy laughed. "No fuckin' way. Father Fenton, maybe, but not Father Raymond. Father Raymond never gave up hope for us, no matter how bad we were. He did everything he could to steer us right. He even put a pool table in the altar boys' dressing room to keep us coming to serve Mass."

Beans and Cosh shook their heads. "Yeah, not Father Raymond," they said in unison.

Cosh laid a dollar bill on the paper cutter and set the slide to mark the blade distance. Then he replaced that with a stack of flash paper and brought down the blade with a swoosh and a thump. "Beautiful," he said, inspecting his work. "We'll finish before morning, then you can bring it back."

"Wait." Gugootz's face fell. "You want me to break back into the school and return it?"

"Of course." Cosh kissed his Saint Dismas pinkie ring. "You wanna curse the whole caper by stealing from the church? We're just borrowing it."

"Grab a scissors, kid," Izzy said. "You can help me cut the bills while Cosh cuts the stacks."

Gugootz slipped his headphones over his ears and pressed the play button on his Walkman. He picked up one of the sheets of flash paper, onto which they had copied images of the front and back of twenty-dollar bills. He went to work cutting out the fake bills.

Beans smiled to hear the distant sounds of Brenton Wood singing, "Great Big Bundle of Love."

• • •

When they had generated enough fake fronts and backs, they placed them on the stacks that Cosh cut and banded them.

Beans finished setting up the remote detonators. He put the incendiary grenades and the C-4 into their boxes, each perfectly sized to two stacks by two stacks by four stacks of bills. He cleared off the folding table he was working on and unrolled the blue stretch wrap by holding the loose end and dropping the roll, letting the weight of it unravel itself along the table. "Okay," he said to the others. "Pile up the stacks on top of the plastic, and let's make our first bundle."

They laid out the first level of the bundle, onto the center of which Beans placed an incendiary device. They placed stacks of the fake money around and on top of the device, building the bundle around it. Beans then brought the blue wrap over the top of the stacks and pulled it tight.

The bundle collapsed, and the stacks spilled onto the table, the box holding the incendiary teetering at the edge. Izzy caught it before it could fall.

"Fuck," Beans said. "This isn't going to be as easy as I thought."

Izzy placed the incendiary at the center of the spilled fake money stacks. "Rebuild it without the stretch wrap. I'll be right back."

Before they were able to finish, Izzy was back, carrying four rolls of clear plastic packing tape. "We use this to seal the boxes at the store," he said. "It's really fuckin' sticky. Wrap it in this first to hold it together, then cover it with the blue shit."

"Hold on a sec." Beans held up a hand and went quiet, contemplating.

The tape would be one more foreign object for forensics to discover. But as of right now, it was the best—and only—option they had. They would just have to hope the thermate would disintegrate everything.

"Okay," he said. "Let's try it."

It worked. They were able to put together eight bundles, seven with incendiaries and one with C-4.

They looked exactly like the bundles in Izzy's pictures.

"So," Gugootz said, "how much are we talking about again? Eight forty-pound bundles of twenties? What does that come to?"

"The way I figure it," Beans said, "it's about three hundred and fifty thousand per bundle. Times eight is two million eight. Divided by four is seven hundred thousand each."

Gugootz replaced his headphones and rewound the cassette.

Beans smiled. *Great big bundles of love. Definitely!*

CHAPTER 30

GO BUGGY

"OKAY. IF YOU can get into the office without anyone seeing you, put this inside the phone." Beans handed Step the bug. "You know how to do it?"

"Yeah, no problem."

The music playing at Dilligaf's was loud enough to cover their voices.

"If you can't get in there alone, you'll have to find the utility closet and figure out which line it is and do it from there."

Big-O was behind the bar, graveling "Here I Go Again" along with the jukebox. "VO, Beans?" he asked.

Beans winked.

He looked to Step. "How 'bout you?"

"Y'know," Step said, "you got a better voice than David Coverdale."

"Who the fuck is that?"

"The guy from Whitesnake." Step circled a finger above his head to indicate the music.

"Never heard of him," Big-O said. "I just like the song. What're you havin'?"

"Gin and tonic."

Big-O plunked two rocks glasses onto the bar.

"Can I get that in a tall glass?" Step said.

Big-O rolled his eyes, put away one of the tumblers, and walked to the other end of the bar.

Step turned to Beans. "I'm pretty sure I can do it in the office. They usually go for lunch in the terminal. I'll figure it out."

"Okay. So that's the bug. This is the receiver." Beans handed him what appeared to be a transistor radio duct-taped to a cassette recorder. "You put this in your locker and make sure the recorder is on. You're gonna have to listen to it at the end of every day and then rewind it. And make sure the batteries are fresh."

Big-O returned with Step's glass of choice, mixed their drinks, and slid them across the bar.

Beans raised his glass with a nod. "Thanks, man."

"Hey, O," Step said. "Somethin' I always wondered about . . ."

"Yeah, and what's that?"

"Why is this place called Dilligaf's? Sounds Irish." Step glanced around the dark little bar. "But just about everyone here is Italian."

Big-O leaned on the bar and narrowed his eyes on Step. "You really don't know?"

"Know what? Does it stand for something?"

Big-O straightened, giving Beans a wink, and walked off down the bar.

"So," Beans said, turning to Step, "you gotta listen to the tape every day, then rewind it. And always keep fresh batteries in it. Then, once we get the call, you gotta keep listening to it to make sure they don't change their plans."

"Got it. No problem."

Uncle Joe, sitting at a nearby table playing brisc with three other old guys, motioned for Beans to come over.

"What's up, Unc?"

"Can I ask a favor?"

"Of course."

"I got a tip on a steamer running tomorrow at Hawthorne. I'm gonna be at the doctor all day. Can I give you something to give to the Wiz?"

"Is the tip reliable? Mind if I put down a bet on it for myself? I don't want to fuck up the tote for you."

"Mortgage the house for this one, kid. Don't worry about the tote. It's going off at twenty-to-one."

Beans laughed. "No problem. I'll drop it off at lunchtime."

"Thanks, kid." Uncle Joe slipped Beans a sheet of paper folded around a twenty-dollar bill.

Beans returned to Step at the bar. "So, you can handle it?"

"No problem."

"How much juice do you have at work? Can you get yourself put on the night shift?"

"Why would I do that?"

"Because this is gonna happen in the afternoon. You'd have to take the day off. That's a red fuckin' flag. They'll shine a spotlight straight up your ass. Just do it for a little while. Then you can say you don't like it and go back to days."

"Yeah, okay." Step stared down into his empty glass. "If I give the foreman a bag of weed, he'll let me do pretty much whatever I want."

"That reminds me," Beans said. "You know you gotta go to work the next day, right? If you're not there, they'll get suspicious.

And you gotta keep working for a few months. Then, if you wanna quit, you can get yourself fired. There's gonna be enough heat on you already. I'm sure they're gonna grill all the employees. Can you handle that?"

"No problem."

"Well, then," Beans said, lifting his glass, "all we gotta do is wait." He drained the whiskey. "Want another?"

Step pulled up his sleeve to check his watch. "Nah, I gotta go."

"Too bad. I was gonna smoke you in a game of darts."

"Next time."

After Step hobbled out, Beans moved to the far end of the bar.

Big-O approached and poured him another drink. "You waiting for him?"

"You better believe it."

"You know you can't win. He's just gonna give you another trouncin'."

"Not this time." Beans shook his head. "Tonight's my night. I can feel it." He leaned in close. "But just in case, how much would you take to slip him a Mickey?"

"Oh no," Big-O said, throwing up his hands. "Don't go gettin' me involved. This is between the two of you."

"Suit yourself. Gimme a deck, will ya?"

After Big-O handed him the cards, Beans picked up his drink and moved to one of the faux-wood Formica-topped tables scattered throughout the place and selected the chair that gave him the best view of the door.

He shuffled the cards, laid out a solitaire hand, and waited.

Two hands and two drinks later, Beans's eyes were fixed on Monk as he sauntered into the bar and took the seat across from him.

"You waitin' for me?"

"Fuckin' right I'm waitin' for you."

Big-O appeared, setting Monk's usual vodka and cranberry down on the table.

"You got a hard head, kid. What're we up to now—twenty-six?"

There it was, that signature smirk. Once a week, Beans met Monk at Dilligaf's to play gin for a dollar a hand.

"It's twenty-seven dollars," Beans replied. "And I ain't goin' home until I'm ahead."

CHAPTER 31

FIRST CALL

STEP HAD BEEN working the night shift for two weeks. It wasn't as bad as he thought it would be. No suits walking around, so that was a plus. There were also fewer flights and fewer fliers, which meant less work and, more importantly, fewer eyes on him. Most nights, he found a quiet corner and slept through the majority of his shift.

When he wasn't sleeping, he prowled around for something to steal.

He had been arriving each day an hour before his shift so he could listen to the tape. He sat on the bench in front of his locker with the recorder inside his jacket. The black wire slithered up out of his collar to a pair of small earphones, and he bopped his head every once in a while to make it appear like he was listening to music.

But this was better than music.

He relished listening to what his boss had to say when he thought no one else was around. Most of it was boring, but the

261

juicy parts made up for that. He was banging a ticket agent from Delta, and the two were in the habit of talking dirty to each other.

The daily sex call had just ended, and the phone rang again.

"American Airlines, Tom Miller speaking."

"Hi, Tom. It's Agent Clark from the treasury."

Step stilled the bopping and pressed the phones firmly to his ears.

"Hi, Frank. What can I do for you?"

"I'm just calling to let you know we'll be sending another shipment this Friday."

"Usual flight, usual everything?"

"Yep."

"Okay. I'll take care of everything on my end. We'll be ready for you."

"Great. Thanks. I'm leaving for Nassau tomorrow, so if there are any issues, you can talk to Barbara Stanton. She'll be running point for me while I'm gone."

"Nassau? I go there all the time. Where're you staying?"

"My travel agent put me at the Hilton. Is it any good?"

"It's beautiful. Not far from where I stay. If you need anything, see Maurice at the Graycliff. He can set you up with the best *entertainment*. If you know what I mean."

Agent Clark chuckled. "I'm going with my family. Probably won't have time for that. Sounds like you get around pretty good, huh?"

"I fly for free."

Step sprung to his feet, cradling the recorder inside his jacket, and ducked into a bathroom stall, where he sat on the toilet and rewound the tape.

He listened again. And again.

It was happening. Fuckin' really happening. *Fuckin' Beans better have a plan.*

He looked at his watch—*10:33*. Not enough time to get to the neighborhood and back before his shift started. But he had to talk to Beans.

Stomach cramps. He'd tell his shift supervisor he had severe stomach cramps and had to go home. He'd believe it. Since Step was already here, he wouldn't think he was playing hooky.

• • •

Traffic on the Kennedy was light at this time of night. Step made it from O'Hare to Hubbard's Cave in nineteen minutes. As he blew through the tunnel, he glanced in the rear-view mirror.

Flashing blue lights.

"Fuck!" He tapped the brake. How fast was he going?

Just past the Monroe Street exit ramp, he moved onto the shoulder and stopped. The cop pulled in behind him, the squad car's headlights illuminating the interior of Step's '77 Plymouth Duster. He fumbled for his license and rolled down the window.

The cop approached, shining a flashlight in Step's face.

Step thrust his license out the window. "I'm sorry, Officer. I know I was speeding, but I'm really sick. If I don't get to a bathroom soon, I'm seriously gonna shit my pants."

The cop took his license, looked it over, and shined the flashlight into the back seat. Then past Step to the front passenger seat. "What the fuck is that?" the cop asked, pointing to the makeshift recording device.

"That's my music. I'm a DJ."

"You were going pretty fast."

"I know," Step said, rocking in the seat for effect. "But I really gotta shit."

The cop looked at his watch. "You're fuckin' up my coffee break."

Step closed his eyes in relief. In Chicago, coffee was the magic word of cops. He whipped out a twenty and offered it. "How 'bout you let that coffee be on me?"

The cop took the bill. "Try to keep it under seventy, huh?"

"Yes, sir. Thank you."

Step was off and going before the cop even made it back to his cruiser.

He made it to Beans's place in just over six minutes.

• • •

"Who is it?"

"It's me, Step. Open up!"

Beans tied the belt of his robe. "What the fuck?" he said, pulling open the door. "You tryin' to break the thing down?"

"Sorry, Beans. We got the call!"

Beans pulled him inside.

As they sat down at the table, Beans couldn't help but be reminded of what had occurred the last time Step had been in his kitchen. His eyes drifted to the spot on the linoleum where he'd exhausted by now at least six cans of Lysol.

He pushed the thought from his mind. "Tell me everything."

"It's gonna happen this Friday." Step set the recorder on the table. "Tell me you got a plan in place."

"Just play the tape."

Step rewound the cassette slightly and pressed *play*.

When Step pressed *stop*, Beans got up and went to the counter for a pen and notepad.

He leaned back against the sink. "Play it again."

This time Beans took notes.

"Tell me you got a plan, Beans," Step repeated.

Fuck off! "I'm right there," Beans told him. "It's Monday. We got four days. I just gotta a few loose ends to tie up."

"What the fuck is there to tie up?" Step was on his feet, his face reddening. "Let's hit these motherfuckers!"

"Shh!" Beans scolded. "Keep your voice down. You want my grandmother to hear you?"

Whoa, Beans. If you lose your head, your ass goes with it. "When we started this," Beans began slowly, "you agreed to do it my way. You gotta let me do my thing. Don't panic. If we can't hit them Friday, we'll hit them next month. For now, you gotta get this recorder back in there and keep listening for any new info."

CHAPTER 32

DROP THE VERNACULAR

IT WAS WEDNESDAY night, two days before the shipment.

Step had been driving Beans crazy since Monday. He sat at the kitchen table, contemplating. Could she handle it? Of course she could. She was one tough chick. A neighborhood girl.

But that wasn't the point.

He'd never involved her before, and had never planned to. It was just a phone call. Still, it made her an accomplice. Would she do it? Of course she would. She'd do anything for him. But he felt guilty even asking.

He heard the familiar jingle of keys outside his door, then a knock.

"Come in!"

Debbie strode into the apartment and into the kitchen, and leaned back against the counter. "What'd you want to talk to me about?"

Beans looked up at his little sister. Since the break-in, she had taken to wearing his old knit Sox hat—the black one with the logo on the cuff—pretty much all day, even in the house and in classes at school. Just until the patch of hair they had to shave to treat her wound grew all the way back. Nobody was going to argue with her, not after what she'd been through.

Beans was seized by a pang of guilt, which had become a familiar part of his routine, anytime he saw Debbie. "Listen," he said. "Ever since we were kids, I always knew you had my back."

"Yeah, and you always had mine. So?"

"So . . ." Beans was experiencing a rare moment of indecisiveness. He elbowed it aside. "So now I gotta ask you to do something. It's gonna put you at risk, and I hate to do it, but it's important. And there's no one I trust more than you."

"You're freaking me out a little," she said, moving into the chair kitty-corner to him. "But you know I'll do whatever you need me to."

"It's not just for me. It's for all of us. I got something that'll change our lives."

She furrowed her brow. "It's not like you to beat around the bush. Just spit it out, Beans."

"I need you to make a phone call. I'm gonna protect you, and I already know how, but if things go sideways, you could be in some trouble."

"I'm Debbie *T.* Trombino. Trouble's my middle name. Wait. Are you asking me to help you on a job?"

"Maybe."

"Like a job. A scam. A score. The real deal?"

Beans shrugged.

Debbie grinned. "I'll do it."

"Yeah?"

"Do you have any idea how long I've waited for you to include me? Do you?"

"I guess not."

"What is it? What do you need me to do?"

He wasn't sure how to take his sister's enthusiasm for the business. Should he be worried or proud? There was no time to think about that now.

"I wrote out a script for you," he said. "I need you to be very professional. Lose the neighborhood accent. Disguise your voice a little." Beans passed her the sheet of looseleaf paper. "You're Barbara Stanton. You're gonna call Tom Miller. I'll be Tom Miller." Beans cleared his throat. "American Airlines, Tom Miller speaking."

"Hi, Tom. This is Agent Stanton with the treasury." Debbie read from the script, taking on an air of secretarial expertise. "I work with Frank Clark." She stopped suddenly and held the paper away. "The treasury? Holy fuck! What are we up to?"

"The less you know right now, the better. When it's all over, I'll explain everything." He continued in Tom Miller's voice. "Oh, yes. Frank mentioned you'd be handling things while he's away. Is everything all right?"

"Everything is fine. We're all set for tomorrow. I also wanted to let you know there won't be another shipment for a while."

"I hope there's not a problem with our service."

"No, no. Nothing like that. It's just that this week's shipment is the tail end of the current batch. We'll likely be starting up again in about six months' time."

Beans and Debbie went over the script a few times, then practiced various ways that the conversation could go. He had to fill her in on some of the details, so she would be able to improvise, if need be.

"Think you can handle it?"

"Nothing to it," she said with a smile. "When do you want me to call?"

"Tomorrow morning. Tom Miller starts at seven. I want you to make the call at 7:05. Find a pay phone located in a nice quiet place—*out* of the neighborhood."

She nodded. "So, how much we talkin' here?"

Beans shook his head, smiling.

CHAPTER 33

LAST CALL

ON THURSDAY, STEP got to work at 10:45 p.m., fifteen minutes before his shift, rather than the usual hour. Why should he bother? Listening to the tapes was a waste of time now. The shipment was tomorrow and fuckin' Beans didn't have a plan.

What's so great about that guy, anyway?

At this rate, they would have to wait until next month, which meant another month of juice to Skinny. He punched his locker. Fuck it! He'd do it himself. Make his own plan. It might not be all fancy like Beans's plans, but he'd get the job done. He dialed the combination to his locker. Or at least he thought he did. It didn't open.

His stomach dropped. Were they onto him? Had they seized the recorder and locked him out?

When he tried a second time, it opened right up. Step exhaled.

He looked to the top shelf where the device sat, staring him in the face, then glanced at his watch. He still had a few minutes to listen to his boss's sex talk—at the least, it would put him in a better mood. He tucked the recorder into his jacket and sat on the bench in front of the row of pale-blue lockers.

He was half-listening and half-daydreaming about killing Beans when the first call began to play. It was Barbara Stanton. *Barbara Stanton.* Where had he heard that name before? He didn't recognize the voice, but she sounded sexy.

". . . tomorrow's shipment is the tail end of this batch. We'll probably roll the presses again in about six months or so and resume shipments then."

Step ducked into a bathroom stall, rewound the tape, and played it again.

"Fuck!"

Six fuckin' months? Skinny would have him whacked way before that. No way he could get rid of Beans, Cosh, and Izzy and plan the job himself in twelve hours. If it didn't happen tomorrow, Step was a dead man.

Time to force Beans's hand.

• • •

Beans lay in bed, waiting.

He had mussed his hair, rubbed his eyes until they were red, and then smushed his face into the pillow.

When the knock at the door came, Beans rose and put on his robe, leaving it untied. "Who is it?"

"Open up, Beans. It's Step."

"Now what the fuck's up?" He dug a knuckle into the corner of his eye. "You gonna make a habit of this?"

"We gotta do it tomorrow. It's the last shipment!"

Beans pulled him in and shut the door. "What're you talking about?"

"The tape." Step held up the recorder and played the conversation between Tom Miller and "Agent Stanton."

"Fuck." Beans shuffled into the kitchen and sat down, dropped his clasped hands between his knees. "I can't wait six fuckin' months." He looked up at Step. "I guess we're doin' this thing tomorrow."

Step's eyes went wide. "Seriously? You're ready?"

Beans nodded. "I got the last piece of information I needed earlier today. Got it all figured. Turns out, it's not gonna be that complicated, after all." He rose and opened the cupboard. "Let's have a cup of coffee, and I'll tell you all about it."

"I don't want any coffee," Step said. "Just tell me the plan."

Beans noticed red blotches on Step's throat. "What are those—hickeys?"

"Yeah, I went to the Show of Shows today. I was makin' out with one of the girls, and she got carried away."

"You were makin' out with a whore?" *Step kisses whores. Figures.* And Show of Shows had the skankiest whores in all of Cook County.

"That's not *all* I was doin' with her."

Beans's stomach convulsed.

If he kissed them, Step likely did the other thing you weren't supposed to do to a whore. Thank God he didn't want coffee. Beans would have to throw away the cup.

Beans had to change the subject to keep from gagging. "Do you think you can handle the two guards with a stun gun?"

"No problem."

"Good. Then my idea for how to do this without getting too rough will work. I've been studying their movements carefully, as well as the loading dock. It's always the same. They drive the bundles from the airport directly to the dock at the Federal Reserve. They never stop on the way. They back into the dock, get out at the

273

same time. Then they go up a little stairway to get to dock level. The driver uses his key to open the back door of the truck, while the other guy goes to a little side room to get the cart. He wheels the cart to the back of the truck, and they both unload the bundles onto the cart. They always look relaxed, laughing and joking. When they've got their guard down, that's when to hit 'em."

"So that's your plan?" Step said. "To try to hit them at the bank? I'd think it'd be better to hit them somewhere on the way."

"Listen to me," Beans said. "The loading dock is off the alley. It's fuckin' desolate back there. I never see anyone else around. If we hit them on the street, there's citizens everywhere—not to mention cops. Our asses will be hangin' out in the wind. The dock is perfect, private, a place we can do whatever we want."

Step leaned against the fridge and crossed his arms. "Go on."

"So, here's my plan. There's a dumpster on the dock, right behind where they unload. You hide in the dump—"

"Hold on—"

"It's not for garbage," Beans said, anticipating Step's next protest. "It's just for paper." *The guy shkeeves garbage, but not VD.*

"Go on."

"You hide in the dumpster. When both guards are at the back of the truck with the door open, you jump out and zap 'em. Make sure it's *after* they open the back door of the truck. Then, once they're knocked out, you handcuff 'em and drag 'em into the room with the carts. I pull up to the docks with a van, we load as many bundles that will fit, and we get the fuck out of there. Simple, easy, and hopefully no one gets hurt."

"How come I gotta go in the dumpster and you drive the van?"

"No plan goes as smooth as you think it will. What if the stun guns don't work right, and the guards don't get knocked out?

I'm just a planner. A burglar. You're more used to that kinda sit-uation. Probably handle it better than me." Playing on Step's ego was almost more than Beans could take.

"So, you're okay with me packin' heat?"

"Yes. But only for emergency. If you don't have to use it and you use it, you and me are gonna have a problem. Use the stun gun. And just so you know, I never carry on a job. That's my rule, so don't expect me to be armed."

Beans caught the subtle shift in Step's expression. He was lining it up in his head. They'd have the money, and he'd have a gun. That's when he'd move to kill Beans and call in Little Man, give him the go-ahead for Cosh and Izzy.

"I gotta admit, Beans," Step said, dropping his arms to his sides, "you live up to your reputation. The plan sounds perfect. Simple and easy."

"It's what I do." Beans shrugged. "The van is all ready. I keep it in a garage on Flournoy Street, across the alley from Fish's house. Meet me there after work at eight a.m. That'll give us a few hours to go over everything." Beans looked at the clock on the kitchen wall. "Hey, aren't you supposed to be at work right now?"

"Yeah, but then I heard the tape. I ran out before I even clocked in."

Idiot. "Not good. If you're not at work, they'll get suspicious. Call your boss and tell him you had car trouble, but you're on your way. A little late at the beginning of a shift should be okay. We hope." Beans wanted Step occupied right up until it was time. Less time for the guy to plan any sort of double cross.

CHAPTER 34

FOR DEBBIE

BEANS SHIFTED HIS weight, careful not to make noise or rock the van. His leg muscles were already cramped even though he'd only been squatting in the back for ten minutes, peering through the eyepiece of his telescope.

What the fuck is he doing?

Beans tried to adjust the focus, but it was at the optimal setting for this distance. He laid it down and put a naked eye to the peephole drilled into the side of the van. From the street, no one would ever notice the small hole in the center of the second *O* of Zoom in the Zoom Messenger Service logo he stenciled along the side of vehicle. He chose that particular business name because he knew the owner of Zoom was duking the Loop cops not to ticket or tow his delivery vehicles. Beans could sit there as long as he needed to without drawing incident. From his vantage point on Quincy Street, Beans could see down the alley and into the entire loading dock area of the Federal Reserve bank.

Right now, he didn't like what he was seeing.

First a head and arm, then a leg and torso. Step was climbing out of the dumpster, where he was supposed to hide until after the armored truck backed in and the guards opened the back door. The truck wasn't there yet, but it was due any minute.

Motherfucker!

His usual rush of adrenaline was accompanied by a dull ache in his gut. Was it simply from having to work with Step, or was it because he knew the end of this job would be like no other before it? He watched helplessly as Step deviated from the plan. Anger and disgust rose in his chest as he watched Step move around to the far side of the dumpster and slink down out of view.

That sick son of a bitch! Just has to take a shit.

Time seemed to stop as Beans watched and waited. What was only a matter of minutes seemed like an hour. The armored car was rolling down LaSalle Street just as Step reappeared and climbed back into the dumpster. The driver pulled onto Quincy Street and made a three-point turn to back into the loading dock.

Beans picked up the detonator marked *TH*.

The guards followed their usual routine to the letter, opening their doors, exiting the truck, and hopping onto the loading dock. Beans was focused like a laser. A second flood of adrenaline gushed into his bloodstream. His timing had to be perfect. The driver walked to the storeroom at the side of the dock to get the four-wheeled cart, while the guard riding shotgun went around to the back of the truck.

Beans's body went numb. The interior of the van vanished. The scene unfolding on the dock was his only consciousness. He couldn't see the rear of the truck, but he knew the back door had been opened wide when he saw its lip protruding past the truck's side panel. The driver rolled out the cart and proceeded to the rear of the truck. The door was open and the guards were in position, facing the money.

Now was the time.

Step nimbly bounded out of the dumpster with a stun gun in each hand, taking the guards by surprise. When they turned toward him, he pressed a gun into the chest of each, simultaneously. One guard dropped instantly. The other convulsed for a second or two, then fell. Step had them both duct-taped and on the cart in under a minute.

The guy's stronger than he looks.

Beans's ears throbbed with the rush of blood and the echo of his pulse. He flipped the toggle on the detonator and a red light came on, indicating it was armed. As Step rolled the cart carrying the guards into the storeroom, Beans pressed his thumb down on the push button of the detonator.

Nothing happened. For a split second.

Then a flash illuminated the darkest corners of the loading dock, and smoke billowed from the truck as the incendiaries lit the flash paper and the fire spread to the real money.

Step emerged from the storeroom, mouth agape. He ran to the back of the truck to find the cause of all the smoke, just as Beans had hoped he would. Beans lifted the detonator marked *C*. His mind raced, wondering if he would ever be the same after this.

Would he be doomed to hell?

Do those doomed to hell see the world differently?

He imagined that everything would be a little dimmer, like looking through dark sunglasses.

Then he remembered Debbie, left for dead, lying in a pool of blood.

He fished into his pocket for the slip of paper. On it, in her childish scrawl, was the riddle she had left for him that morning.

He read aloud, "Where do pencils come from?"

He didn't get it earlier, but it came to him now in an instant.

In one single motion, he flipped the toggle and pressed the push button to set off the C-4.

"Pencilvania!"

The shock waves rocked the van and knocked Beans backward from his squatting position. The armored car exploded into mangled chunks of steel and bits of shrapnel, which sailed through the air mixed with money—and Step, in pieces.

CHAPTER 35

IN THE DOGHOUSE

THE PREVIOUS MONDAY, just before midnight.

"Y'ello."

"It's me."

"What's up?"

"It's showtime."

"When?"

"Friday."

Cosh looked at his watch. "For sure?"

"Yep. He was just here."

Cosh kissed his Saint Dismas ring. "Perfect. We're on it." He hung up and called Izzy, then Gugootz, after which he slipped into his Member's Only jacket, dipped his hand into his coffee can full of coins, filled a pocket, and hustled out to his car.

He drove to Paulina Street, eyes darting repeatedly to the rear-view mirror, and parked. Once inside St. Luke's Hospital, he located a pay phone in a secluded area.

He drew a deep breath, popped in a quarter, and said a little prayer.

One of the biggest variables of the plan was making sure they got on all the correct flights. He called American Airlines and made a reservation for Friday on flight 311 from DC to O'Hare for himself and Capo, or rather, "Frederic Barnes" and "Fritz." Next, he called back and made arrangements to ship the crates from DC to O'Hare, making sure that those, too, would be on flight 311. Then he called United and booked a one-way flight for Thursday from O'Hare to DC for himself and Capo, or rather, "James Gonzales" and "Pepito." Lastly, he called Southwest and made a one-way reservation for Thursday from O'Hare to Washington DC for Gugootz, or rather, "Victor Vogelmeyer."

When the task was completed, he drove home and called Beans. "Yo, it's me."

"How'd it go?"

"All good."

"That's great. Admittedly, I was a little worried. When do you leave?"

"Thursday."

•••

Wednesday, just before midnight.

Cosh let himself into the empty club, and flicked on the lights. Capo, curled up on the sofa, opened his eyes but didn't move.

"This what you do when no one's around?"

Cosh pulled a bandana from his pocket and tied it over his nose and mouth, then pulled on a pair of black leather gloves. He petted Capo's head.

The dog yawned and rolled onto his back.

"A belly rub? Now? We got work to do, boy."

Capo stared up at him with pleading brown eyes.

"Okay, okay. But just for a minute." Cosh lowered himself to the sofa, scratched the dog's middle, then wiped his gloves on the upholstery to remove any dander or saliva. He got to his feet. "Okay, boy. Let's go."

Capo rolled over and back into his curled-up position.

"So that's how you're gonna play this, huh?"

Cosh went into the kitchen, snagged a Heineken from the fridge, and popped open the can. Capo leapt from the sofa and trotted into the back and to his bowl. Cosh poured in a few ounces of beer, and while Capo was lapping it up, he latched the leash to his collar.

"Suh-marter than the average bear. And dog too." Cosh reached into the box of Milk Bones and plucked out a biscuit. Capo took the treat, crunched three times, and swallowed. Cosh pulled the back door ajar, so that when the club members noticed Capo was missing, they would assume someone had left the door open and Capo ran away.

He then took the dog to Geraldi's to sleep until morning.

• • •

Thursday morning, bright and early.

Cosh and Capo waited in Geraldi's Garage until they heard the short toot of a car horn. As the overhead door rattled open, Gugootz climbed out of the van's passenger side and coaxed Capo into his crate in the back of the van.

Cosh jumped in the shotgun seat next to Izzy, who was behind the wheel.

As Izzy drove toward the highway, Cosh and Gugootz put on their disguises—a simple hat and glasses would suffice for the flight to DC, just enough to make a witness question himself if viewing a lineup. Cosh wore a Cubs cap and metal gold-framed glasses, Gugootz a newsboy cap and tortoiseshell horn-rims.

"Don't forget your mustache," Cosh said, glancing over his shoulder to Gugootz. "Gotta look like the photo on your ID."

Gugootz held the mustache in his palm and dabbed glue onto the back. He pressed it above his upper lip and came forward to use the rear-view mirror to adjust and straighten it before the glue dried.

He turned his head to Cosh. "How's it look?"

"Perfect," Cosh said. "A real Victor Vogelmeyer if I ever saw one." He snorted and sneezed and scratched at his neck. "Fuckin' dog." Before his head had a chance to fill with mucus, he located a Benadryl in his pocket and popped it in his mouth.

Izzy turned right on Jackson Boulevard and headed for the Kennedy Expressway. The van lurched and belched, then backfired like the sound of a gunshot. Then it died.

Izzy steered it to the curb. "Motherfucker!"

"What the fuck was that?" Gugootz asked.

"That was a Dirty Dave special, that's what." Izzy turned the key in the ignition.

The engine cranked and sputtered, but wouldn't start. He tried again. Same result.

"He was supposed to check the vans out," Izzy said, his head finding the top of the steering wheel. "I swear Dave got his mechanic's license from a box of Cracker Jacks. The son of a bitch couldn't fix a fuckin' ham sandwich."

"Good thing I was a Boy Scout." Cosh reached behind the driver's seat and yanked up a metal toolbox.

"I hope you can fix it fast." Izzy looked at his watch. "We gotta be at the airport in forty minutes."

Cosh got out of the van and set the toolbox on the seat. "Izzy, pop the hood and give me a hand up front. Gugootz, remove the doghouse."

Izzy and Cosh went around front, poking their heads around the engine, looking for the problem.

"Hey, Gugootz! How you doin' with that doghouse?" Cosh felt something brush up against his leg.

"All good here." Gugootz was standing beside him, holding Capo on his leash.

Cosh peered down the side of the van to where Capo's crate sat on the pavement.

Capo nuzzled his nose into Cosh's crotch.

"Get out of there!" Cosh pushed Capo away. "What the fuck's he doing out of the van?"

Gugootz's brow knitted. "You said to take him out."

"What? Are you fuckin' with me? No I didn't." Cosh had to think for a second. "I said remove the dog*house*, not the dog crate."

"Doghouse, dog crate, what's the difference?"

Cosh led Gugootz around to the driver's side door and slapped the center console. "The fuckin' doghouse of the van! This thing, right here, over the fuckin' motor." He slapped it again. "Don't you know what the fuckin' doghouse is?"

"There's a motor under there? I thought the motor was under the hood."

"Izzy, give me a hand, please." Cosh turned to Gugootz and pointed to a taxicab down the block. "Go tell that cab driver not to go anywhere, we might need a ride to the airport."

Cosh put the gas filter in his mouth and blew through the nipple. He turned his head and spit out the taste of gasoline, then put the thing to his lips and blew again.

"Hey, guys," Gugootz yelled as Capo dragged him back to the van. "The cab driver says he won't take the dog."

"Izzy, go talk to the guy, will ya?" Cosh said. "I'll keep working on this."

Izzy strode to the open driver's door window of the cab and rested his forearms on the cab door. He put his face close to the man. Cosh couldn't hear much of what he was saying, but he heard the cab driver well enough.

"No dogs."

Izzy retrieved a hundred-dollar bill from his pocket and held it out to the guy.

"Okay," he said. "But no dogs."

Izzy went back to his pocket again, took out another hundred, and thrust that and the other in the man's face.

"No dogs means no dogs!" the driver insisted.

Izzy shoved the money back into his pocket, reached into the window, and grabbed the driver by the throat, his giant hands encircling the entire circumference of the guy's neck.

Cosh rolled his eyes, jumped behind the wheel of the van, and said a little prayer. The cab driver was halfway out the window when the van roared to life.

He blew the horn. "Quit fuckin' around! We gotta go!"

Izzy shoved the driver back into his cab and jogged back to the van. Together, he and Gugootz loaded Capo and his crate back into the van, while Cosh moved back to the passenger seat. Then they hopped in themselves.

"You see," Izzy said to Gugootz, "that's how easy things can get fucked-up. Nothing ever goes as smooth as you plan it. You gotta be prepared and be able to flow with the conditions. Remember what Beans says: 'Expect the unexpected.' What if we break down on the return trip, on the highway, when the van is full of zort? What if some state trooper comes and offers assistance and looks in the van? We all go to prison."

They spent the rest of the ride to the airport in eerie silence.

Gugootz slipped on his headphones, while Cosh stared out the window, able to hear the faint melody of "Keep Your Eye on the Sparrow"—the theme from *Baretta*. His thoughts zeroed in on Debbie. Once he got the money, he'd be able to give her a good life, the best life, anything she wanted. Beans would know that his sister would be taken care of. But what if things went wrong and he got caught? How much time would he get? He'd have to start from scratch after he got out. He had a nice little pile of cash saved, but the fucking lawyers would eat that up in a hurry. Would Debbie wait for him? He heard Beans's voice in his head: *Don't do the crime if you can't do the time.* He kissed his Saint Dismas ring and prepared mentally for prison life. He looked over at Izzy, then back to Gugootz.

It wasn't hard to see they were all thinking similar thoughts.

• • •

Izzy dropped off Cosh and Capo at the United terminal. "All right," he said. "Good luck. I'm gonna drop off the kid at Southwest. I'll see you tomorrow."

Cosh's flight was uneventful. As planned, he met up with Gugootz at the DC house—a furnished townhome in Foggy Bottom with a garage for the van.

"How was your flight?" Cosh asked him.

"All smooth. No problems. But I'm fuckin' starvin'."

They ordered two pizzas from Famous Luigi's. Capo finished what they couldn't.

For some unknown reason, maybe it was their full stomachs—or, in Cosh's case, the Benadryl—they slept like three little babies.

CHAPTER 36

THIS IS IT

GUGOOTZ FELT HIS stomach rumble.

"Okay, kid. This is it." Cosh pulled the van onto the gravel shoulder of the road. The American Airlines freight terminal was just around the corner.

Gugootz's stomach rumbled again—this time louder.

"Was that you?" Cosh asked. "Are you nervous?"

Gugootz shook his head. "Nah. I shouldn't have put that hot giardiniera on the pizza last night. It gives me agita."

Cosh nodded. "You got everything?"

"Blanket, oxygen, flashlight." Gugootz unfurled a finger for each item. "I even brought a beer for Capo."

"Heineken?"

"Yep."

"Good. We don't want him shitting all over the money. You got your gloves?"

"Fuck!" Gugootz frantically searched his pockets. He went to the back of the van and opened the lid to the large wooden crate and riffled around inside. "Fuck!"

Cosh threw up his arms. "Well, we're fucked now. We can't do it. I gotta turn around. We're gonna miss our flight. You just blew the whole caper."

"What?" Gugootz searched his pockets again. "Don't you have a pair of gloves I can use?"

"I have *my* gloves," Cosh said. He held up a pair of Wells Lamont leather work gloves. "But I need them to wipe the van later."

"Beans is gonna kill me."

Cosh went into his pocket and came out with a crumpled handful of surgical gloves. He dangled them in the air. "Gimme a sawbuck, and I won't tell him."

"Phew! You're a lifesaver, Cosh." Gugootz snatched the tangled ball of latex from Cosh's hand and stepped into the crate. He squatted and curled into a fetal position on his back, with his knees bent and his feet against the end wall.

He closed the lid. Pitch-black.

He felt the van pull back onto the road to the freight terminal. Riding inside the crate was bumpier than Gugootz had expected. He had spent hours practicing inside the crate, but not in a moving vehicle. He had gotten used to the cramped position and the utter darkness. What was new was the motion and the noise. Some of the sounds outside the crate were muffled, but others were amplified. The crunch of rubber on gravel. The occasional stone being thrown up into the wheel well. The steel springs of the van creaking as they rolled over a dip in the road.

A gaping pothole caused an earsplitting clang of wood against metal as the crate bounced on the floor of the van. The momentum changed from forward, to left, to back, as Cosh made a three-point turn to back up to the special van-height loading dock. The van crept back gently until its chrome rear bumper kissed the rubber bumpers on the dock. This caused the wooden crate to slide a few inches closer to the rear door and squeak loudly against the metal floor.

Gugootz was surprised at how calm he was. It was actually kind of fun.

He resisted the urge to put on his headphones and listen to music. He wanted to hear as much as possible of what was happening outside.

The driver's side door opened and closed—Cosh getting out. Even though it was dark inside the crate, Gugootz closed his eyes as if that would allow him to hear better. Three tinny clangs—Cosh climbing the diamond-plate metal stairs up to the dock. Garbled voices—Cosh talking to the dockworker. Then the rear doors of the van opened. Cosh stepping inside. The scrubbing and screeching of wood against metal as Cosh dragged the four smaller crates across the van floor.

The van wobbled as Cosh lobbed the crates onto the dock.

"You need a hand with that one?" Gugootz was able to hear the dockworker clearly.

"Nah," Cosh said. "Just wheel the dolly to the end of the dock, and I'll slide it onto it." Cosh slid the crate to the end of the van. "You okay in there, kid?" he whispered.

Gugootz began to answer, but stopped himself when heard the dockworker's voice.

"Who are you talking to?"

"Oh," Cosh said. "Just the dog."

"You deliver animals too?"

"I'll deliver horse manure if they pay me enough." Cosh tilted the crate and spanned the distance between the van's floor bed and the dock. He slid it onto the dolly.

When the dockworker tilted the dolly, Gugootz pushed his feet and elbows against the walls of the crate to brace himself. As they rolled, the wheel of the dolly squeaked intermittently like an annoying chirping bird. For some reason, Gugootz found himself counting the chirps. He was pretty sure there were seventeen. The dockworker lowered the crate and slid out the dolly.

Silence.

It would be at least an hour until the crate was loaded onto the plane. He could listen to music until he felt movement again.

• • •

Steve Miller was singing "Jet Airliner" to Gugootz through the Walkman's headphones when he stopped the tape. "Get rich or get busted." *Damn, Steve Miller's a prophet.* He lay on his back in the dark, feet pressed against the wall of the crate, contemplating both scenarios. He tried to focus on the getting busted part, like Beans advised, to prepare himself for the worst. It didn't work. He couldn't stop his mind from going to the money. There would be eight bundles. That makes two bundles each. If the bills were unpacked and thrown loosely, they might fill a bathtub. Gugootz imagined himself falling asleep in a bathtub full of money.

The squeaking wheel of the dolly shattered his reverie like BBs shot at a car window. A slight tilt. The tongue of the dolly scraped against the concrete floor of the dock and slid under the crate. Gugootz braced himself with his feet and elbows. A forty-five-degree tilt. *Chirp, chirp, chirp.* Nineteen chirps. Probably at the end of the dock. Upward movement, then forward and down with a crash. Probably on the transport now. No movement, but multiple crashes as the other freight was loaded around him, then on top of him. Rolling forward—smoothly at first, and then bouncing and rattling all the way to the plane. He could hear the engines

292

whine and roar. Stopped moving. The scraping of wood on wood as a smaller crate was dragged across the top of his crate. Scraping and dragging all around him.

Then backward movement as he was loaded, headfirst, onto the plane.

• • •

Beans had told Gugootz to use the landing gear as a signal. After takeoff, wait to hear the wheels go up. Only then was it safe to climb out of the crate and switch the bundles. He could remain out of the crate until he heard the wheels descend for landing. It was a short flight, but that would give him plenty of time to take care of business and limit the time he had to spend cramped in the crate. He resisted the urge to put his headphones back on. There were some good songs lined up on the tape, but he didn't want to miss the sound of the wheels.

He waited anxiously.

Time dragged inside the crate. For some reason, the smell of fresh-sawn wood was stronger than it had ever been. His nostrils stung. He shined the flashlight to check his watch and turned it off quickly to save the battery.

His stomach gurgled.

The fucking peppers on the pizza last night. When it gurgled again, he felt his lower abdomen rumble. This could be bad. Very bad. If he shit his pants inside the crate, the smell—not to mention, the mess—would be unbearable.

Gugootz began to sweat.

He waited a while, then checked his watch again. Only two minutes had gone by. *Are you fucking kidding me?* It had felt like half an hour. He tried to relax and not think about it, but his sphincter wouldn't let him.

"Shit!" he said aloud, then immediately regretted it. *Fuck!* This was one contingency he hadn't planned for.

He felt the plane roll forward, stop for what seemed like an eternity, then roll again. He had to get out of this thing. He couldn't shit his pants now. The guys would laugh their balls off. And probably give him a new, even less pleasant, nickname. Cah-Cah instead of Gugootz, or Jimmy Shitty Pants, or something stupid like that. The engines roared, and he sensed the speed and the incline as the plane took off. The plane leveled out, and Gugootz heard the high-pitched whirring of the electric motor that raised the hydraulics of the landing gear. The noise grew louder and more high-pitched, then stopped abruptly with a rapid series of loud knocks.

At last, the wheels were up.

He rotated the catch on the crate's interior locking device and raised the lid slowly. The lid was heavier than he remembered. He pushed harder, and the lid rose about six inches and stopped. He lowered the lid and tried again. But again, six inches and it stopped. He held up the lid with his knees and slinked out an arm. He was able to bend his elbow upward and grope the top of the lid.

Fuck!

One of the smaller crates had been loaded on top of his crate and was hitting the ceiling of the cargo hold whenever he lifted the lid, preventing it from opening all the way. He pulled his arm back in and lowered the lid.

His stomach gurgled. Now what?

Gugootz lay quietly, curled up in the darkness, and gently bounced with the turbulence. *It's over.* A beautiful plan foiled by a little wooden crate. And he'd have a ridiculous nickname for the rest of his life. One particularly jerky bounce caused the crate above to jump up and come back down hard. He raised the lid with his knees and slinked out his arm again. He tried to push the crate off, but couldn't get it to budge. In this position, he had no leverage. He pulled his arm back in and lowered the lid. More turbulence. Another jerky bounce, and he could hear the small crate lift up and slam back down.

Turbulence! He could use the turbulence!

Again, he raised the lid with his knees. He had to raise it just right. Enough to get his arm out, but not so much that it wedged the smaller crate against the ceiling. He had to give it room to bounce.

A stabbing pain in his abdomen. He prayed for more turbulence.

Each time the plane rose and fell, the crate above him floated for a split second. He had to time his pushes to each float. He felt the plane rise and pushed as hard as he could as the plane fell back down. The crate moved a few inches. He waited. The plane jerked upward again, and he pushed. A few more inches. Three more pushes and the smaller crate crashed down onto the floor of the cargo hold. He froze and imagined the pilot and copilot talking above him.

"*Did you hear that?*"

"*Yeah.*"

"*What was it?*"

"*Just some freight settling. Nothing to worry about. That new flight attendant is a doll, isn't she?*"

"*Yeah. If she has a layover, I might see if she wants to have a drink.*"

Gugootz wriggled the surgical gloves over his fingers one hand at a time and stretched them up to his wrists with a snap. He felt around in his jacket pocket for the headband flashlight that Beans had given him. He slipped it onto his head and flicked it on. He raised the lid and poured himself over the side of the crate.

How much room would he have to move around?

He could feel the cold of the metal floor on his knees, through his jeans. He raised and lowered his head to illuminate the ceiling and then the floor, gauging the height. He stayed on his knees. Not enough room to stand unless he bent over. He turned slowly in each direction to shine light on the rest of the cargo hold. Thank God there wasn't much other freight. Just his crate and the four smaller ones, a cardboard box sealed with duct tape, and some puffy white bundles that looked like bales of cotton. He was separated from the rest of the hold by a curtain of black netting. Past that, Capo's crate and the baggage, then another curtain of netting.

Past that second curtain would be the money.

He was able to slink out between the end of the netting and the cargo-hold wall. He worked loose the top and bottom buckles on one side of the netting, and the curtain drooped off to one side. Now he could see Capo in his crate. The dog was lying down in his sphinx position, ears erect and eyes wide open, watching. Gugootz inched his way around on his knees and tossed suitcases to one side to pile them out of his way. Capo had his nose pressed against the wire-grate door of the crate, the wet black tip of it poking through one of the square openings.

"That looks like it hurts, boy." Gugootz stuck his finger through the opening above and stroked the bridge of Capo's nose. "I brought a present for you, but you gotta wait."

He continued piling suitcases off to one side to clear a path to the money. The only thing in his way now was the curtain of black netting.

He worked loose the top and bottom buckles on the right side of the netting and let it swag to the left side. He shined the light ahead and bathed it onto the blue bundles. They glistened and glowed in their shiny plastic-wrapped magnificence, and he imagined a choir hitting a high note at midnight Mass.

A chill crawled up his spine, and he froze. *This is really fucking happening!*

He clasped his hands behind his neck and rolled his eyes heavenward. *Thank you. Thank you.*

Gugootz shuffled on his knees toward the bundles. "Move one bundle at a time," Beans had told him, "so you can't fuck up."

He put his face close to each bundle to check the denomination. Get the twenties. Beans said twenty was the best. They would have a hard time spending the hundreds. But so far, only hundreds. He lifted one of the bundles to move it out of the way. Are these really only forty pounds? They felt heavier. He piled the bundles out of his way as he went.

Hundreds. Hundreds. Hundreds. "Shit."

Shit? Don't even say the word.

He puckered his sphincter tight and continued. More hundreds. Each time he strained to lift a bundle, he felt the hot peppers move farther down his intestines. His face flushed, and sweat dripped from his nose as he examined the bundles one at a time and struggled to heave them out of his way. Each one was heavier than the one before it. He couldn't lift them anymore, couldn't stand the strain it put on his bowels. He pushed them and slid them back and to the side, out of his way. He worked his way through the pile of bundles to the end.

Hundreds. Hundreds. Hundreds. *Fuck!*

No twenties. Only hundreds. A whole load of hundreds. What

the fuck should he do? The pain in his bowels became unbearable. He couldn't think. Sweat rolled down his face and neck. Was the pressure in his bowels preventing him from thinking, or was the strain of thinking putting pressure on his bowels? He couldn't stand it anymore. He knee-walked to the end of the cargo hold, unfastened his pants, and squatted.

The stench rapidly overtook the cargo hold. Gugootz didn't care. Relief at last. Now what? How would he clean himself? What did he have in the crate that he could use? He reviewed the inventory in his head. *Flashlight. Oxygen tank. Two cans of Coke. Baggie full of candy bars. Sleeping bag.*

The sleeping bag! He could cut it into pieces. But then he'd have to knee-walk all the way back to his crate with a dirty ass. He fumbled his hands into his pockets two at a time. First the jacket, then the front pants pockets, then the back pants pockets. Nothing he could use.

He mentally worked his way down his body. He pulled off his shoes, and then his socks, and used those to clean himself.

Now he could think. No twenties. What should he do?

As to the money, he had no choice. He had to take the hundreds. He cradled a bundle to his chest and inched his way back over to the wooden crate. He laid it down in front of the crate and went back for another and carried it over to the crate. He pulled the lever of the secret catch under the lip of the lid, and the lid opened with a click. He removed the two bundles of fake money and replaced them with the two bundles of real money. Then he pushed the crate as far as possible out of the way and placed the two fake bundles on top of it.

One crate done. Three to go.

He knee-walked back to the real bundles and continued.

By the time he had finished loading the second crate, his knees ached. Four more trips to go. If this wasn't so much fun, he'd be miserable. Had the stench subsided, or had he gotten used to it? He sat back on his rump and stretched out his legs.

Should have brought kneepads.

He got up onto his feet and into a squatting position, then duckwalked back to the money. Four more duckwalk trips and all of the crates were full of real hundred-dollar bills. Four crates, two bundles in each crate, forty pounds per bundle.

Holy fuck!

Three hundred and twenty pounds of hundred-dollar bills. They were supposed to get twenties, but got hundreds instead. That's five times what they were expecting. Gugootz couldn't even think that high.

His thighs and calves ached. He got back to his knees to put the fake bundles in with the rest of the real money and stacked them all up neatly.

CHAPTER 37

TIME FOR CHAMPAGNE

"YOU OKAY IN there, kid?" Izzy asked over his shoulder. Despite all of his jokes, he was genuinely concerned for Gugootz.

A muffled "yeah" came from inside the crate in the back of the van.

Izzy sighed in relief. The back doors were open to the dock, and Cosh was loading the other four crates into the van.

"Don't come out yet," Izzy said. "Wait 'til we hit the highway. I'll let you know when." Izzy checked his mirrors as he neared the end of the on-ramp. "All right, kid. You can come on out now."

The secret latch clicked open, and the lid rose. "Motherfucking fucker." Gugootz climbed out of the crate. "That was fun. Hi, Capo. It's me again."

Cosh looked at Izzy. "This fuckin' kid is crazier than you."

"So, what the fuck?" Izzy said. "Did we do it?"

Gugootz fished into his crate. "I brought something, just in case."

He turned his back, shaking and struggling with something in his hands.

Izzy exchanged a worried glance with Cosh.

Gugootz turned back around, gripping a bottle of champagne. He turned and twisted the cork, which launched out of the bottle with a loud pop and bounced off the windshield. Champagne gushed from the neck of the bottle and spewed throughout the van.

"Holy fuck!" Izzy said. "We did it? We did it!" He drummed his palms on the steering wheel while dodging champagne drips from the roof liner above.

Cosh kissed his Saint Dismas ring. "Un-fucking-believable." He knelt backward in the passenger seat, pulled Gugootz close, and planted a giant kiss on his forehead. "Good job, kid." He reached into his back pants pocket for his handkerchief and blotted the champagne from his face, then handed the hanky to Izzy.

Izzy laughed and wiped his face as he motored along the Mannheim Road exit. He glanced in the rear-view as Gugootz opened Capo's crate and let him lick the champagne from his hand.

"I can't fuckin' believe it," Izzy said. "There's three million dollars in this van right now. Three million dollars!"

Gugootz cleared his throat. "Not exactly . . ."

"What do you mean, 'not exactly?'" Izzy's eyes moved back to the rear-view.

"I knew it was too good to be true," Cosh said, turning in his seat. "What happened?"

"I couldn't help it, guys. There was nothing I could do. There were no twenties in the whole shipment."

"Don't even tell me we got four crates full of singles," Izzy said.

"Not singles. Hundreds. The entire shipment was hundred-dollar bills."

Izzy did the math. "Fifteen million dollars? Is that what you're telling me? That there's fifteen million dollars back there?"

"I guess so," Gugootz said. "But Beans said we can't spend the hundreds."

"He didn't say *can't*," Cosh said, turning in his seat. "He said it would be difficult. But we'll figure it out. Gimme that champagne." He took the bottle from Gugootz, chugged from it, and handed it to Izzy.

"Ho-lee fuck!" With his left hand on the steering wheel and the bottle in his right, Izzy chugged some bubbly, then handed it back to Gugootz.

He drove south down Mannheim Road, past North Avenue.

"I gotta get rid of this fuckin' beard," Cosh said. "It's itching the fuck out of me. Did you bring the alcohol?"

"Now you're allergic to beards?" Izzy said. "It's in the glove."

While Cosh reached into the glove compartment for the rubbing alcohol and washcloths for him and Gugootz, Izzy turned left at Soffel Avenue, made a quick right down the alley between Mannheim Road and Fortieth Avenue, and stopped in front of a garage.

"How come we rented a house in Stone Park to take the money to?" Gugootz asked.

"'Cause it's a straight shot from the airport," Izzy explained. "And it's out of the neighborhood, and we know all the cops in this town."

"Okay, but did we have to pick a house right here?" Gugootz pointed across the alley to the parking lot of the Stone Park Police Station.

"It's the safest place to be. You could beat a murder rap in this town for two grand." Izzy chuckled. "I wonder how Beans is doing?" The question had been nagging just below the surface of his consciousness all day.

Cosh looked at the Movado on his wrist. "The truck's probably not even there yet. It's gonna be a while 'til we see him."

Izzy pressed the button on the remote control, and the garage door opened. "Pretty nice that the house comes with a clicker."

Izzy backed the van into the garage. When they got out, Cosh pressed the button on the wall to lower the door.

"Capo probably has to piss like a racehorse," Izzy said. "Gugootz, why don't you take him for a walk while me and Cosh unload the crates."

Izzy and Cosh brought the crates inside, opened them, and placed the bundles on the kitchen table. When Gugootz returned with Capo, each of them took a seat and stared at the bundles like children at a birthday party waiting for someone to cut the cake.

Gugootz opened his mouth to say something, but nothing came out.

Cosh tried to answer him, but he had no words either.

Izzy was mesmerized, peering at the stacks of hundreds through the blue plastic. "Should we open one up?"

"We should wait for Beans," Gugootz said.

"Yeah." Cosh rubbed at his chin. "But maybe just pull back some of the plastic on one, so we can see it better."

Izzy smiled. His heart raced as he dragged the tip of his pocketknife across the top of one of the bundles, scoring the blue plastic wrap. He dug the point of the knife into the center of the scored line, made a slit big enough to fit two fingers, then worked each of his index fingers into the slit and ripped the plastic back.

There was another layer of plastic under it, but at least the money was less blue than before.

"How's that?" Izzy asked.

"That's good," Cosh said.

Gugootz nodded. "Yeah . . . good."

Cosh set his elbows on the table, steepled his fingers, and rested his chin on his fingertips. "Maybe . . . do it again," he said, his eyes locked on the bundle.

Izzy scored the second layer and pulled back the plastic. His heart raced even faster. The top stacks of hundreds were bare.

They sat again in silence, staring at the money.

"Can I touch it?" Gugootz asked. "When I was handling it on the airplane, it didn't seem real. Maybe because it was blue."

"Sure," Izzy said. "Go ahead."

Gugootz stood and stroked one of the stacks with the tip of his index finger and then quickly sat back down.

"How's it feel?" Cosh asked.

"Good. Real good."

Cosh stood and ran the tip of his finger across one of the stacks. He sat back down, returned his elbows to the table, and interlocked his fingers, so that this time his chin rested on his knuckles. "Maybe we should just pull out one of the stacks. Y'know, so we can count it . . ."

By the time Beans came knocking, there were loose hundred-dollar bills scattered all throughout the kitchen, and they lay over the tops of the unopened bundles—on the table, chairs, windowsills, and even the floor, like the remnants of a tickertape parade.

• • •

The first thing Beans saw when Izzy opened the door was Gugootz lying on his back in the middle of the kitchen atop a bed of hundred-dollar bills. The kid's eyes were closed, his headphones over his ears. The volume was high enough that a faint, tinny version of "Money for Nothing" could be heard throughout the room.

Beans turned his head to Cosh, who sat at the kitchen table, laughing maniacally as he scooped up loose bills and tossed them into the air.

Izzy pulled Beans close, wrapping his arms around him, and squeezed with all of his might. Beans was on his toes, gasping for breath. Somehow he managed to squeeze Izzy back and kiss him on the cheek.

After Izzy released him, Beans gazed around the room and then walked into the kitchen. "I guess it worked," Beans said, turning back to Izzy.

"We're good on our end. How did it go with you? Is it done?"

Beans felt a twitch in his spine. "Just like we planned."

"You good?" Izzy asked.

"Not sure. Kind of numb. Time will tell."

Cosh, as if he only just realized Beans was there, stood up from the table and rushed him, throwing his arms around Beans and lifting him off the floor. He spun him around three times and then kissed him on the forehead. "We did it, Beans," he said. "We really fuckin' did it."

As if in a dream, Beans turned in a circle, scanning the bills strewn throughout the room. He moved close to the unopened bundles and examined them. *What the . . .* He cocked his head. "They're all hundreds?"

"The kid'll tell you." Izzy pointed to Gugootz, who had, thus far, remained oblivious to his arrival—eyes closed, feet clacking together to Dire Straits.

Beans kicked the sole of his left Ked, startling the kid from his afterglow.

Gugootz sprung to his feet and threw off the headphones. "Beans! Are you okay?"

"I'm okay." Beans laughed. "Wanna tell me why there are no twenties here?"

"Beans, I swear, the whole fuckin' load was C-notes. No twenties, no tens, no fives. I had no choice."

"Beans," Izzy said, setting a hand on his back, "there's five times what we thought there would be. Fifteen million dollars. That's a good thing."

Beans, still in a daze, could only shrug. "Could be good. Could be bad. We'll just have to see."

CHAPTER 38

THE HOT PEPPER PROBLEM

"**UNBELIEVABLE.**" **PAT GIBBONS** cut open his crab Rangoon and drenched it with sweet-and-sour sauce. "That close to all that money, and he blows himself up? What a fuckin' moron."

The mounted televisions at opposite corners of the Lucky Star blared, as usual, and the cacophony of patrons' voices echoed off the restaurant's dingy yellow plaster walls. Beans imagined every conversation was about the Federal Reserve explosion.

He speared a thin slice of his Hong Kong steak with his fork. "It doesn't make sense. What does the G think?"

"Best they could come up with is that he somehow set off the explosives accidentally while unloading the money."

Beans nodded. That's exactly what he wanted them to think.

"But they're confused about a few things," Pat said.

"Like what?"

"Well, he had the guards subdued, and he was all alone on the dock with a truckful of money. If that was the plan, why the fuck would he even *bring* explosives?"

Beans swallowed down the steak. "Maybe in case he had to

blow open the door of the truck?"

"Maybe. Another thing is, so far as we knew, he always worked alone, but they think he might have had an accomplice for this one."

Beans put his fork down. This could be bad. "Why would they think that?"

"I think they're just being careful," Pat said. "Since the money got burned up, they don't know if any of it is missing. Now they're sending out alerts to all the banks to keep an eye out for the serial number run."

Beans felt an ache deep in the pit of his stomach. The G was supposed to presume that any missing money was burned up in the explosion. That was the whole point, so they wouldn't look for the missing money. "Okay, but . . . any thief with an ounce of brains would know better than to take the money to a bank."

Pat dabbed his lips with his napkin. "Doesn't matter. Wherever he spends it, it's gonna end up in a bank eventually. Then they'll trace it backward. But one thing that's really got them confused, and me too, is if he was working alone, how was he able to be in two places at the same time?"

"What do you mean?"

"You know how he used to take a crap at the scene of the crime, right?"

"Yeah, so?"

"So, they found a pile of shit on the dock at the Federal Reserve, but they also found one in the cargo hold of the plane."

Beans stared at him blankly. He couldn't process this. "I don't understand."

"Neither do I," Pat said. "And neither does the G. So now they're gonna keep the case open until they figure it out."

"What if they can't figure it out?"

"Then the case stays open."

"For how long?"

Pat cocked his head and looked askance at Beans. "I don't know, I guess five years."

"Why five years?"

"That's the statute of limitations for bank robbery."

Beans resisted the urge to get up to walk out. He had to tell the guys the bad news, but if he left now, it wouldn't look good. Forcing himself to sit calmly and finish his meal, he searched his mind for a way to change the subject. "I'm sorry it's taking so long to find a gas tank."

Pat had a mouthful, so he made a sweeping gesture with his hand, as if to say, "No hurry."

"I just haven't come across a seventy-eight Buick wagon for you. I even talked to a friend at a junkyard. No luck."

Pat swallowed. "It's my second car. Just a junk I use to drive to work. You'll get it when you get it."

Sara came by the table with their tabs—separate, of course. Beans snatched them both out of her hand.

"Hey, what the hell are you doing?" Pat asked.

"Listen, you buy every time. Let me get it for once."

"Fine. If I knew you were buying, I'd have ordered the steak too."

Beans laughed. If there was one thing Pat was not, it was a cheapskate.

"I gotta go," Beans said. "There's a Buick wagon out there somewhere, and I'm determined to find it." He scuffled between tables and chairs and made his way to the counter, where Sara was standing behind the cash register. He handed her the two checks and a fifty-dollar bill. "Keep it." It was too big of a tip, but he didn't have time to wait for change. Hopefully she wouldn't interpret it as him hitting on her. Or maybe, hopefully, she would.

"Thanks, Hon." She gave him a wink. "See you soon."

He wasn't sure how to decode that exchange, but he didn't have time to think about it. He jogged to his tow truck, hopped in, and proceeded to run every light all the way to the gas station at Canal and Twenty-Sixth Street, where one of his preferred pay phones was tucked into a corner.

"Geraldi's," Cosh answered.

"Hey, is the other guy there with you?"

"Yeah, he's here. You okay?"

"Where's the id-kay?"

"I dunno. Maybe down the street."

"Go get him. I'll be there in ten minutes."

Beans hung up, and out of sheer habit worked the coin return lever and poked his finger into the chute. Nothing.

He drove down Canal Street to Taylor, then down Taylor past the projects. He parked the tow truck at the hydrant on the corner of Taylor and Loomis, in front of the Chiefs Club. Geraldi's was across the street. He jogged to the door and opened it. Despite everything on his mind, the little bell at the top of the door made his mouth water. He threaded through the invisible cloud of husky aromas and into the back room, where Cosh, Izzy, and Gugootz—rallied from the club—were seated at the table.

"What's up?" Izzy asked.

Beans took a seat across from Gugootz and laid his fists on the table. "Is there something you want to tell us?" he asked, looking into the kid's eyes.

Gugootz paused. "No. why?"

"Your answer is no, then?"

Cosh stood. "C'mon, Beans? You gonna tell us what's going on?"

Beans ignored him and kept his gaze locked on Gugootz. "How well did you know Step?"

"I dunno, from the club, around the neighborhood. Not very well."

"You never worked with him?"

Gugootz looked genuinely insulted. "No."

"Did he ever talk to you about work?" Beans asked. "Give you advice, teach you stuff?"

"No," Gugootz shook his head. "I don't even think he knew I was kinky. I never talk to anyone about what we do."

"Are you genetically related to him somehow, maybe?"

"What the fuck, Beans?" Izzy threw Cosh a bewildered look. "Just tell us what's on your mind, and we can help figure it out."

"What's on my mind is that the G is keeping the case open. They think Step had an accomplice. And they're sending out alerts to watch for the serial numbers of the missing money."

"Aw, no!" Cosh said. "Why?"

"Because either Step had an accomplice who's as fucked-up as he was, or he managed to be in two places at the same time."

Beans returned his attention to Gugootz, whose face had turned beet-red. Sweat was beading up on his forehead.

"What are you talking about?" Izzy asked.

"You know how the sick bastard liked to take a shit at the scene?"

"Yeah, so?" Cosh said.

"So, not only did they find a pile of shit on the docks at the

Federal Reserve, they found one in the cargo hold of the fuckin' plane!"

Gugootz lowered his head.

"Kid," Beans said, "are you sure you don't have something to tell us?"

Gugootz raised his head and looked at Cosh. "I told you fuckin' giardiniera gives me agita! Why'd you let me eat it?"

"Wait . . ." Cosh stared the kid down. "You didn't . . ."

"What the fuck was I supposed to do?" Gugootz said. "I tried to hold it. I did. I couldn't. There's no fuckin' bac'ouse in the cargo hold!"

"And you didn't think to tell us?" Beans asked.

"I was embarrassed. You don't go around telling people stuff like that."

"Does this mean what I think it means?" Izzy asked.

Beans sat back in the chair. "I hate to break it to you guys, but we've got fifteen million dollars that we can't spend. At least not for five years. If we don't get busted for it before then. After that, they can't prosecute."

"So, we gotta stash it away for five years?" Cosh was on his feet. "What are we supposed to do in the meantime? Damn it! I had plans!"

"We all had plans," Beans said. "But you know what they say about best-laid plans. We just gotta go about business as usual. Keep our jobs. Go on a nice quiet caper here and there to get by."

"You think we could find a way to wash it now?" Izzy asked.

"It's too hot. Nobody will touch it. Plus, if we start putting out feelers, Uncle Skinny will get wind and try to muscle us out of it."

"Fuck." Cosh paced beside the table and then stopped. "Okay, then. That's what we gotta do. Bury it for five years. All agreed?"

They all nodded.

Gugootz slumped forward until his forehead hit the table.

Izzy and Beans stood.

"All that planning," Beans said. "All that work. Shot to shit because of some hot fuckin' peppers." He smacked Gugootz on the back of the head and walked out of the room.

"Peppers. Pfft," he heard Izzy say. Then the blunt sound of another smack.

Cosh followed suit. "Fuckin' peppers," he muttered. Then the loudest smack of all.

On that day, Jimmy Gugootz became Jimmy Peppers.

Only four people would ever know why.

CHAPTER 39

ONLY HUMAN

SIX MONTHS LATER . . .

Cosh downshifted into a turn, almost toppling the half-empty box of fresh figs that sat in Izzy's lap. Izzy had dozed off in his usual position in the passenger seat of the truck, with his feet on the dashboard.

The sudden change of momentum jarred him awake. "You sure you don't want one?" Izzy gripped the stem of a fig and held it out to Cosh.

"I'm good. Thanks."

Izzy held on to the stem, lowered the entire fig into his mouth, and bit down. Only the stem remained between his thumb and forefinger. "Four years and six months to go," he mumbled with his mouth full. "If we don't get pinched, that is. Then you'll be a rich man. Still thinking about that yacht?"

"I dunno," Cosh said. "There's a lot to think about now. I'm worried about Beans. Does he seem different to you?"

"Maybe a little quieter. Wanna spar today?"

• • •

Beans sat alone, smoking a cigarette on the front stoop of his family's greystone. When he was alone with his thoughts, he occasionally had splashes of remorse for killing Step.

It was a ton of zort. Life changing. But was it worth whacking someone?

But when he thought about Debbie, he felt justified.

That sick fuck almost killed her.

And then there were the people Step actually killed. The girl in Chinatown. The poor family he tortured. Little kids!

Would Beans go to hell for being a murderer? But wasn't it right to kill someone who was evil?

Well, if he had to go to hell, at least it was for Debbie.

Was he a different person now? Maybe. Maybe a monster, maybe more of a man, definitely more human. A natural-born sinner. Did the world appear darker, like he thought it would? Not really. Just a bit more serious. He actually felt stronger, almost invincible, fully confident in his ability to do whatever it took to protect the people he loved.

Mrs. DiMarco came rolling up with Mickey.

"Hey, Mick." Beans stood and put his hand out for his old friend to shake.

Mickey was still. Didn't even look at Beans.

Beans honked Mickey's nose. "Hey, Mickey. Is that your nose, or are you eating a banana?"

But Mickey just sat, emotionless in his chair, staring blankly ahead.

Beans turned to Mrs. DiMarco. "What's wrong with him?"

Her eyes filled and tears ran down her face. "Can you watch him for a minute, Beans?"

"Sure, Mrs. D."

She ran into her house next door and returned a minute later. Her arms were folded across her chest, only partially concealing the envelope she held there. She sniffled, composed herself, and sat next to Beans on the stoop. "I have to talk to you. About Mickey."

"Whatsa matter?"

"He started with a new physical therapist last week." Her face contorted, and once again the tears began to fall. "He came home with blood in his underwear, and he hasn't spoken since."

Beans sat, stunned. He let the implication sink in. "Are you telling me . . ."

Mrs. D nodded. "Uh-huh."

"You're sure?"

"I confronted him—the therapist. He practically admitted it. Said I couldn't prove anything. He actually laughed."

"Mrs. D, I don't know what to say."

She set the envelope in his lap. "This is my life savings. Almost ten thousand dollars. I want you to say you'll take care of it."

Beans stared at her, unblinking. Was she asking him to do what he thought she was asking? How was this happening?

He looked down at Mickey, silent in his chair on the sidewalk. "Mrs. D, I can't . . ."

She buried her face in his chest and sobbed. "He hurt my baby, Beans!"

Beans gripped her shoulders and looked into her eyes. "You don't understand. I can't take your money. Go back in the house and hide it somewhere. Somewhere good. Then I want you to come back out with a piece of paper with a name on it."

THE END

AARON PALMER is a retired sociologist living in Phoenix, Arizona. He lived in the Taylor Street/ Little Italy neighborhood of Chicago for twenty-five years, from 1972 to 1997. During that time, he conducted more than four hundred in-depth and confidential interviews with the neighborhood people, as well as interviews with Chicago Police officers and FBI agents. The knowledge and insights gleaned from these interviews became the basis for his fictional stories.

Printed in the USA
CPSIA information can be obtained
at www.ICGtesting.com
LVHW041558031123
762989LV00002B/207

9 781960 378088